HOW'S YOUR
ROMANCE?

OTHER FICTION BY ETHAN MORDDEN

How's Your Romance?

Concluding the "Buddies" Cycle

ETHAN MORDDEN

ST. MARTIN'S PRESS ☎ NEW YORK

www.stmartins.com

Design by Jamie Kerner-Scott

Library of Congress Cataloging-in-Publication Data

Mordden, Ethan.
    How's your romance? : concluding the "Buddies" cycle / Ethan Mordden.—
1st ed.
        p. cm.
    ISBN 0-312-33330-7
    EAN 978-0-312-33330-0
    1. Gay men—Fiction.   2. Male friendship—Fiction.   3. Manhattan (New
York, N.Y.)—Fiction.   I. Title.

PS3563.O7717H69 2005
813'.54—dc22

                                                    2005046577

First Edition: September 2005

10   9   8   7   6   5   4   3   2   1

To Gregg and the Boys

ACKNOWLEDGMENTS

To my agent, Joe Spieler; to copy editor Benjamin Dreyer, relentless in pursuit of Fowler's "sturdy indefensibles"; to production editor Meg "I've never seen a book without italics" Drislane; to my editor, Keith Kahla.

CONTENTS

INTRODUCTION: IN WHICH NOTHING HAPPENS

WAS RECRUITED DURING INTERMISSION at a performance of *South Pacific* at the Brandywine Music Circus in Concordville, Pennsylvania. My father, a building contractor, had taken me along on an inspection trip of his sites—the motel outside Waretown, New Jersey; the torpedo plant in New London, Connecticut; rest stops along some turnpike; and the new court house in Concordville.

These trips were great fun because of the incidentals, such as amusement parks, afternoon tea-dancing at the hotels, and especially summer theatres, generally "in the round" inside a great tent. These are virtually extinct nowadays; however, decades ago summer theatre was a mainstay from Maine to Virginia and from Long Island to Minnesota, most often featuring the so-called "package tour." This offered some show-biz star or merry has-been leading a company of unknowns in new plays or old musicals. Tallulah Bankhead never missed a season; she always claimed it was this or debtor's prison. At various times, Dolores Gray, Kitty Carlisle, and Jane Morgan tried *Lady in the Dark*. Norma Terris and Allan Jones exhumed themselves and operetta. Gypsy Rose Lee took over Ethel Merman's role in *Happy Hunting*. To a Broadway veteran like me, this was a hodgepodge. Still, a musical is a musical.

Anyway, Concordville had one of those tents, and our visit coincided with a week of *South Pacific* starring Don Ameche and Betsy Palmer. My girl-in-every-port father saw a dating opportunity in depositing me at the Brandywine Music Circus, and I was alone in my seat waiting for the second act to start when a nondescript but dapper character slipped into the place next to me, set a new sheet atop his clipboard, and asked, "Name?"

Now, I should warn you that *South Pacific* is a Joshua Logan show, Logan being the co-librettist and director of the original production. A lifelong hibernating gay who was unwittingly out to everybody but himself, Logan habitually dressed his musicals with shirtless hunks in, for example, a swimming-pool scene and even a physique parade in a college football team's locker room.

South Pacific's hunks are Seabees, one of them, by Logan tradition, a Hercules. I was trying to decide which one I preferred—yes, even then I knew—when the clipboard guy joined me. He asked for basic data only, yet was clearly weighing my answers. I said, "What's all this about?"

"Your contract. Last question: who do you like the most?"

Impulsively, I made my mind up: "The blond on the end. With the shoulders."

"No. In the world."

"Oh. Barbara Cook."

"You made it. Sign here."

I signed, he handed me a carbon, and he bustled off to quiz an avid youth sitting across the aisle in a Peter Pan collar, surrounded by aunts.

Looking over the contract, I was mystified by all the sexual boilerplate—what was "rimming"?—but I wasn't too young to see the immense advantage in two exemptive clauses, one from marriage and the other from military service. There was a rider advising that wearing green on Thursday was now optional and—most interesting to me—a kind of sermonette at the end on the importance of friendship.

It's interesting because while gays supposedly have a lot of sex, what most of them really have is a lot of relationships, including odd ones. My odd ones are uncountable, but my close odd ones are with the former Little Kiwi, now known as J., and Cosgrove, the two juniors in my personal gay family. Playmates, business partners, and allies against the world, they sometimes turn into rivals in a competition whose prize is unknowable and whose rules are unclear. Tension can break out at any moment, so let us proceed to another intermission at a musical. For his birthday, J. had asked me to take him and Cosgrove to *Les Misérables*. Most people pass the interval just sitting there, finding the bar, or visiting the belasco (my mother's euphemism, when we were kids and out in public, for the toilet). J. spent the time testing Cosgrove on the plot, and what he thought would happen next.

"What if I don't know?" Cosgrove fearfully asked.

"You must understand what each story is about," said J., "if you want to learn how life is."

"It's about love," said Cosgrove, none too sure.

"Everything's about love," replied J., with a patronizingly reassuring smile. "Let's be specific. Guess who divides. Guess who conquers."

I butted in and offered J. fifty bucks, silvershine on the barrelhead, if he could recount the show's plot thus far. He couldn't, of course. Hugo's novel has tons of plot, tons even that the musical had to omit, including a touching relationship between the street urchin Gavroche and two homeless and very young brothers whom he temporarily takes care of, none of them aware that Gavroche is in fact the boys' brother, too. I shared this bit of intelligence with the kids, who were fascinated. "How come they didn't know?" Cosgrove asked.

"They are all progeny of the novel's villain couple, les Thénardier, who only raise daughters. The boys they dispose of."

"Did Gavroche and his brothers ever learn the secret?" Cosgrove asked.

"Gavroche is killed during a battle between revolutionaries

and Authority, and Hugo leaves the other two fending for themselves in the 'great monster,' Paris."

Cosgrove was quiet, but J., irked at my crabbing his act, huffed out, "I don't see what all that has to do with a trip to the theatre."

"Theatre is education," I pointed out. "That's why gay boys are born theatregoers." To which I added, "Theatregoers and runaways."

"How so?" asked Cosgrove, as J. decided to study the actors' bios in the playbill and make angry little fooing noises.

"Well," I said, "like Gavroche and his brothers, we're cut off from our families of origin and the social system they champion or simply stooge for unthinkingly. We make our own families, invent *our* system. You need smarts to do that. So—education. The older among us kind of take care of the fledglings."

J. turned a page of his playbill so brutally that it ripped.

"Well, don't we?" I asked.

"Did anyone take care of you?" Cosgrove asked.

"I didn't need it, because of all the theatre I'd logged. But if I had been needy, someone would have seen to it. It can be an informal thing, you know. People looking out for you without your even noticing. Or it can be very structured, as with you and J. Have the two of you ever had sex, by the way?"

Cosgrove's eyes widened, and now he, too, began touring tensely through his program.

"I've been wondering from the beginning," I went on, "and there would be a kind of symmetry to it, as everyone else in the family has had carnal knowledge of the rest of us at least once that I know of. And . . . well, runaways will do that when they first meet, if only to . . . what? Discover the size of the commitment?"

"Here's all about the plays that were seen in this theatre eons ago," J. announced.

"I now know who the wardrobe supervisor may be," Cosgrove put in.

"You've had plenty of opportunity and a bond of spectacular proportions," I went on, rather enjoying myself. "This is weight-lifted love, or at least it was."

At that they momentarily glanced at each other, then went back to their reading. "But what's wrong with a little cheating now and again? One of the worst aspects of hetero marriage is this absurd belief that one should—even *can*—live without sensual variety. One can't, of course. So, already, every breeder is lying all the   "

"At last!" cried J., as the houselights dimmed.

"Let's enjoy the heartrending second act," Cosgrove almost begged.

I can't. I want to know what is true in the world. I already understand why Gavroche is killed: in war. But I don't understand why love is killed. J. used to be the life partner of my best friend, Dennis Savage; and now he isn't.

Okay. Okay, another change of scene, to the little park at the eastern end of our street, overlooking the river.

"He went astray," I tell Dennis Savage. "Then he saw how wrong that was and came back repentant. Why not forgive?"

"He is not repentant," my buddy tells me, quite casually. He doesn't care to extend himself about it. "He'll find a new daddy in due course, and it won't be the likes of me. That little tyrant of the heart has had all the middle class he can use. He's heading for the margins, where nothing is forbidden."

I try this: "One, He hurt me by leaving. Two, He is so changed that the fit is off. Three, I was tiring of sharing every aspect of existence. Four, Other, please specify."

Dennis Savage sighed as a Circle Line boat glided past us on its cruise to nowhere, ever in quest and ever ending up where it began.

"You two were such . . . such friends!" I say.

A moment. The boat. The vast emptiness before us. The breeze. A vagabond on a nearby bench having a rowdy conversation with, it turned out, Lee Harvey Oswald. A New York moment.

I try this: "Do you miss him?"

"I miss what he was."

Back in our building, we parted in the elevator, and I wondered whether I would ever get to miss what Cosgrove had been, which, right now, was Very Domestic: carefully following a water-blurred index card bearing Dennis Savage's recipe for Stuffed Rigatoni, an intricately brilliant dish in which homemade pasta is filled with the most finely chopped spinach, raisins, walnuts, bacon, and chicken, and the sauce is . . . It takes hours. But it was Thursday night, time for J.'s weekly dinner with us, which Cosgrove instituted out of fear that, on his own, J. wouldn't eat right.

"Does Dennis Savage really get all this slice-up mush into these little things?" Cosgrove asked me when I looked in on the prep.

"I think you're supposed to stuff the pasta before you cook it."

Cosgrove stopped stuffing. "*Now* they tell me! How will J. come back if we don't show him the best of everything?"

"He isn't coming back," I said. "Last week, when you brought out those tiny handmade pretzels as an appetizer, he hardly said a word. Once he would have raved."

"It's possible," said Cosgrove wistfully, "that he doesn't realize that I'm the Pretzel King of Fifty-third Street."

Surveying the kitchen, which lately had the look of the Versailles bakeshop on the night Louis XVI married Marie-Antoinette, I said, "I wonder if he's worth this trouble."

"It's not the same," Cosgrove agreed. "But you have to hold on, out of family honor and secret sadness for what it was in the old days."

"Are you ready to say if you two ever had sex or not?"

"Yikes, my sauce is thickening at a frantic rate!"

"You can't dodge me forever. I'll have the secret before this saga is over, I swear."

J. duly arrived, as perfunctory as always in his greeting and conversation. He seemed like a relative, someone you see because you're supposed to, not because you want to.

Is he *trying* to make it awkward? I thought, as he and Cosgrove ran through the latest indie movie hit, the way spring was being stalled by a cold front, and the supposed feud between Blur and Oasis. Distracted and aimlessly changing subjects, J. grew keen but once, when Cosgrove said he was looking forward to a Pines weekend and J. wanted to know who was inviting us out.

"Someone I know," Cosgrove replied, as he fetched another of those little Perrier bottles for refills. "He has an excellent house on the ocean, and as he is quite the international gadabout he is often away and the place is empty for his friends' use."

"You never mentioned him before," said J., with the tiniest suspicion of complaint.

"No?" said Cosgrove, attending to J.'s glass.

J. turned to me, hoping for information without having to ask for it: Have I a rival? Can I be replaced? There was a time, after all, when the only someone Cosgrove knew was J.

"Cosgrove's become something of a socialite," I said. "I expect to find a paparazzo or two hanging around outside the building any day now."

"How'd you meet a rich guy?" J. asked Cosgrove.

"It was a bike accident in the Park. Oh, did you see my new GT Palomar? It has twenty-one speeds."

"I saw it when I came in," said J. flatly. That basket of fun.

"So we wouldn't have to share my old Raleigh three-speed," I said.

"It's so glamorous at last," said Cosgrove, crossing over to where the new bike leaned against the piano. "Though I'm never happy about leaving it alone with Bud's junkmobile." Cosgrove caressed the GT's crossbar as Fleabiscuit came over and nuzzled the front wheel. "You know how territorial Raleighs are. Especially the three-speeds."

This fanciful line of humor was, once on a time, J.'s stock-in-trade; now he simply ignored it.

"What bike accident?" he asked.

"Well, it's because of all the speeds on the GT. I was crossing between the big fountain and the roller-skate place and I couldn't decide whether third gear or eighteenth, so I wasn't looking and I crashed into this guy in a beret. But he wasn't hurt, and we got to talking, and he said I could use his Pines house sometime."

"Just like that," said J. sarcastically.

"No. During lunch."

J. looked at me again. "Did this guy have sex with Cosgrove?"

"Did you?"

J. made an exasperated face. "What kind of household is this, when you do a bike accident and then have sex with the victim?"

"I didn't have sex," said Cosgrove quietly. "He was just being nice because he liked me."

J. steamed over that in silence for a bit, then suddenly rose and apologetically put his arms around Cosgrove and held him. Breaking, J. said, "I'm just cranky because of my day job."

"Why don't we eat?" I suggested.

It was Potage Saint-Germain to start, which I must admit is Campbell's split pea soup with crushed bacon and onion slivers on top; but it fools almost everyone.

Again, the conversation was fitful till I commented on how constantly gay life seems to fill with ever new friends. One drops some people along the way, true. But what was that dowdy piece of propaganda they used to print on the boxes of Girl Scout cookies my mother would order? Ah yes; and I quoted over the soup: " 'Make new friends and keep the old. One is silver and the other gold.' "

J. seized his moment. "*I* have a new friend, even if he's no great millionaire with a Pines house and a beret."

"Who could it be?" Cosgrove politely wondered.

"It's my roommate, Vince. I didn't believe we were going to be friends at first, because he's so big and hairy, not to mention his whole right side is covered with body art and he smokes those disgusting cigars. But then he's like this big dog crazy for attention. He's always bringing the ladies over, as you might well guess, and I can tell by their breathing gasps and happy screams that they are glad to be with him. But they don't come back, except for, like, Shona, who even says she doesn't like him but just has to be fucked right and she can count on him. He complained to me about her but he dates her anyway. That's how he says it—'dating.' He means just fucking, because he doesn't take them out or anything. He tells me about these girls he meets and says, 'I really want to date her.' He doesn't mean dinner and a movie. Just his dick and tattoos. He means well, though, I think. Vince."

"What's his last name?" Cosgrove asked.

"He's Vince Choclo."

"What kind of strange name is that?"

"Well, he *is* strange. Sometimes his mother calls, saying, 'This is Mrs. Choclo,' and all I want to tell is how he fucked a girl so completely last night that she drowned out *NYPD Blue*. I very almost said, 'She was touched to the root, Mrs. Choclo.' "

Out came that torturously prepared rigatoni. J. failed to compliment the chef, though he scarfed up the pasta and was not shy about asking for seconds.

"Now this interesting kink," J. went on. "Vince keeps a little wooden chest of Polaroids that he will always take of each of his dates, with their measurements penciled on the back. He measures them all up and down, including parts you didn't expect, like their nipple size or even their honey box. That's what he calls it. At night he likes to lie in bed nursing a bottle of beer and going over his Polaroids. He says their names out loud. You hear 'Brenda.' 'Candy.' 'Gina.' It's like humming. Sometimes he comes into my bedroom when I'm reading. He brings his chest of Polaroids to show me. Guess what he calls them? *'Valentines'!* He picks them out and tells me what they were like. 'Chicks,' he says. He has many Polaroids of chicks. I told him he should have Polaroids of him and these chicks at the same time, especially when he's fucking them and coming and his eyes go all crazy and his teeth would be seen. He said, 'Who would take these pictures?' And I told him I would."

"I'm reading *Watership Down*," said Cosgrove.

"What's that about?" asked J.

"Rabbits."

"How can a book be about rabbits?"

"Well, how can someone be Vince Choclo?"

"It happens. And when he comes in with his Polaroids, I manage to slide the bedcovers low, so he can see me in my skin, way way down. I know he is looking. He *sees* me, Cosgrove. So what are all his dates about? How come he's sitting on my bed at night calling me 'Sugar Boy'? Just how he walks around after a shower with his dick out tells that he wonders about me. I want to quit this day job and just keep house like you. I want the freedom of gay life, where a pretty boy gets his way. So I go out of the shower just as nude as Vince. He offered to towel me off once, but I said no. You don't rush a guy like Vince. They get scared to know what they are. I'll wait till he's crazy about me—right now, he's just curious. And guess what? I take money off his dresser and he doesn't say anything."

"Stealing is crummy," I observed.

"It's just little coins. Besides, I'm worth it. Don't I bring joy into his life? He is fascinated to talk to me, I notice."

"Does he know about us?" I asked.

"It is too soon for Vince to know about us."

Cosgrove absorbed this, then said, "It's apple-and-walnut salad for dessert."

"Bring it on," said J., expanding and patting his stomach like Falstaff. "In this mood I'm in now, I will love everything set before me."

"HE STEALS A GUY'S CHANGE?" said Dennis Savage, when I told him a few minutes later, at his place. I always report in, partly to give Cosgrove privacy time with his former mentor and partly to learn if Dennis Savage could relate the present and somewhat reproachable J. to the boy who was once a pleasure to know.

"Did he ever steal from you?" I asked. "Maybe at the very beginning?"

He shook his head.

"Thing is," I went on, "he actually seems manipulative now. Shrewdly calculating, even. He was so *impulsive* before. Can people so change their natures?"

"Is he hurt that I don't want him back? Or does he perhaps enjoy his new freedom?"

"Can't tell yet. How did he seem the night of What Happened Upstairs?"

"Like a defendant at one of Stalin's show trials—totally innocent but resigned to being found guilty."

"And how did you seem?"

"Like Stalin, I guess."

"Obdurate?"

"No, just endless. Like God in the Old Testament. You know—too much destruction is never enough. Yet somehow I had thought that if you can slide past the third-month bad-habits-getting-on-your-nerves thing, and the year's-end don't-you-give-me-orders argument, and the second-year malaise, and the seventh-year cheating scandal—"

"With Cosgrove?"

"That wouldn't be a scandal. No, with a sailor."

Indeed, I was scandalized. "I didn't know they still *had* sailors. I mean, in the Gulf War, yes, but not around here. Not in that gay thing of late-night pickups of uniformed trade."

"Anyway, I figured if you can work past all that, you're a cinch for long-run stats."

"You had ten fine years. How long should it be, after all?"

"For life," he said, simply, openly, mildly.

"Nobody gets that. Goethe didn't get that. Ken Ryker won't get that."

Cosgrove came upstairs then, to return Dennis Savage's garlic press and colander. A certain animosity on both sides usually keeps Cosgrove from venturing up here except on state visits, but this time he seemed in no hurry to leave.

"J. went on forever about his new roommate," said Cosgrove, wandering around the room looking at things. "And all crazy stuff. Like the roommate beats off by fucking the bed."

"Is this some cynosure?" Dennis Savage asked me.

"Some straight guy who would appear to have an angle on picking up women."

"J. says it's a total pussy house over there," said Cosgrove, pausing at the bookshelf. "He's writing porn stories now and sending them to magazines to earn extra money, and he says I should, too. But I guess I ought to read up some, to get smart first. What books do you recommend to smarten me?"

"Byron's *Don Juan*," said Dennis Savage. "It's the smartest work of the smartest century. The nineteenth."

"Of course, that's my favorite century of all."

"Well, then . . . you'll enjoy this simple test. What nineteenth-century figure wrote stories, composed music, is the hero of an opera, and had Mozart's middle name?"

"*You?*"

"Boys, boys," I said as they moved into skirmishing positions.

"How long do *you* get?" Dennis Savage suddenly asked me. "You and our abradant little Cosgrove here?"

The silence that followed that one was so fine we could hear the roaches discussing their itineraries.

Then Cosgrove said, "If we were straights, we would never be in this room together, or returning a garlic press."

"If we were straights," Dennis Savage countered, "none of our lives would have happened, including 'and' and 'the.' Straight life is about your relatives—demanding mothers, clueless fathers, idiot uncles. Gay life is about your friends."

He's right, of course. Let me show you a very defining straight relationship, of the kind I term "Beauty and the Beast." Some years ago, in the summer, research took me daily to the Lincoln Center Library, and I was timing my crossing of Columbus Circle to the lunchtime appearance of two men employed in construction on the Fordham University campus nearby. Rigorous union timekeeping meant they would materialize hungry at exactly

12:01, nosh somewhere, and then hang out at the war memorial to the *Maine* at the southwest entrance to Central Park at about 12:20, waiting till their break ended.

One guy was a study in nondescript: a face one forgot even while gazing at it. His buddy, shirtless in crispy-clean jeans and Timberland boots, was a looker: tall and total with one of those long-waisted, big-shouldered physiques that load on muscle easily. His face was no more than okay, but the unusual steel-gray hair and a tense mustache gave him extra presence to match the come-on build, and his bright eyes, looking everywhere but at no one, seemed to celebrate the knowledge that people were aware of him.

I sure was. Day after day, I'd take a perch close by and monitor their conversation while pretending to check over my notebook. And what I heard was the looker constantly belittling his friend. I distinguished three patterns. Pattern 1 was:

> LOOKER: What a time last night with Deena.
> SIDEKICK: She's not so great.
> LOOKER: Oh, yeah? So what dog did you fuck?

In Pattern 2, the sidekick would fight back:

> LOOKER: Check out the classy redhead with a fine two-
>   piece set.
> SIDEKICK: Like maybe you got a chance.

Pattern 3 called up ontological considerations:

> LOOKER: All you get is my leftovers.

It was a horribly unequal relationship, but men like this looker have the advantage. There's an excitement about them, a vitality

that comes of having all the first choices in life, so a lot of ego val-
idation lies in sharing their company. For some people, it is the
famous who wield this redemptive power. But whether the room-
tilter is a movie star, or rich, or lovely to see, he must treat one
with a sense of welcome or his strength becomes one's punishment. Like your parents when you're young and vulnerable, he
has the authority to judge you as worthy or unworthy: and to
make you believe it.

One day, I arrived at the meeting place (so to say) to find the
pair going at each other near the newsstand. The looker was trying out a new style, going not only shirtless but beltless with the
two top buttons of his jeans open, an unforgivably captivating
touch. I studied the magazine covers while he hammered away at
his partner, trying to borrow twenty bucks.

"I loaned you twenty last week," the sidekick complained.
"Didn't see that one come back yet, did I?"

"You don't think I'm good for it?"

The sidekick stood there and steamed, his face set and his
body rigid.

"You don't trust me, is that what?"

"Christ, how do I maybe *should* trust you if you borrow and
don't—"

"This is about Lauren, right? That night she stood you up?"

"What's *Lauren* got to do with twenty real dollars you owe me?"

The looker sunshined out a grin real slow, turned his body
slightly away from his friend, and nodded sardonically, knowingly.
Playacting.

"She broke her date with you to be with me," the looker explained. "Didn't she tell you?"

The sidekick took it straight on, full horror but no flinching.
His mouth starts to work: "You got to bring *that* in?"

"So give me the twenty and we'll say no more."

"I'm not giving you no twenty after that, am I? First twenty, then Lauren?"

"So what are you good for?" Two beats, then: "I'm asking you *what* are you *for*? Chicks don't dig you, guys don't respect you, your own buddy you don't trust—full of resentment, I would guess, because Lauren prefers a handsome guy *and so where the hell are you going?*"

The sidekick had taken off and was now crossing the street; in the comic-book version, they would print a big black square before his eyes.

The looker watched him go for a bit, then turned to me with a half-mocking smile; of course, he had figured out my game. "What do you say, chief?" he asked. Disconcerted, I stared at the idol and finally got out, "I expect he'll be back for more in due course."

"Think so?" he replied with a grin. And off he went.

Now, that sort of relationship is much less common in gay life, which is an essentially civilizing force, like prep school or Peggy Lee albums. I want to show you an example of this in someone who might easily have ended up quite badly had he not stumbled into the Scene, been befriended by it, and become one of its poster boys.

I first saw him quite some years ago, when I was fresh out of college and attending—is that the word? but it did seem like theatre—my first gay bar, the Eagle. It stood at the Hudson River edge of a then ungentrified Chelsea, and it maintained a "leather and western" theme, meaning no admittance except to "cowboy," "biker," or fifties "straight" in jeans and white T.

The Eagle gave a rake-off on your beer if you went shirtless, and Dennis Savage partook of this discount during his trashier-than-thou gym era. He even entered the Eagle's Navel Contest one year, unbuttoning the top of his jeans like our straight friend in Columbus Circle and lowering his beltline obscenely. One had to: because they weren't judging navels per se but rather that body area centering on the midsection, where the waist starts to V up to the shoulders even as it makes that jump downward over the Venus girdle to start the legs. Remember, too, that in this vanished age no gay guy could be taken seriously (or home) if he wore underpants.

Dennis Savage might have won the contest, for he supplemented weight lifting with swimming laps, and his waist was so tight it squeaked when he walked. Still, he placed second. The winner was the man I wish to tell you of, a devastato beyond even the exacting standards of this Temple of Mars: about six foot two and molto heavy in the style of the day, when bulk was everything and no one had abs. He was also alarmingly handsome. Or no: rudely, roughly handsome. Prince Charming as a hangman. His smile had edge. When he won, he warily allowed the bartender-judge to pull down his pants to reveal one of those sensory-overload dicks that already is huge rather than gets huge.

"Who is that guy?" I asked Dennis Savage after the contest, in the routine question of the day.

Regarding the winner, Dennis Savage said, "He's kind of a thug, actually."

"Do you know him?"

"As slightly as possible."

Nevertheless, the guy came over to shake hands with Dennis Savage. We were introduced—his name, which I had missed during the judging, was Rip—and after a bit of this and that he clumped off into the bar's other room.

"You know that guy?" I said, not trying to hide my awe. "Do I get the story?"

Thinking it over, he said, "You do remember that I was graduated summa cum laude from Hamilton College on a full scholar-ship. You know I'm made of better stuff than this."

"I'd rather respect you for this."

"They're all the same story, though, aren't they? The tale of the Law of Beauty, superseding all those other laws. The ones your parents follow, and your pastor follows, and the president follows."

He gestured at the rest of the bar, at the cowpokes and leathermen and James Deans.

"Are we still trapped in a system that someone else invented?" he asked.

Eric ran up to pound Dennis Savage's left arm and cry, "I'm speechless! You won the Navel Contest!"

"I came in second."

"You're shameless," Eric went on, genuinely impressed.

"Tough is hot," said Dennis Savage, to me. "But sweet is hotter."

Eric balled a fist and thrust it into his mouth while uttering a thrilled noise, then raced off.

Rip came back into the room, looking about himself.

"Be careful," Dennis Savage warned me as he joined some brand-new fan for a little talk. Very little: it was considered un-manly to converse at length before going home with someone. Sex was looks, not character.

I watched the big guy for a while, thinking that Rip was a great name for him, then left the bar.

Now. A few days later, I was coming out of a movie in our strip of theatres along Third Avenue in the Sixties when I found my-self walking next to Rip. We both did a take at the same time, and we both laughed. I asked him if he'd noticed a hitch in the movie's dialogue, something alluded to in reel 10 that was apparently cut out of reel 4 or so. He jumped at that.

"I surely knew there was something disconnected there," he

said. He sounded glad. It seemed that his second favorite nonsexual activity was moviegoing, but his first was discovering a film's storytelling errors, accidental changes of outfit within a scene, or any other fraud in the realism, because then he didn't have to take movies seriously, and for some reason he didn't want to.

We were discussing the something disconnected outside the theatre in that awkward situation in which the two of you might formalize the socializing but at least one of you is afraid to suggest it.

"You live around here?" Rip suddenly asked me.

So we went to my place for coffee. Shockingly, while I ground the beans and set the water up for heating, Rip pulled open the refrigerator and snacked without permission.

Clearly, he'd come out of a different culture; or maybe this was another case of beauty taking over the world. He never scheduled a movie date in advance; he just showed up, telephoning from the corner. He had no steady job, hustling or working short-haul moving when he needed money. He only sort of had an apartment, even. Subletting it was another source of income, so he was forever moving in with some trick. He had no property, no groceries, no ambition. The everyday of his life was generic; the romance of his life was uniquely pumped to the max. I would see him stalking through the Eagle, raw and magnificent, fast, impatient. Once I got so engrossed that he was startled and came over to me and said, "What?"

I just replied, "Are your eyes really black?"

"I'm dark on my father's side," he replied, turning to note the passing of some dazzler, and to follow.

DENNIS SAVAGE FOUND IT bizarre to learn that Rip was visiting our building.

"What incongruity!" he cried one evening, ladling out dinner. "Here we are, collegiate, cultured, debonair . . . and here's this . . . what? this *specimen* in our midst. In looks, he's absolute clarity. But what is he in content? Remote and troubled. He's mining something dangerous. He's deep. Not as in intelligent—as in *hidden*. You know what he'll do to the guy who tries to discover him? And all *you* see is the black hair against the red lips."

"He takes movies apart like Darrow questioning Bryan at the Scopes trial. You'd like him if you knew him."

"I know him."

"Do you know yourself? Who *also* entered the Navel Contest? Who fucked Helmut Schmidt in some porn theatre, onstage, right in front of the screen only four days ago *as we speak?*"

Stunned with his serving tray, he paused. Then: "I'm going to *kill* Eric!"

"No," I told him, "because that's what's great about us. We're not entirely middle-class any more." Runaways. "Last weekend, when you came out to my folks' and we found you a bathing suit in the pool house . . . You were on the diving board, showing off, and I caught my mother looking at you wearing that undersize *pour-la-plage* or whatever it was that was maybe last worn by Booth Tarkington, and you were more or less coming out of it altogether. And you didn't care, and you looked so hot like that. I caught her eye, looking at you, and she quickly looked away. And I thought, Lady, you don't know anything about it. Gays are the men who have fun being men. We're inventing the wheel."

We were inventing a sex manual, and professions so we wouldn't have straights bossing us around, and styles for leisure, and even a politics. But most of all we were inventing a method by which men could relate to and support and enlighten and perhaps love each other. Maybe it's my mistake, this late in the first piece, not to set all the book's narrative throughlines into motion.

Many of you will doubtless feel relief when Vince Choclo shows up with his bizarre buddy Red Backhaus, two straights ready to tumble into gay, though I still don't believe there is such a thing as a bisexual. And our old comrade Peter Keene, that stalwart disciple of excess, will fall for the most poisonously appealing of Beefalo Boys. We'll go to a farm to meet my old high-schoolmate Evan McNeary, learn new gay styles from Chelsea twentysomethings Davey-Boy and Tom-Tom. A certain Nesto will befriend Cosgrove, who must grow free of J.'s influence, though I am going to put into rotation a porn story they co-wrote. All this will busy us for many pages, whereupon I will finally bring this saga to its resolution, this time (as Bullwinkle used to say) for sure.

But please bear with me while I scrutinize what I believe has been the identifying feature of Stonewall gay life. I'm going to look in on a significant moment that many relationships undergo, when the two of you realize that you have moved from airy to dense.

It was after another movie. Rip ate his way through my fridge—cold spaghetti, two apples, and a frozen Milky Way— then said, "I'm going to tell you a little something."

"Okay," I said, fussing around at the sink.

"Leave that and come here, now. You come along nice to me."

"I'm always nice to you," I said, drying my hands.

"This'll may need some extra nice. But I got to tell you all the same."

"Shoot," I said, joining him on the couch.

"You recall my speaking of Quincy, this big old guy I have been known to boff on occasion? We sometimes play basketball at that court on Second Avenue, in the park. It's pretty much come-one-all, so there's always new guys around, and I enjoy to see my buddy Quincy taking a shine to one of them and going all team spirit if somebody scores so he can grab the guy and dance with him.

"We have this deal that if he doesn't pick up anyone, I go to his place, where we shower up and then figure out if there's some new position for me to fuck him in. We got fourteen so far."

"Does he ever actually pick up anyone?"

Rip laughed. "That'd be hard to do, with everyone all around on the court there. But he can dream."

"Do any of those other guys know he's gay?"

"I don't believe *Quincy* knows he's gay."

"But he lets you fuck him?"

"He can't help it, 'cause he loves me so." He smiled. "He's a big boy, kind of gruff on the surface. But he's got a secret soft side that he shows only to me. You know I'm right fond of that style of boy, I guess."

True enough. Though he occasionally traveled the official circuit, Rip tended to cruise outside the parish. No doubt he had a special clause in his recruitment contract.

"Well, this one time Quincy and I go at it for a nice long session, and it's near midnight when I leave. Some of the streets are kind of empty, and there's all those dead buildings. The burnouts and such."

He got up then, looking around the room as if wondering where he was.

"Could I have a cocktail?" he said.

I want you to see this: he's in dark green cords and a white T-shirt so thin you can read his parts right through the cloth, and he's got all the power in the world to redeem or reject you. Yet he looks, for once, a little unsure.

"A cocktail?" I echo, wondering where this farmboy heard the term.

"Whatever you'd drink. Quick, my friend."

I splashed some vodka over ice and gave it to him. He drank, wiped his mouth, and said, "This one place, halfway down the block, one of those crazy street ladies comes out of nowhere, shouting, 'Tramp, you stole my life! You called the agency on me!' and all that stuff they say. She's got this stick and she comes at me with it. So I grab it from her and toss it."

He took another swig of the drink, wiped his mouth again, and said, "Taking ahold of wood while someone's firing it at you, you're going to cut yourself, so I was pretty mad. So when she came at me kicking, I just punched her a sweet one right in the face. Down she goes."

He stopped, looking at me, the two of us standing in the middle of my living room.

"Think it's over yet? I get maybe four steps down the street, she's on me again. I didn't hit her hard enough? Okay. *This* time."

More vodka, and now he wipes his mouth not on his hand but roughly all the way up his arm, showing me that he's getting mad all over again.

"Because why do I have to come to hurt if *she* wants to start something? 'Tramp, you have struck me!' and all. Oh, *I* have struck *you*? Miss, you are truly going to discover what struck *is*!"

Silence.

"So?" I asked.

"So we're now in front of some, I don't know, school or church. It's a goddamn wall of nothing there, so I grabbed her by the hair and swung her as hard as I could into that wall, three times."

Taking my hand, he wrapped it around the glass to hold it for him so he could show me how he did it.

"Now that *cunt* is *down*, and that's *all* she *wrote*!"

He was almost panting with anger, his face flushed, his eyes fireworks.

"That's *all she wrote*," he insisted, retrieving his drink. "And let's hear from you now."

"I'm happy you're here," I told him. "I'm happy you raid my fridge when you're hungry. I'm happy you trust me."

Taken aback, he slowly wound up to "Say something about what I told you."

"It's good that you weren't hurt."

Thinking that over, he pressed the glass into my hands. "You drink," he said.

"It's too early."

"Just a sip, real personal, as a favor to me."

So I did.

"Right," he said, reaching over to take the glass and put it down.

"Can I get away with this?" I asked, putting my hands on him. I wanted to know what something that big and free felt like. His heart was still pumping heavily, but otherwise he was still and almost welcoming.

When we broke, he said, "I have to be somewhere."

I smiled. "Quincy?"

"Business." And off he goes.

I went right up to Dennis Savage, who had finally invested in a photo album and was sorting through an epoch of loose photographs.

"Should it run chronologically?" he asked. "By categories? Relatives, trips, tableaux vivants, tricks? Does one organize it by type, do you think?"

"The big guys, first of all," I suggested. "Especially the ones with big personalities."

He gives me his satiric look as he starts arranging his pictures in piles. "Someone's been on another coffee date with Ivanhoe and got all amazed again. Here's one of you in drag."

Horrified, I grabbed it—no, it was just the Grand Canyon and some Boy Scouts, young Dennis Savage among them. Recounting what I'd just heard in my place, I began helping him sort.

"He was testing you, of course," said Dennis Savage.

"That story, you mean?"

Setting down a series of family shots, he said, "Midwestern farmboy from a very narrow society where everyone has the same value system arrives in the total city where society is a mix. Where some people treat values they don't share with savage attacks. He has an evil run-in with a street crazy, and when he tells of his adventure, some react unsympathetically. With accusations, even. How dare he not show compassion, tolerance, or the leftist's favorite posture, passivity? Why, his...his *violence*, isn't it? His moral primitivism! His outrageous act of self-defense! It is forbidden in the total city."

I said, "Why is *he* so special? It's Stonewall, and we're overrun with tall and handsome and built and hung. Some nights in the Eagle, it's like—"

"Hair. Nipples. Forearms."

That stopped me.

"Your friend so special why is he?" he went on. "One, he's got crazy hair that's smooth and soft yet seems to edge up into the air so that it more or less shimmers over him. It's wonderful. It's implausible."

He shuffled through the visual record of his family life for a moment. Aimlessly, just doing it. Punctuation, maybe.

"Two, his nipples are big red circles with heavy white spiking. Is it sexy or freakish? He's *too* something. As if he'd sprouted out of the earth, like a carrot. And three, where did he get those gigantic forearms? He's Popeye. He's a cartoon. *In fact*...he's a fantasy. Quick, what's his name?"

"You say Rip," I replied. "But he told me to call him Carlo."

"See? Ripley Smith is his name. Carlo's his hustling name. That's what you want to connect with—a fantasy."

"Or is fantasy the gay equivalent of what straights call 'sin'? Isn't it simply that he has a lot of sexual content?"

"He has a lot of emotional content, which he is using sex to explore, as blindly as possible. He is, I repeat, a fantasy."

"He's not a fantasy. He only looks like one."

"What else *is* a fantasy but he looks like one? I really need to introduce you to some nice gay attorney, some ... stockbroker or something. Someone you could have gone to high school with."

"Introductions are inconclusive."

Suddenly gathering up all the Kodak to drop it back in the box that had held it lo these many years, Dennis Savage proposed to tackle the photo album project another time. "What we mainly should do is consider my outfit for the Black and White Party. Do you think I can get away with this?"

"This" turned out to be a stoker's mesh top over the kind of black leather britches favored by men whose workplace is a torture chamber.

"You really ought to stop attending Gilles de Rais' garage sales," I observed.

"But what footgear goes with it?"

"Boots, surely?"

"I can't dance in boots." Moving to the mirror, he held the outfit against himself. "I know it isn't me. Just tell me I'll look good."

"You'll look terrific."

"Kenny Reeves is going in white ducks and a striped T. So sensible, he says. But won't everyone come that way? How do you make an entrance dressed off the rack?"

"Carlo would."

"Oh, her," he said, moving into the bedroom.

Following him, I said, "You know, the key thing about us run-aways is that we can all come to Stonewall not because of our education but because of our hunger for freedom. Gay life isn't about class. It's about feelings. We enter it to be obliged not to people we resent but to people we adore."

He was rooting around in a drawer of his bureau, and he may not have heard me.

1

TELL
THEM
ABOUT
THE FLIP

TWICE A YEAR, EACH of my publishers mails a financial statement, indicating how many copies of each title have been sold and including a royalty check—that is, my percentage of the gross.

These checks can be pathetically small, yet they arouse Cosgrove's interest. As he cannot absorb the concept of royalties, he believes that somehow, somewhere, somebody is accidentally paying me for work that was compensated for years ago. And as this is clearly found money, Cosgrove feels that we should bank it in a special "rainy-day fund."

"Meaning," I said, as he handed me the mail, containing two pieces of what he has come to recognize as publishers' accounting department communication, "you want to use it to buy CDs."

He said nothing but sweetly whistled "We're in the Money" as I opened the envelopes and examined the statements.

"One of these checks is for twenty-eight dollars," I told him. "You want it? It's yours."

He clasped his hands at his throat like an opera diva going for high C as I endorsed it over to him.

"What's the big deal?" I said. "You don't even have a checking account."

"I know someone who will cash this for me," he explained, tucking it into his wallet.

"If you really want extra money," I said, filing the bills and dumping the junkmail, "why don't you write porn stories like J. and sell them to the slicks?"

"Would they publish my stories?"

"Here's a secret that was confided to me some years ago by the porn king himself, John Preston. One day a month, an editor assumes control of the pile of submitted manuscripts and makes the following deductions: everything handwritten, out; everything on both sides of each page, out; everything with no margins, out; everything entirely in capital letters, out; and so on, till three stories are left. The editor accepts those three stories."

"But how do you write porn?" Cosgrove asked, following me into the bedroom.

"By idealizing. Bring together two hot men of a very disparate type who in real life would never meet, much less have sex." Changing my clothes for some imminent socializing, I went on, "Banker's car breaks down near farm, farmer invites banker to spend the night, both go *whee!* Or: high-school teacher meets former student, the two repair to teacher's apartment, student reveals titanic gym development and longtime wish to ball teacher, both go *whee!*"

Cosgrove looked doubtful. "It isn't hot to say *whee!,* though, is it?"

One pats his head or rubs the back of his neck at such moments. "Figure of speech, pal."

Buzzer: Doorman: Peter Keene coming up.

"Look, I'll help you," I said. "Give it some thought, then I'll show you how to outline it. Remember, though: you don't start with a situation. You start with *characters.*"

"Could I start with Vince Choclo? Except what type is he?"

"Why Vince Choclo?"

"Because it's such a good name. It's so dumb and dippy, he'll have to be hot. He will be pleading in the big scene, where everything's at stake and the crowd are fearful as the Zombie Contessa goes into her monkey dance." After a moment he added, "I may be writing postmodernesque porn."

Peter came in wearing running shorts, a sleeveless muscle-T, and a do-rag; I think he would have failed the dress code at a dog fight.

"Hey, pirate, where's your doubloons?" Cosgrove asked him.

"You go make coffee," Peter told him. "For I have news, friends. I have fallen very, very heavily for a fellow man, and if I could only—no, you mustn't congratulate me, for this is a wondrous yet terrible thing. You feel so enlarged, so re-created . . . but you, yes, *mope* with joy, you worry . . ."

He sat on the couch, excited and flustered, wanting to spill thirty secrets at once.

"Could this be just the slightest bit premature?" I asked. "I mean, you picked up some guy in the street for the three hundredth time and—"

"No, no, my—and I don't blame you—cynical friend. I've been a glad slut. But I never mentioned the 'L' word before, did I? For the last three weeks, I've been trying to . . . well, yes, to shape this lecture I knew I'd be giving you, yet I still don't know where to—"

"Let me call Dennis Savage down," I put in, going to the phone. "If it's that serious."

Peter went right on talking, ignoring the fact that I was briefly speaking to Dennis Savage and completely missing the appearance of the head of Fleabiscuit from under the couch, deftly to teethe on one of Peter's shoelaces and pull the knot open. It's his latest trick. Through all of this, I caught snatches of the time-honored phrases. You know: ". . . when I realized I couldn't wait the required three days . . ." and "He wasn't going to get out of my apartment alive" and "We just held each other and . . ."

Absently retying his shoelace, Peter mused, "If I told you his name, would it . . . or if I tried to describe the taste of his . . ."

"Week-old underpants?" said Cosgrove from the kitchen doorway.

Peter was quietly beside himself, running down like a fake Rolex. "Where do I even start?" he bleated. "It all comes out at once. One . . . raves."

" 'That is the usual method, but not mine—*My* way is to begin with the beginning,' " said Cosgrove.

Peter paused, then asked, "Isn't that Byron somehow?"

I nodded. "Cosgrove's studying *Don Juan* in preparation for a writing career. He's starting with porn, but who knows? Maybe one day you'll publish his first novel, perhaps a high-society whodunit."

Cosgrove agreed, and even offered a working title: *The Secret Diary of the Zombie Contessa.*

"The beginning . . . His name is Lars Erich Blücher. His family came here when he was six, so he speaks fluent English with the sexiest little accent and blunders that bewitch one fatally. I met him in Sheep Meadow three Sundays ago, and we haven't been apart for a day since, because he's life itself. Around him, everyone else becomes . . . meaningless. But then, you two must know what I . . ."

Regarding Cosgrove and me, Peter stopped, decided not to go there, and as he dived into a rhapsody on Lars Erich's looks, he again failed to notice that Fleabiscuit had poked his way out from under the couch and untied his other shoelace.

"Wait a minute," I said. "I'll be the last to discount the importance of a healthy physical appearance in gay courtship etiquette. But what's this guy's personality like?"

"If you saw the way that tiny waist draws up to those en garde shoulders," said Peter, retying his shoelace, "you wouldn't ask."

Then Dennis Savage came in, and Cosgrove served the coffee as Peter tried to bring Dennis Savage up to speed. But the Master simply held out his hand, saying, "Let's view the evidence."

"What evidence?" Peter asked.

"You must have a selection of photographs for us to consider. George Bush wouldn't. Rudy Giuliani wouldn't. You do."

Peter hesitated, blushing, then dug a few snapshots out and passed them around. An opulent silence filled the room as we examined and shared.

Cosgrove asked, "What type is this?"

"Big blond boy," I said. "With intelligent eyes. It's a seventies build with nineties details. Or no— "

"You cannot type him," said Peter. "He is beyond type."

And yet. Lars Erich Blücher belonged to *some* category; every beauty does. He was in his early thirties, with a Teutonic face at once buoyant and hard. His hair was a blend of yellow and light brown, cut short around the ears but thick on top; he sported one of those lean torsos, all the muscle packed into the arms and thighs, and, in these snaps, he was clad only in dark green Lederhosen and kitschy suspenders. The silly clothes on the astonishing person created a paradox: the grinning man, the authoritative boy. He respected the taxonomy while outwitting it, which made him impossible to categorize.

"If you knew what it is to love as I suddenly know it," said Peter as we studied the pictures, "you would flee from love."

"Why is it," asked Dennis Savage, "that everyone who finally falls in love thinks he's discovered radium or something?" A sip of coffee, then: "And when do we meet the prodigy?"

"*Gradually*," said Peter. "You know? He had me to dinner two nights ago, and I thought it would be we two and a meat loaf. Well, ha!: seared tuna, spinach almondine, silver on the table, and six of his friends. I felt very, very auditioned, my pals. *Inspected.* At least they were mainly gym bunnies. The most incredible stomach crust but very little between the ears."

"How did you know they have crust?" Cosgrove asked.

"Well, they're always pulling each other's shirts up and holding mini-contests, aren't they? If I weren't so hefty myself, they . . . well, they'd turn quite against a fellow. Now, imagine plopping Lars Erich among you intellectual cut-'em-ups all at once. What would occur?"

Cosgrove said, "I dread to think"; and Dennis Savage snapped back, "Everyone knows you dread to think."

Without shifting his seat on the couch in the slightest, Peter held them apart while continuing, "So I thought, let's not have a general scrutiny of my . . . Yes, Lars Erich wants to expand his CD collection. Weak in his classics, it seems, though like all Europeans he's horribly brisk on the rudiments. Knowing how many symphonies Brahms wrote and even the D Major or e minor part. Does the key matter, one wonders?"

Taking advantage of the altercation between Cosgrove and Dennis Savage, Fleabiscuit had slithered out from under the couch to reopen Peter's right shoelace.

"A symphony in D Major," I observed, "really is a different type of music from one in any minor key. *Boys,*" I then warned Cosgrove and Dennis Savage, who were winding down anyway. "Each type creates a different drama."

"Yes, but so *I* thought if you *alone* went with Lars Erich and me to Tower Records for an expert's buy, it would smooth my friend's way into the . . . well, coterie. I was thinking this Sunday, with lunch after."

"This guy with the gym-bunny friends and the Lederhosen," I said. "What does he do for a living?"

"He trains seeing-eye dogs."

That so startled us that even Cosgrove and Dennis Savage shared a *wow!* look. Fleabiscuit sought to celebrate the moment by opening Peter's left shoelace.

"You found some hero?" I said. "A good guy?"

"Would I fall for a ribbon clerk?" Peter countered.

"But what is his type?" Cosgrove insisted, holding up one of the Lars Erich photos.

"His type is love," said Peter, retying his shoelace.

"You've hooked up with a man in a charity service industry," said Dennis Savage, incredulously. "Why did I foresee a liaison with a soap-opera stud? A circus strongman?"

"Because you think all gay men are materialists."

"No, just you."

"I want to come to Tower, too," said Cosgrove. "This guy could model for a character in my series of porn stories. Only there is no desk for Cosgrove in this apartment. Some may ask, Does he have a theme? Yes. Yet there are those who will fear the dire mythology I unveil."

"I would need a decoder ring to even begin replying to all that," said Peter. "Except this first time it really should be just Bud. The rest of us are so . . . unpredictable?"

Followed then a bit of scurrying around. Dennis Savage went upstairs, Cosgrove set out on household errands, and Peter took a refill on coffee.

"It's okay about Tower, right?" Peter asked me, relaxing a little, as, I've noticed, he always does when a group boils down to a two-some. He doesn't like having to Hold the Stage. "I can't wait to see how you . . . But that's gay life, isn't it? Presenting your new boy friend, and your buddies hold this pep rally thing, and deep bonds are forged. Why do my shoelaces keep coming undone whenever I sit on this couch?"

"Would you please finally take that ridiculous thing off your head?"

He did, and that was even worse: he was bald.

"Christ and Judas!" I said. "*What* are you *doing?*"

"Well, it's a look. The hair'll grow back. Haven't you ever wondered how you'd seem without . . . Some men find it attractive."

"I've never wondered how I'd seem being eaten by wolves. I've never wondered how I'd seem going down on the *Andrea Doria*. And I've never wondered how I'd seem bald."

"Lars Erich digs it."

The next few seconds hosted a gently rapturous moment, as Peter contemplated his great good fortune.

"Just to . . . to talk to him," Peter finally fluted out. "His smile as he dives into little German phrases. The fierce way he pushes me onto my back, his hair falling across his forehead and his mouth frowning like a little boy's. Can I whisper to you?"

Not waiting for a reply, he leaned over and quoted, in a synthetic German accent, " 'Now it is my Peter who is being fucked, you will see that!' "

Retying my right shoelace, I set up the logistics for the Tower trip in a tone designed to conclude the visit, but Peter appeared to have one more thing on his mind.

"Yes?" I said, stopped while working my way to the door.

He rose; he didn't follow. "I need to say this, but I'm afraid you'll think I'm crazy."

"I already think you're crazy."

"It's a sort of . . . yes, a . . . a dream, you see, that I, you might say, entertain. You'll find it strange. I don't know where it came from, but it's in me somehow. I can't get away from it, shocking though that . . . But I have to tell you, or someone. It's funny how concerned one can be about appearances, then . . . suddenly . . . you aren't at all."

"Sure you are—you've just changed the appearances."

"It's about a sacrifice ceremony. Drums and feathers in a sacred grove, the Maria Montez thing. And *he's* the sacrifice, struggling in the grip of burly guards...or why use that silly vague straight term, 'burly'? No, they're lavish dynamite, as hungry to fuck him as to...You see how *frontal* it gets? As if a boy this beautiful cannot simply be loved. He must be done to on the highest level, an ultimate worship, with a sort of ...death love... like Tristan and Isolde?"

"Snuff fuck."

"Bound and crying out and looking around for help that will not come and he has never been more beautiful. He's too splendid to live, almost. It's like that exposé on talk radio, did you see that? Where the black voice said, 'I want to kill a pretty white boy.' It's all so..,. Oh, wait till Sunday."

As we walked to the door, Fleabiscuit came running out from under the couch, began to frolic, suddenly realized that he was About to Be Left Alone in Bud's Sadistic Grip, wurfed, and raced into the bedroom to hide.

"Thank you for listening to me," Peter said. Then, impulsively, he gave me our first hug.

"Now, that's gay life," I told him as I opened the door. "Someone is willing to hear what you need to say."

IT IS WORTH REMARKING on Lars Erich's unique sophistication of looks, because we have been graduated from a time when everyone in gay was either a type or invisible. Nowadays, most guys are not types; and the whole typing system has grown so complex it's meaningless.

It was so simple before, in the early days of Stonewall. Fantasy cartoonists proclaimed the styles: on the one hand Tom of Finland's dangerous giants, and on the other Toby's plunderable goslings. I kept wondering whether these artists were tapping into something universal or were outlining a vision dear only to them-

selves. But the porn stars were not kids: hairy-chested Richard
Locke, one of the first gays to take a tattoo (a butterfly on the
right thigh); an eerily handsome galoot named Paul something
who Colted under the billing of Ledermeister; and an angel-faced
hoodlum named Jimmy Hughes who won *The Advocate*'s Groovy
Guy contest and was almost immediately after convicted of multiple counts of sexual assault upon women he supposedly ab-
ducted from supermarket parking lots.

So you could not be a kid, it seemed. You could not even be
you. You had to be big, rough-hewn, surprising. Bright and
funny—the essence of urban gay—was unhot. But what was hot?
Abducting women from supermarket parking lots?

"I hate this," Dennis Savage would wail, coming back from the
gym in his early days there. "It is so sheerly punishment." Still, his
mesomorph structure took on the extra flash easily, and he so enjoyed the results that he upped his program. Then, too, the
gym—Profile for Men, just down Second Avenue from our
building—was notoriously cruisy. Orgies were known to break
out in the steam room.

One day, as a shirtless Dennis Savage flexed and paraded
around in his apartment with a sinful grin, I asked, "Are gays having so much sex simply because it's pleasurable? Or is it part of a
psychological transaction?"

"You have to teach a guy to like himself," said Carlo, coming
out of the kitchen munching an apple.

"How do you do that?"

Carlo thought it over while examining Dennis Savage's waist-
to-shoulders ratio. "You will show him solutions to his problems,"
Carlo began. "Always side with him against the world.... Now
you want to work the delts extra-heavy, my friend. Give yourself
the wing look. Extra wide at the top is best. And not so much
arms now."

"But they notice those first," Dennis Savage protested, moving to the mirror to see for himself what Stonewall had made of Jane Austen's Eligible Young Man: the hunk.

"Main thing they see is the shape of the torso," said Carlo, coming up behind Dennis Savage to demonstrate like an academic at a chart, pointing, underlining, savoring. "You want this long V above all. Big chest for those fine buttons to ride on. They will not just be there—they will stand out."

From across the room, I said, "To just be there is not permitted in gay life."

"You will keep on heavy in the legs," Carlo went on. "Big thighs are a lovely sight to see."

"They only show in summer," Dennis Savage complained, but gently now, going under Carlo's spell as he touched and murmured.

"Summer's when most tricking occurs, I do believe," Carlo told him. "I want to fill my summertime with lively strangers."

"What about the haircut?"

"Short's best on you, so that's just right."

"What does all this have to do with teaching some guy to like himself?" I asked, coming over to them as Carlo ditched the apple core in an ashtray and started working from behind on Dennis Savage's shoulders, enjoying the feel of them while Dennis Savage relaxed and went with it. "Imagine that guy heading for the Eagle tonight, dreaming of . . . of being loved like that. He's planning on something other than a hot date, isn't he?"

"How would you truly plan on something other?" asked Carlo, clearly amused at the way Dennis Savage responded to the massage. He even sighed.

"He wants a personality he can . . . something to respond to that responds to him."

"Oh please, do I have to be judged on my personality, too?"

said Dennis Savage. "Isn't the looks competition hard enough? I've got to be fabulous company? When does it end?"

"Hush, now," Carlo told him, rubbing Dennis Savage's tummy and growling sex telegrams into his ear. Dennis Savage's eyes were closed, and he mooed a bit as Carlo opened his pants. As I've said, fashion decreed in that time that no one hot wear under-clothes, and Dennis Savage's cock came surging out. It was call of the wild in your living room, going naked in the city. Dennis Savage's is an exploratory and importunate cock, also a very long and fat one ringed with veins. Or, as Carlo said, reaching around to feel and admire, "A piece like so will truly taste, and that's what I call a man."

I CALL A MAN anything in pants, but you see whither this view was tending: to weight, to power. Gays wanted to co-opt the authority claimed by heteros as the natural order. *They* said, The Fathers shall rule; *we* said, The sons shall be their own Fathers. Thus, we remade ourselves in our own God's image.

Then created we the **Clone**, unassailably hot. Dark-haired, preferably tall, well-built though not necessarily double-pumped, and bearing the masculine warranty of thirty-five or so, the Clone was early Stonewall's essential erotic figure, concocted (for few took his form naturally) to incorporate the manly arts. That is: few words, slow motion, big hot. What a paragon to live up to! Moreover, there remained the irony that gay culture reveled in what I call "the Knowledge"—basically, all that Broadway, old Hollywood, and opera, with glitzy trivia thrown in—yet wanted the Clone innocent of it.

This was a bequest of pre-Stonewall, the world of johns and hustlers. Sex occurred between a piece of trade and a piece of fruit; there were no "gay men." By the understanding of the age, the very idea was an oxymoron. Thus, when we decided to cease being fruit, we tried to turn into trade.

Of course, trade screwed women, whereas Clones didn't even know any. Clone was a look: the build, the clothes, the hair. If a mustache was de rigueur, beards were the bonne bouche. Hair was virile. Ironically, today smooth skin is phallic.

The smooth **Blond Boy** was in physical style the Clone's opposite, partly because blonds are expected to be young, not to mention dumb. It's a compliment, in a way: it expresses the wish that blonds *were* stupid, because if intelligence is complicated, then stupid is vacant and therefore directly connected to its appetites. Calling blonds dumb is no more than the verbalization of the desire for someone whose sexual expression is limitlessly efficient.

While I'm at it, the third of the classic Stonewall types is **Trash,** the stupid thing combined with a class thing. Trash not only lacked the Knowledge but didn't know how to behave—not just at a dinner party: at a urinal. The trashy man laughed at things that weren't funny, or made disturbing confessions. Gordon Fay, a fixture at the Eagle's half-price-beer-for-shirtless-guys nights, looked like many another raggedly pretty, awesomely chiseled boy. But Gordon, after hours, would share with you his fantasy of visiting Central Park some midnight to seek out the sleeping homeless and "lop off a few heads."

Trash made porn, spent nights in jail, and held down dimwit jobs. And *their* opposite was the **Natural.** This type was totally middle-class, but at any rate he was cute. The least "created" of Stonewall's personalities, the Natural wore clothes, not an identity kit. For some reason, the Natural was always younger than you were, though he had to make certain adjustments when he faced his first aging crisis, usually at twenty-four. I remember running into Tadhe O'Connor for the first time after several months to find him swollen with build, a graduate from sweetheart to red-hot muscleboy. "I was turning twenty-seven," Tadhe explained, "and I figured I needed an angle."

This emphasis on appearance has led some—in what the social and art critic Robert Hughes has termed our "culture of complaint"—to call love of beauty "divisive." This is akin to calling it "divisive" to favor Debussy over rap. It's called taste. The smart, the swift, the determined will always get ahead: and the beautiful as well. Outstanding figures are not divisive but unifying, showing us what to aspire to.

So the **Bodybuilder** could be thought of as the democratic invention of the gay world, for virtually anyone can join the corps if he works at it. A very few people are handed everything at birth; the rest of us have to bargain with devils.

The Bodybuilder may not be cute, for the eroticization of physique makes face something that almost doesn't matter. True—as Peter Keene once told me—"face never doesn't matter." He meant in gay life; but it never doesn't matter, period.

"No, but among *us,* my disputatious friend," he would characteristically go on, and indeed did so: "the handsome thing ensnares and exhilarates. One gets so terribly worried."

We're back in the present, as he and I aimlessly nosed around the classical section of the downtown Tower Records, waiting for Lars Erich Blücher.

"Worried?" I said.

Eyeing the entrance doors, Peter said, "Well, who can know how mutual the attraction is? Who loves more? Who's just asking you for a tango?"

I am the simplifier. I said, "Couldn't you go into one of those ... they used to be called 'modern' relationships?"

"We'll have to. A moment of monogamy would crowd Lars Erich. He's so purely what he is, it's scary. No, wait, I mustn't lose my mind in the classical department. . . . Yes, I'll consider buying a CD of . . . Look, there's a composer named Sauguet. And *is* he? So gay? Because Lars Erich changes one's mind about what gay is. I hope you're ready for that."

"He just walked in," I said.

Okay. Dress: snug but not strangling T over khaki shorts, tiny light gray socks in sneakers.

Eyes: purple, it turned out—they had read as merely dark in his photographs. It's a color I'd never before seen live.

Greeting: "Kommt ein schlanker Bursch gegangen!": Here comes a cutie!

That he was, smiling and confident; and why hadn't Peter mentioned that Lars Erich was six foot five?

"Yes, you are Bud," he said, almost pointing at me. "Peter is there," he added, gently applying pressure from his thumb and forefinger upon the nape of Peter's neck. "And I am wondering which is my purchase of CDs at last. These will educate me and fascinate many friends. We should start by Mozart? French orientalia? But what is trendy now? What is Technicolor?"

"You are," I said.

Peter made the official introduction and Lars Erich treated me to that horribly squeezing handshake that Europeans favor. As he smiled at me, his eyes seemed to lose some color and glow a bit— probably, I thought, an effect of the store's lighting facilities.

"It is so interesting," Lars Erich said, quietly, very nearly to himself. "Peter's friends."

"Let me go," I told him, because his handshake was lasting as long as *Siegfried.*

"You will excuse me," he said apologetically. I'm not attempting to duplicate his accent, but contrary to what Peter had said, it was heavy, though Lars Erich's English came flowing forth without a pause. "I am very grateful that you assist in this collection of music for the home."

We talked about that for a bit—what repertory he liked, son-ics and price, and so on. All the while, I watched them together—the way Lars Erich kept taking hold of Peter as if claiming him and the way Peter loved it but tried not to show it. The way Lars Erich carefully waited for my sentences to end before ignoring them in pursuit of some tack of his own. The way he flirted, touching your forearm as if for social corroboration but then lingering there, feeling you. Then he'd withdraw his hand and I do believe his eyes *would* brighten. And he'd stand in such a way that his biceps would expand. You couldn't not look.

"Do you like the big romantic stuff?" I asked. "Piano concertos with cascades of melody? Or the slashing modernists? Think of it as a choice between doing it smooth and doing it rough."

"Ja, that is a nifty American joke," said Lars Erich, his attention distracted by a dark-haired Chelsea Boy in a striped vest over a bare torso, his jeans pulled up to emphasize the genitals. "Na, prima Bursche," Lars Erich whispered. "Mein Arsch braucht dein Fick": Wow, hot guy, you want to fuck me?

I was shocked, and Lars Erich noticed. "You speak German?" he asked, in a neutral tone.

"Ein wenig": a little.

He glanced at Peter, then at me, his eyes now gone dark—not menacing or anything like that; they had simply changed color again, to a kind of red-blue.

"Is something wrong?" I asked.

Taking a final look at the Chelsea Boy, who was rummaging through the Bach CDs, Lars Erich started over again: "Now I choose the most super opera singer of all," he cried energetically. "Because that is what you will play at the dinner party, yes? And this is who?"

"Maria Callas."

"In *Fidelio,* I am hoping, Beethoven's holy work, ideal for the festival. I have it now, but not such a fine performance."

"Callas never recorded it, but she does have a *Parsifal.*"

"You think all Germans like Wagner?" he countered, pausing as a kindly, bearded nerd approached to say, "Wayne Fischer died."

"Oh no," I said.

He nodded. "It was on the news this morning." Turning to move on, he added, "Get out your red ribbons."

"Do you know that man?" Peter asked me, bewildered.

"He's probably just a well-meaning town-crier type."

"Who is dead?" asked Lars Erich.

"Wayne Fischer was the local TV news channel's AIDS poster boy," I explained. "They were running a series on his battle with the disease, and now—"

"Ja, I regard this. He is a whiner, always worrying and easily conquered. They make a mistake to show this man as a symbol."

"All AIDS victims are equal," I said.

"Yes, it is sad how it happens to each person. But for such a series on television, it is better the heroic figure to show, where otherlanders then see that gay men are worthy of admiration. It is never good for a cause that—" He stopped to touch a hand to his ear, then looked up. "There is a water leak in Tower Records?"

"Let's check out the Callas section," Peter suggested. Then he, too, felt a watery discharge on his head. I turned just in time to see a shape dart out of sight at the end of the aisle leading to the budget discs—but Peter grabbed my hand and started pulling me along after Lars Erich, who was heading in the wrong direction. I took out a short list I had made of some of the essential opera sets—the Georges Thill–Ninon Vallin *Werther,* the Joan Sutherland–Janet Baket *Rodelinda* in English, the 1962 La Scala *Huguenots,* and so on—and handed it to Peter and Lars Erich while aiming them at the opera section. I then went off after Cosgrove and his water gun. Of *course* he had decided to come along, against orders; have I learned nothing yet?

However. Not only did he elude me, but when I was all the way over in the C composers he reappeared, sashaying past Peter and Lars Erich wearing a joke-shop big-nose-and-mustache-with-eyeglasses disguise and, it at first seemed, the world's deepest set of abs, bubbling up under his shirt like lava. At second glance, the abs looked more like half an egg box taped onto his stomach, bottom side out. As I started over, Cosgrove scurried away and disappeared into the Historical section.

When I rejoined Peter and Lars Erich, the latter told me, "In Europe, they are always saying how the first thing to know about the States is that the people are eccentric."

"Especially that people," said Peter.

"Is he a crazy stranger, too?" Lars Erich asked.

I quickly rerouted the conversation to the business at hand, but the talk kept sliding into the personal. It was as though Lars Erich could approach a topic only through his opinion of how people function. He doesn't believe in History: he believes in Napoléon, Stalin, Hitler, the terrible consequences of the particular man in the place at the time. As I, too, see the world this way, I was immediately drawn to him.

He was certainly easy to advise in the buying of CDs. "No," he said to all my questions about his requirements. "You choose it, I buy it."

Handing him a copy of the Cetra *Don Carlos,* I was reassured to observe that Cosgrove had parked himself at one of the listening stations, where customers sample the latest issues through headphones. He can become quite engrossed, and has been known to spend more time thus than the employees do behind the counter.

"What about *Scheherazade?*" Peter asked. "Shouldn't he have that?"

"What is music to fuck to?" Lars Erich put in, not caring who overheard. "They tell me Ravel's *Bolero,* but that is such cliché."

"Isn't there something called 'The Sabre Dance'?" asked smirking Peter.

"That's too short," I said, "unless you're fifteen years old."

Peter went off to rummage through the *Scheherazades,* and Lars Erich, watching him go, said, "He is so beautiful. The skin and taste of him, it is all so correct for me. But he is not strong inside. A man should not worry what others criticize. I am not worried that you review me, that you approve of our friendship."

His tone was even, unchallenging. Yet there was something lavish in the once again darkened eyes, rigid and pugnacious, defying disapproval on the chance that there should be any.

He went on, "I know my living style is not what some respect. Is it all jealousy? There is always resentment of the extraordinary. Every day, I see in the mirror how I am a little bigger, a little more beautiful in the curves and tight fit. It is immodest? But it is true. You have been not once failing to look at my body this whole time. You think I do not see? My body sees. I hear walking behind me on the street, this looking. In the States, you work so hard on the parades and the laws of protection. But what is the real passion? What can we ask for, all of us? It is das Faustrecht zur Freiheit, you know this term?"

It's untranslatable, literally "Fistright to Freedom" but essentially meaning "If you have the power to overwhelm your enemies, you deserve to."

"What happened," I said, "to You are very grateful that I assist in this collection of—"

"Ja, ja, I am too abrupt." His eyes searched for Peter, still hunting through the Rimsky-Korsakof bins. "It is what I mean, but I should discover not such a sharp way to express it. Oh, here is another American doing the impossible."

It was Cosgrove with a paper bag over his head, complete with not only eye and mouth holes but ear hinges.

"It is maybe your buddy, ja? Peter has warned me."

"Do you get air sickness up there?" the bag asked Lars Erich.

Lars Erich took the bag off Cosgrove, saying, "Now see what a nice boy comes through, who wants to tease us with an American surprise."

"How about this one?" asked Peter, coming up to show us the old von Matačić *Scheherazade*.

"That is not a competitive performance," said Cosgrove. "The classics are Sir Thomas Beecham and Fritz Reiner, acceptable modern readings are Bernstein and von Karajan, and the greatest of all is the Russian Svyetlanof with the USSR Symphony Orchestra."

"You will please find me that one," said Lars Erich, "and one good Bartók, also the postwar Frenchman who sounds like clouds parting over the edge of the world."

"Messiaen," said Cosgrove, more or less. Even the French find that name tough to pronounce.

"And then we will already have lunch."

"Can we go to the green-pea place?" Cosgrove asked me as he marched off to fetch Lars Erich's CDs.

"This will be what?" Lars Erich asked me.

"We generally go there after, because they have the best split-pea soup in the city. It's a dive, but it's quite close by."

"We go there," Lars Erich decided.

There was silence then, as Lars Erich reviewed his opera boxes and Peter just drank him in. Isn't he beautiful?, Peter was, I believe, thinking. Wouldn't you give up anything to have that on a platter? Isn't he the prototype?

Yes, no, and *arguably* are the answers. Meanwhile, I was thinking that more striking than Lars Erich's body-god looks was the fact that he had a body-god personality to match: expansive, captivating, bossy. This is real danger. A beauty with nothing to offer but physical charm is no more than a date; a beauty who is *personally* gifted will have you risking your self-esteem trying to have impact on him.

Cosgrove reported back, Lars Erich made his acquisition, and we fought our way through Tower's irritatingly overcrowded ground floor into that strange neighborhood outside. This is lower Broadway, bordered by commercial establishments of no importance yet thronged every day of the week, especially by the young and built. One thinks of the Beach Parade out at the Pines: a show. Walking beside the bursting Peter and Lars Erich and the youthfully trim Cosgrove (who had that paper-bag head back on), I felt like the actor hired to supply jests in a college musical while everyone else in the cast has romances, models hot styles, and introduces the New Dance Sensation.

What a relief to duck into the green-pea place and wrestle with those gigantic enplasticked menus.

I launched the scene. "Peter says you train seeing-eye dogs," I told Lars Erich.

"You must say 'guide dogs.' The 'Seeing Eye' is a certain brand. A copyright, one will tell you."

"How did you get started on such a . . . well—"

"Back in Germany, when I am growing up, my family are raising puppies which will be educated as guides. You know, they cannot be trained so young. They are a year first, and *then* trained. So we raise many, mostly shepherds, a few white Labs. Always, it is so sad when they leave, for it is necessary to surround them with love, to strengthen them for training. Without love, a puppy has nothing to live for, and then how is there the incentive for train-

ing? But we have put in the love, and then they go from us? It was
a regular day in our lives, with my little brother and sister weeping and clinging. They are saying, 'Can we just keep this one?'
Once, Harry hid puppy Törless' toys, he is thinking that without
the toys they wouldn't haul the dog away. But they did."

"I have a puppy," said Cosgrove, still in the paper-bag head,
"and his trick is to untie shoelaces."

"Yes, it is so funny, how a little dog will understand all his
rules but still can make mischief in a moment. As when everyone
is asking, 'Where is puppy Hanno?,' and then he pops up with all
the family's missing socks in his mouth. Or when my brother and
sister are running through the neighborhood to find puppy As-
terix, and we all come back tearful as if he must be lost forever.
But he is in the kitchen, wagging his tail. And two weeks later,
they take him away, and he cries so that Harry cries, too, and we
all three break apart with crying, because he thinks we let him go
without caring.... I will stop here."

His eyes were wet.

The waiter was hovering, and Lars Erich brisked us out of the
sad moment with "Now we must order our American platters,
where the food comes like the Grand Gardens of Babylon."

We ordered, did a little number on this and that, and then, at
my guidance, returned to Lars Erich's profession.

"Well," he admitted, "it is so strange that examples of each
breed will look alike, but each subject has a different personality.
We call it 'the subject,' the dog we are training. You may think it
is always a male, but both genders will be found useful. And you
know what is so odd, that these heroic dogs are given to people
who so often do not appreciate them or will even mistreat them.
This is a great secret, of course. One of those many things that
one is forbidden to say in America."

His arms bent and swelled as he said this, and Peter helplessly grabbed one to feel. It's a little annoying: don't they get enough at home?

"Do the dogs have any idea of their heroic role?" I asked. "Do they ever wish, do you think, that they were the merest household pets, without responsibility?"

"A dog does not know choices. In Alaska, the sled dog does not wonder, Why am I not pampered Lassie of the movies? A dog knows only who feeds him and what the rules are to be still more fed then. It is mankind only that conceives of possibilities, of changing one's position. It is why the gym, so popular now even in Europe."

"When you spoke before of the resentment of the extraordinary," I said, "that really caught me. Because I think homophobia is based on that—or maybe more a fear of the unconventional. That is, not counting the Religion Nazis, who turn Christianity into a hating machine. But the average homophobe simply doesn't like *anything* he isn't used to."

"They are afraid of too much everything in the world," said Lars Erich, with a shrug. "Just a few things they can understand—house, food, jobs, vacations. But ideas"—here he held up a warning finger very close to me, leaning in, flirting and teaching—"are mysterious. Mystery is troubling. They want to kill what troubles them, ja?"

Peter interrupted by asking Cosgrove, "How are you going to eat with that paper bag on?"

"By magic," Cosgrove darkly replied, though in the event he simply removed it.

"So a folk," Lars Erich went on, "that lives entirely in its own way is very troubling, very to be killed. Being gay is not just different language, religion, king. It is different in every way."

"Please," said Peter, "enough Citizenship 101."

"Instead, let's name our favorite actors," said Cosgrove. "Mine is Andrea Thompson, Jill on *NYPD Blue.*"

Lars Erich smiled. "Mine is Aiden Shaw," he said. "Handsome like a wonderful schoolteacher who is also leading the hiking club on forest trips. Then he is stripped in a movie and it is a very mysterious idea."

MUCH LATER, BACK UPTOWN, Cosgrove asked me, "So what type is the German guy?"

That was hard to say now, for despite the gay emphasis on looks, personality overwhelms all calculations, and Lars Erich's personality—his restless intelligence in particular—seemed bigger even than his looks. I've known smart hunks, humorous hunks, surpassingly talented hunks, brilliant hunks, and even a hunk with such finely nuanced democratic principles that he'd give a mercy fuck to anyone who asked. But not till Lars Erich had I met a hunk so stimulating in his worldview that he made me reconsider my beliefs.

"How can I write porn," Cosgrove grumped, "if I don't know what anyone is?"

"Well, *you* describe him."

"He's a big young guy. He's a cute authority figure. He's like your minister but then he takes you to the prom for your first secret kiss. What kind is that?"

"It's *type,* not kind. And what type he is: I don't know."

"Last week, when you were being extra reproachful of Cosgrove who forgot to pick up the laundry, you said you know everything."

God, am I turning into a parent?

"Anyway," Cosgrove went on as he tended another batch of

pretzels, "get ready for more types. Because now J. said he would bring his roommate to dinner this Thursday."

"Vince Choclo? You've got to be kidding!"

"And Cosgrove is not unhappy to meet him after all these tales we've heard. I may be seen taking notes."

"Wait a minute," I said. "Is he ready for us?"

"J. thinks their relationship will soon reach critical mass. They're up to the massage stage."

I was hunting for the big orange household scissors, which are *supposed* to be in the flatware drawer but finally turned up inside the carriage of the pasta machine.

"How would you feel if I canceled this dinner?" I asked.

"You *can't*! I have to meet Vince Choclo for myself!"

"Why?" I said, going to my desk to wrap Dennis Savage's birthday present, a cashmere sweater he had fallen in love with in Bloomingdale's and had alluded to perhaps 387 times in the last four days. Cosgrove, having coated his pretzels with honey and salt and laid them in the oven, followed me, wiping his hands on a dish towel.

"I need to see," he told me quietly, "what J. wanted instead of Dennis Savage."

I was wrestling with the gift wrap, an insufferably thin and easily crinkled paper in a baby motif.* "You mean," I said, "you need to see what J. wanted instead of us."

And *that* brings us to a final type, marginal yet timelessly essential to the gay world: what I call the **60–40.** You won't find this genre of man hanging around Splash, but he might have turned

---

*I found a pile of this stuff remaindered at ten cents a roll in 1983 and bought twenty-five rolls. We've got three rolls left as I write. (We would have had six rolls, except Cosgrove used a few to go out as a baby mummy two Halloweens ago; the costume took two hours to build and fell apart before Cosgrove had reached the first traffic light.)

up in a bathhouse in the old days, on a night when his wife had taken the kids for an overnight to visit her mother.

The 60–40 is apparently straight, actually. (For an even truer statement, switch the adverbs.) Sixty percent of him is attracted to women, enough to make a marriage on and, if he is a willing stooge of homophobes, stick with it. However, 40 percent of him seeks carnal knowledge of men, and that is a hefty fraction of one-self to control. The healthier 60–40s find outlets on the sly and may even leave the marriage; the more damaged 60–40s go through life insane with frustration at all the Hot Guys down-loaded into the American consciousness by advertising, movies, and real life, hating what they were born to be and, sometimes, heading "family preservation" groups for the Religion Nazi com-munity.

Generally, 60–40s never enter gay life in any true sense. You may meet a few describing themselves as "bisexuals." But most 60–40s don't describe themselves at all. Like the freedom-fearing people whom Lars Erich cited, they feel perilously sub-merged in choices. The true 60–40 is a shadow figure, one piece of him maintaining a profile existence as a round-the-clock het-ero and the other piece frantically darting in and out of a fan-tastic existence: ours. A single honest moment and he is destroyed.

But now I'm going to have to give Vince credit—he was hon-est to a fault at our dinner. True, if he was a 60–40, he concen-trated on his 60 side, rapping endlessly about women, whom he treated as a genre divided into three categories. *Gash*, his favorite, loved sex and asked for no more than a good lay. *Princesses*, whom he resented, would put out only after "dinner and a show." *Brides*, who mystified him, did not have sex at all, at least not with Vince.

"I'm just some mutt to them," Vince told us, sitting on our

couch, congratulating us for having Beck's Dark beer and thanking Cosgrove for giving it to him in a glass, looking around at the stuff on the walls as if he'd never seen *Wizard of Oz* frame enlargements or a *Billion Dollar Baby* poster before.

He was very tall, with long, shaggy brown hair and the heavy, loose construction of a thirtysomething who doesn't consciously take care of himself but spends his days delivering those great bulbs of water-cooler water and picking up the empties. I'd call him ordinary but for a saving grace: his eyes grew extra warm and wrinkly when he smiled.

J. walked in a bit later, and I stopped him at the door with a whisper: "Just give me the ground rules here—are we supposed to be gay?"

"Make your choice," he said, brushing past me.

Vince looked up gladly as J. approached. "Your friends are treating me real nice."

"They can show a cruel side," said J., joining Vince on the couch. "Yet I love them as brothers."

"Friends, sure," said Vince. "Can't fuck with them, can't fuck without them. Like my buddy Red Backhaus. Him and me, we're special-close, all the way back to second grade. Screwed our first gash together, side by side. Put him up when some bitch threw him out after hours. He'd do anything for me, Red. But there's always this, like, contest, when he disagrees with what I say and betting me a fast ten I'm wrong. Then he tries to forget to pay. But I love his soul."

"Does he have red hair?" Cosgrove asked.

Thinking it over, Vince said, " 'S'more brown. He doesn't take to the color, keeps it short. And his body is all freckles, which also he don't take to. But chicks'll notice colors, and that can be useful."

J.'s failure to explain the reason for this visit worried me. Were

Cosgrove and I supposed to represent the normality of gay life, thus to correct Vince's preconceptions and advance his seduction by J.? Yet J. had, I learned, told Vince nothing of us save that we're all longtime friends. Vince even asked Cosgrove where he lived.

"Right here" was the answer.

Vince nodded. "So you're like me and J. here."

"You aren't yet," said Cosgrove.

"Yeah, now, with my real good buddy Red Backhaus, we both know the same things, so there's no surprises. Huh—'less Red shows up with some slick new babe and I steal her away." Chuckling here. "He'll bet on it, the girlfriend tango we have. He'll lose. But he could steal gash from me anytime he wanted to. He's a five-alarm guy, Red. A beautiful, beautiful guy to know about."

Fleabiscuit's snout came ever so slowly out from under the couch, just to the right of Vince's shoe.

"I told Red he should establish some Polaroids of himself, show his charms. Not to no princess, you know, who would just pretend to be horrified, like she's been taught to show. But gash love to know what's in store. Now, what are *you* up to, short stuff?" he suddenly asked, swooping down to pick up Fleabiscuit. "Where'd this little flyboy come from?"

Fleabiscuit, content in Vince's grasp, closed his eyes and went limp.

"That's right, now," said Vince, setting the puppy to rest on his lap. "Anyhowsle, though, I took a few shots of ol' Red to show him how it goes. Had him pose in just a pair of dress pants I lent him, which gives it class. We opened them up so to show off his racy boner and he looked real good. But I don't expect that Red takes those pictures out at the right moment. Red'll get confused or drunk. He prefers to do a triple, where two ol' friends share the gash and everybody's happy."

Fleabiscuit awoke, shook himself, and jumped back down under the couch.

"Now, with J. here," Vince went on, his eyes winningly wrinkling, "it's always a surprise. He made me get a VCR and he's teaching me all about the movies. 'S'funny, with friends, 'cause you don't want a buddy like Red too smart or he'll go all boss on you. But I like J. being smart, you know. He showed me this one attraction I would never have known was okay didn't J. explain it to me. It looked stupid, but J. says it's *supposed* to, so then you can enjoy it. Two old bags going at each other, greasy fat guy and all." He thought for a moment. "*See What Happened to Lady June.*"

"*Lady Jane,*" said J.

"*Baby Jane,*" said Cosgrove.

"Yeah. Movie's older'n I am, could almost be a silent. You know, where all the actors was posing while passing fifi remarks and it don't seem real. Like, we sure could use Harrison Ford here. But J. says it's this whole world of entertainment I could get into, with strange music and jokes, and it gives you a new life."

" 'You will be assimilated,' " said Cosgrove, quoting *Star Trek* in hollow tones. " 'Resistance is futile.' "

"You haven't said much, mister," Vince told me.

"Cosgrove went to special trouble over this dinner," I replied as the little chef returned to the kitchen. "He's trying out some first-time recipes of great complexity."

"Yeah? I don't cook myself, except for you heat a can of tuna and stir it into spaghetti. Some butter, grated cheese. Company coming, you can sprinkle those French's fried onions over the top, it's fancy. Right, J.?"

"Vince and I are pals," said J., "so what he says, goes."

"Here's the appetizer," Cosgrove announced, bringing in a platter. "I call it"—he had to concentrate to get the sounds out smoothly—"*biscuit assaisoné.*"

"Say, little pretzels!" said Vince. "Fresh and hot, too, like you can't get on the street."

I was watching J., wondering if he'd make a disparaging comment. He seemed about to, but then he simply took his pretzel and ate it.

He'd seen me watching him, too. He didn't care. He's busy retailoring Vince as a suitor, stooge, and meal ticket. Why should J. worry what judgments I draw?

Was all that Little Kiwi–Dennis Savage love affair a fraud? No, of course not. But J. deeply resented having to work— especially after Cosgrove moved in with me with only the family chores to do. Straights want laws, constrictions, social pressures. Gays want freedom. J. may well be the gayest of all. He yearns for irresponsibility. (That's a joke, my brothers.)

I was riding my train of thought with such concentration that I didn't realize that I had reached a conclusive stop and opened my mouth at the same time:

"You're a little gold digger," I blurted out.

J. coolly considered me. Vince was once more fondling Fleabiscuit. Cosgrove was back in the kitchen.

Silence.

Finally, Cosgrove came out with his risotto of greens and sea scallops, cooked to a T. As he and I had made sure that Vince's glass was never left empty, the guest of honor was soon buzzed, which led him to confide in us his dating secrets. These included how to tell gash from brides; how to speed a princess; and how all women want to be fucked by their fathers.

"Not their main and true father," he added. "The husband of their mother. But someone *like* that, with the power to love them

or not when they were, like, four years old. That totally huge guy
who can give or take *everything* from them, you know? And they
don't care what he looks like. He's got the tall and the making
rules and the heavy dark thing to him. That's daddy to them, and
they need daddy so."

Cosgrove distributed the plates, his face blank.

"No, sure, they don't admit to it." He laughed. "Start with
whispering in their ear, the puppy kissing, the daddy talking. My
pal Red, he always backs off at the time. He don't have the script.
But it's not poetry, it's anything, like. Just so you're gentle, 'cause
they'll do anything to get that from daddy. Daddy love runs the
world, you know."

"Does anyone like the food?" Cosgrove asked, patiently.

"Delicious," said J.

"Yeah, it's so . . . Then you work them to the bed, always daddy
and his girl, using how bigger you are to sweeten them along. No
forcing, but always control. They love it so like that, give you anything you want."

My brother Jim has this quality: a talking blueprint for the seduction of females. To such men as Vince and Jim, a date is successful when a woman is cajoled, persuaded, lured into sex; a date
who shows up wanting it takes all the fun out of it, robs them of
their male magic. But then, given the byzantine etiquette of het-
erosexual courtship, what woman ever shows up wanting it? This
is one reason why gay romance is easier to manage than straight.
When a gay date shows up, he's counting on having sex. It's all
over but the shouting.

"Vince," said J., "tell them about the flip."

Smiling, Vince set aside his empty plate and took a sip of
beer. "Oh yeah," he said. "The flip, huh?" More chuckling. "See,
even prime gash don't really want to give it up to you, not right
up front. They got to be wiggled into it, somehow, kind of

daddied-up. Hands all over 'em when you're standing behind, nudging them with your little wonder. Steamy liplock, which if you do it right is a form of fucking. But all with the greatest respect. They could be the cheapest ho in Clancy's, you treat 'em like a royal queen. Look 'em over with, like, you can't believe this loveliness. It's an honor, you know? Say, 'Baby, let me flip you.' Say, 'You got the flops, I feel it in your skin. Let me give you a look-see.' "

"Would anyone like more lemon squeeze on their fish?" asked Cosgrove.

"The look-see, well, that's your plain old eat-'em-out, which also gets you to the bed, where grease and condoms are displayed." Another sip of beer. "That prepares the romantic mood, so you got to remember to lay them out in advance. You know what I mean?"

He was looking at me, and I nodded. "In the theatre," I said, "they call that a 'pre-set.' "

"They do that live in a theatre somewhere? Fuck shows?"

"Vince," J. put in, "tell them about Shona."

Cosgrove asked, "Vince, would you like seconds?" And Vince, without missing a measure, extended his plate to be taken off and refilled.

"Shona lady?" Vince went on, nodding rhetorically. "*Loves* the flip, but she also loves pretending she don't got the flops. I say, 'You got the flops, sweet love,' and she's like, 'Not yet, taste a bit more.' " He grinned again. "You got to eat her out so total it's like—"

"*Vince!*" Cosgrove yelled from the kitchen.

Vince paused.

Cosgrove appeared at the kitchen doorway. "Do you like what I made or not?"

"Sure, I like it. What for did you cry out at me?"

Cosgrove said nothing and did not move.

"It's like when ol' Red Backhaus gets perturbed all a sudden, and what'd I do? I apologize, just the same."

"Go on, Vince," J. urged him. "Shona gets eaten."

"Well, yeah, she does. She can play you just as you play her, you know. She's rising to it, getting set for daddy time, and she's all flopped up and so hungry she's just swinging away on your dick. Oh, thank you, my man." This to Cosgrove, for his food. "And I always start 'em eyes down, but the great moment is when you flip 'em for the ice-cream treat of eye contact big-time. If you fix their legs right, you can kiss 'em while fucking, which is so racy, you know? That is what I call the flip, a noble thing between man and woman, and if it wasn't for marriage fucking up the chicks' heads, we would all have a beautiful time."

I had noticed that Vince used certain adjectives—all positive ones, like "wonderful," "lovely," and "beautiful"—as if making love with them. They came out slow and breathless, with his melting-eyes smile, and I could see why women might like him. He was crude with us, but to a working-class female, used to the strenuous style of the neighborhood guys, Vince might come off as flatteringly extrasensory, with his absurd language of love and his father fantasy. My brother Jim was no different in the long run: and Jim made out like a bandit.

I didn't give J. the slightest chance of restructuring Vince's sex life with a homosexual episode. I know the sound a hetero makes when trying to intellectualize his grunting, and Vince, for my money, was straight. Yes, there was all that suspiciously fond stuff about Red Backhaus. But remember the two construction workers I spoke of in the Introduction? That's testosterone jostling, loving but not *flesh*-loving. The pair could fuck and it still wouldn't be gay. They could even kiss. But let one comment on the quality of the other's skin tone and you have 60–40 crossover.

After our Vince-meeting dinner came cappuccino, from our own cappuccino maker, another of Cosgrove's prides.* He also treated us to his prize car-chase and talk-show fight clips, which Vince particularly responded to. I risked a few fifi remarks. Fleabiscuit came out a few times to romp and hide. We got a high on, especially Vince, who was chain-guzzling his beer. With me at the piano, J. and Cosgrove reprised their old cabaret act, improvisationally updating their version of "Let's Call the Whole Thing Off" with

> *You say 'Caucăsus,' and I say "Caucāsus';*
> *You like the Blur boys, but I like Oasis.*

I thought that was brilliant, and so did Vince, who had no idea what the Caucasus, Blur, or Oasis might be. J. and Cosgrove, so long divided, embraced and kissed; Vince looked on unmoved. Not pretending it didn't exist: uninterested in it. So what did all this mean?

J. left with Vince. At the door, Vince told Cosgrove and me, "You guys should be in show business."

And Cosgrove said, "We are."

---

*Cosgrove really has become the kitchen master. At any given moment, the fridge disgorges tuna salad, shrimp cocktail portions in individual plastic containers with tiny appointments of cocktail sauce and lemon wedge on lettuce doilies, chicken drumsticks marinated in fruit preserve and broiled to extra-well-done perfection, and miniature salmon–cream cheese sandwiches on pumpernickel. I have to hand over my Chase Visa Rewards checks, which Cosgrove, aided by the usual "someone I know," turns into his favorite thing, Tower Records gift certificates; but at least I no longer have to go out hunting for food every day like a lion in the jungle.

2

THERE ARE ONLY THREE KINDS OF LOVE

THERE ARE IN FACT many kinds of love, almost as many kinds as there are people. There's blind love, summertime love, desperation love, love on the rebound, least-horrible-available-partner love, imaginary love, academic love, weekend love, puppy love, career-move love, voodoo love, love for revenge.

Nevertheless, three kinds in particular seem to me essential to gay life: **Hungry Love, Buddy Love,** and **True Love**. Some gays taste of them all, over and over. Others specialize. A goodly number of gays may never know the roaring, frustrated ecstasy of hungry love, preferring the spacious intimacy of buddy love. And who among us has penetrated true love in all its baffling contours? With this chapter, I hope to solve some small mysteries and at length flirt with a few of love's conundrums as they pertain to gay life. Now back to our story:

It was that spring of 1997, when something like thirty-five Broadway musicals opened within a single week, and Peter thought we could pursue the introduction of Lars Erich Blücher to our circle with one of those theatre evenings. The chosen show was *Titanic*, then still in its troubled previews; and a friend of Lars Erich's, not in the actual theatre party, was to host an after-theatre dinner.

"Someone's not welcome at the entertainment but invited to prepare the reception?" Dennis Savage asked me.

"Peter says it's this odd thing," I replied while fastening Cosgrove's tie, which bore the ghoulish figure of Edvard Munch's *The Scream*. He'd found it at the Museum of Modern Art Shop, the one that used to be on Fifth Avenue. "Lars Erich's friends are apparently so devoted to him that they supply whatever is wanted. Money, trips to where, parties."

"This guy must really be something, huh?"

"Too much so, in a way," I said, combing Cosgrove's hair. "I've known lookers who were smart and interesting, but has there ever been someone *so* beautiful who's *this* big and *that* fascinating? You can't be just in love with that, you have to be in idolatry. *There!*"

Standing behind Cosgrove, I presented him to Dennis Savage. "Neat," I said, my hands on his shoulders. "Tailored," moving down his sides. *"Charmant,"* at his waist.

"Very handsome," said Dennis Savage neutrally.

"And yet I come like night," Cosgrove diabolically intoned.

"That isn't Byron, surely," I said.

"It's a Cosgrove original."

We three met Lars Erich and Peter outside the Lunt-Fontanne Theatre, where the former assured us that the saga of the world's greatest ship was celebrated in German- as in English-speaking countries.

"Georg Heym, 'Die Seefahrer'!" he cried. " 'Aber wir trieben dahin, hinaus in den Abend der Meere' ": Yet on we drifted, out into the evening of the sea. "It is quite the story to put to a musical, ja? So much at stake, so much love and life! It is thrilling to be here, more to know of Peter's coterie. But I, too, have friends, which we are meeting later at a soirée."

Lars Erich troubled to draw Dennis Savage out—"What are you doing as a career?" and so on—while Cosgrove explained J.'s new life to Peter and I stepped back a bit and took stock.

One, Peter was underpowered, almost quiet. Not tired because of an exacting schedule, not too busy listening to talk: without force, as if something had been drained out of him.

Two, Lars Erich was wearing unreproachable slacks and impressive dress shoes, but his top was a Very Designer form-hugging thing in off-white that wasn't see-through but looked as if it should be. Quite classy but so hot: as if Lars Erich won't be one thing without being another thing as well.

Three, Cosgrove was discussing J.'s travails—or was it schemes?—as if they were events in a television series, something one views rather than experiences.

Four, I was visualizing myself as a contestant in one of those pageants where you get a chance to hope for something important, such as World Peace. All I hoped for was for my friends to be happy: meaning that the Family would hold together.

Inside, we sat up close, thrown right into the heart of this resplendent show, the last of the great operettas, in which grace, wit, and comedy (and a grand theme) accompany the Big Sing that too many cheaply operatic musicals have debased for us. *Titanic* is the real thing—and Cosgrove knew it at once, when the prelude of water music moved from gentle to rough, like a date that slips past teasing into rape. Just after, the action begins not with the expected harbor scene but with the ship's architect wandering on in front of the curtain, phlegmatic, optimistic, concerned . . . and Cosgrove turned to me and *nodded*.

I never fail to get a kick out of the uncanny sense of *communitas* that live theatre provides: all those people, silent and motionless in the dark, yet at their quickest as they fix upon the stage to absorb a single entertainment each in his fashion. Of course, it was in the theatre where I signed my gay contract; I'm sentimental. Still, theatregoing is gay life in miniature, isn't it?—all in the same playhouse, each admiring the show in his unique way.

Cosgrove certainly admired this one. As the first-act curtain fell on the now famous view of the little model of a *Titanic* crossing the stage to meet the (unseen) iceberg, Cosgrove almost jumped out of his seat with excitement. During the intermission, he tried singing snatches of the score as the rest of us milled about and exchanged the odd pleasantry with acquaintances. Peter and Lars Erich were huddling and cooing in that new-kids-on-the-block manner that I find a bit irritating, though I did enjoy watching Lars Erich angling his torso this way and that to display his shockingly expansive V-slope. Peter couldn't keep his hands off the guy.

"I just love having a Lars Erich Blücher in our gang," Dennis Savage was whispering to me. "Everyone should have three names and a nineteen-inch waist and quote Hammacher Schlemmer, or whoever that was."

"Georg Heym."

"Okay," said Cosgrove. "It's all ready." And he sang:

> You say 'angelic,' and I say 'satanic';
> You crave a boat ride—oh, let's take Titanic!

"Is that from this show?" I asked.

"Perhaps it was in the interscherzo."

"*What* interscherzo?" Dennis Savage countered. Then he impulsively tousled Cosgrove's hair, and blushed.

"The crab's going soft!" Cosgrove crowed. "At last I win!"

There came, just then, a sharp report, like the slap of something against something, and we all looked around. Yet we saw nothing but these two tall guys staring at each other: Peter and Lars Erich. Peter had his hand to his cheek, and Lars Erich had grabbed him close. His voice menacingly low even as he smiled, Lars Erich said, "Na so werden wir zu Kumpels then, and you see what becomes if I do not like what I am hearing."

Most of the audience was out lobbying and smoking, and the few people around us either missed it or were but half-intrigued.

So our two friends enjoyed privacy as Lars Erich continued talking, his voice trickling into a whisper and Peter too stunned to do anything. Then Lars Erich released him, immediately turned to find us, nodded, and said, "He is all right, you see that, so I will get for myself a drink of water," and went up the aisle.

The three of us looked at Peter.

Peter shrugged.

Moving closer, I asked, "Are you okay?"

Feeling the angry red blotch on his cheek, Peter said, "It's nothing. Sheer rhetoric. Playacting. It's the . . . well, the craftsmanship of love. That, and . . . the, yes, troublesome topics that just *may* gang up on one in the first—"

"What topics?" Dennis Savage asked as he and Cosgrove joined us.

"Same old thing, really. Bareback sex as opposed to Should one use condoms when tricking outside the—"

"*Peter!*" cried Dennis Savage, genuinely appalled. "You don't discuss the use of condoms—you *use condoms!*"

"Yes, old chap, I know that. At least, I learned it, under your . . . tender . . . guidance. *No,*" he forcefully went on, for Dennis Savage was starting up again. "No, it's *not* that simple, because if two fellows have been going bareback already, what's the point in their now denying themselves the all-night delight of—"

"Don't say any more of that," Dennis Savage put in. "I really like you, so make your own choices. Just don't tell me about it."

As Dennis Savage went back to his seat, Peter said, "Everything's a moral question in your family. It's so *judgmental.*"

"Peter," said Cosgrove, "would you like to hear my new *Titanic* song?"

" 'Judgmental' has become an attack word in this culture," said I. "As if all behavior were equal. A culture without judgments is amoral."

People were streaming back to their seats for the second act, Cosgrove sang his ditty, Peter declared it the best thing in the score, and we settled in. Lars Erich didn't join us till three minutes after the curtain went up, though as he was on the aisle it created no disturbance.

No, *that* he saved for dinner after, in one of those showplace East Side apartments that every East Sider but me has, with two bathrooms, dream kitchen, and dazzle views. Our hosts, a straight couple, were also German, apparently friends of Lars Erich's parents, and there was a spread of Western Civilization among their other guests. Dinner was served buffet-style, centering on a gigantic lasagna that smelled so good that Cosgrove ducked around everyone to avoid the handshaking, grabbed a plate, filled it, and ran to a couch to feed. (He was quickly joined by a Turkish guy—at any rate, a guy wearing one of those hats shaped like a huge thimble with a bookmark at the top—who talked and talked while Cosgrove silently dined.)

Doing my writerly job, I collected some raw dialogue from various guests, then got Lars Erich aside. "Who's gay at this party?" I asked.

"Oh, it is this usual European *assemblée* where no one says, I am gay, I am not gay. It depends on who is there and how I am feeling. One can make bisexual choices."

"Do you ever make bisexual choices?" I asked.

"Not so much, it is true. Not maybe ever. But it is always possible, no? Oh, there is Peter making conversation with that tedious French professor who quotes Chateaubriand. I rescue him."

Off he went, as Cosgrove pulled up to comment acidly on how poorly J.'s beloved A *Chorus Line* compared with *Titanic.* "A *Chorus Line* was fun and moving, okay. But how small and tidy, when this show tonight is the Great Floating City of Nevermore."

Neatening his hair with my trusty X-Men pocket comb, I

said, "You don't have to disdain J.'s favorite show to ease him out of your life, you know. If he's going, he's going."

"But why is he going?"

"I think he got exhausted with all the performing he had to do—being cute and unpredictable and conceiving outlandish projects and making sure everyone found him seraphic. It's just a guess, but I believe he would like nothing more than a little place of his own and no one to come calling. A nice long vacation by himself."

"Look," said Dennis Savage, suddenly there and indicating Lars Erich and Peter, earnestly conversing in a corner with their hands on each other's shoulders. They could have been models, in one of the "cutting edge" poses that fashion favors today, Peter in an ultra-light gray suit over a white turtleneck and Lars Erich in that too-sexy-to-live outfit of his.

"Breathtaking," I said.

"Supreme," Dennis Savage agreed.

"Barky," said Cosgrove. "Something's funny about that Lars Erich."

"Wrong," said Dennis Savage. "*Fifty* things are funny about—"

"He's on something," said Cosgrove. "He's *doing*."

There was a pause.

"Like when he jumps from one subject to the next," Cosgrove continued. "Not changing the subject—losing it. He goes fast, then he's slow."

Another pause.

"You don't notice that?" he concluded. "Someone comb my hair some more."

Dennis Savage did the honors as I pursued this line of inquiry. "Are his eyes dilated or something?"

"It's not that kind of high. Not in his head. It's deeper. Oh! Look innocent, he's coming!"

Dennis Savage and I looked innocent; Cosgrove slipped on his novelty-store eyeglasses with the bulbous nose.

"I appeal to you," Lars Erich began. "Peter says it is so sad for so many gay teenagers, they kill themselves from fear of homophobia. Their parents, friends, the folk. I say it is so loathsome to throw away the one life, our only time on earth, when we could make so much of it. Sixteen, seventeen . . . dead. Why? Because Mutti won't like me? *You* have respect for this? Bud?"

"I don't, in fact."

"Why?"

"Because the culture is loaded with liberated gay images. Sitcoms are virtually made of homophilia. It wasn't like that when I was growing up, yet I had no problem with it. If I can, they can."

"Oh, is it that easy?" Dennis Savage asked.

"It isn't easy at all," said Peter, coming up. "Think of all the propaganda you get from everyone around you."

"But you weren't put on earth to please their idea of what you should be," I said. "This is the part I never get—why does anyone care what some jackass thinks?"

"You hear?" Lars Erich asked—told—Peter.

"I only—"

"It is *disgusting* to sympathize with suicides of such a young age! Not finally ill, in pain, without hope. Yes, for these, of course—but youths, just undertaking their life and work, and they will *believe* homophobia? They say, I must be worthless if Mutti says so?"

"Mutti," I offered, in my usual soothing style, "is a stupid bitch."

"*Yes!*" Lars Erich shot back. "Now I, a German, tell you for instance of Jewish people in Deutschland, when the Nazis are in power. Did the Jewish people think they must be unallowable because the Nazis say so? No—they think the Nazis are unallowable. And so I must feel that anyone who does this, who lets the bigot persuade him to hate himself, must be *disgusting* and *deserves* to *die*."

"Lars Erich," Peter began.

"I *say this!*" His eyes blazing. *"Disgusting!"* Turning to Cosgrove, he said, "You, the boy who loves mischief. We have a name for you, it is Till Eulenspiegel. You did not let parents force you to go a suicide, ja?"

"Perhaps his emotional constitution is stronger than—"

"That is bullshit *excuses!*" Lars Erich muttered, really angry now. "Where you say the ones who didn't surrender didn't have to, they were born stronger. We were *all* born the *same!* And so the sensible ones overrise!" To me, he added, "You have this word?" Before I could supply an English equivalent, he said, "I could gladly murder about this surrender to bigotry."

He was so fierce that we just stood there, till Dennis Savage said, "I almost killed myself. Or ... I considered it. Really, I was that afraid. Don't be angry at the victims; be amazed at the persuasiveness of these particular bigots. Like, why do Jews simply resist anti-Semitism while some gays virtually embrace homophobia?"

Polite to us, Lars Erich shot visual bullets through Peter as the conversation continued. We got out of there soon enough and hailed our separate cabs, Peter holding his hand to his cheek as if he'd been slapped again. We Fifty-third Streeters held conference on the ride home.

"You see?" said Cosgrove.

"He's right," Dennis Savage agreed. "The way Lars Erich leaps from nodding at us to whacking at Peter. It's like the stupendous carvings of his physique, so demonstrative. Hysterical, even."

"Amazing guy," I said. "His insights are stunning. Ten minutes with him and you see the entire world more clearly. I haven't met many people like that."

"When do I get a secret *Titanic* tape?" Cosgrove asked. "I know we'll get one, I just want to know how long."

"Soon."

"It better be," he said, kind of nuzzling his body deeper between Dennis Savage and me till we were nearly a ménage à trois. Dennis Savage didn't mind; later, he asked if he could be the one to present Cosgrove with the *Titanic* cassette, which a friend got for me from the underground. Dennis Savage wrapped it in his special Mondrian paper (from the Museum store again; it's only four blocks away), and Cosgrove was immediately suspicious.

"Could this be a letter bomb from some fiend?" he wondered when I pointed him to it.

"Dennis Savage left it for you."

"My point exactly."

"It's *Titanic*, from early in previews, complete with the dropped numbers and the audible groans of the audience when a new scene is to begin and the lights come up on another technical failure."

Stunned with excitement—I mean, frozen yet grabby—Cosgrove gave himself over to wonder as he gazed upon the tape. Then: "What does Dennis Savage have to do with it?"

"He wants peace between you two."

"Ha," Cosgrove observed, moving to the stereo with the present, whose wrapping was shredded in a moment. "He wants sex between us."

"He's already had sex between you."

Slowly he turned.

"I happened to come upon you two in the act, all that long ago at the beach," I explained.

"That was a hologram," he pleaded. "It was all done with strings."

"It was you and he fucking. I don't mind, because you were

desperate to get off the streets and he was so hot for a seductive
tyke in a Speedo—who had, if I know anything, worked himself
up at just the right moment—that he lost all sense of proportion.
People have a right to slide here and there. Love is not a bank account. I'll never mention it again, but I want something in return."

"Never," he said, impatient at the PLAY button; *Titanic* must
sail forth. "What?"

"Tell me if you and J. have ever—"

"That again?"

"This is the final volume, and my readers have to know. No,
don't turn to the machine. Turn to me."

After a while, he did. He said, "I'll tell at the last story."

Our Thursday night dinner with J. really had
become a chore, though at least he did continue to entertain with
the ongoing saga of Vince Choclo.

"Two nights ago it happened," he was saying, digging into Cosgrove's Mushroom Soup Surprise as heedlessly as if it were Campbell's. All right, it is Campbell's—but Campbell's with the classy
alchemy of red wine, cooked spinach, thyme, and melted jujubes.

"No, it won't be long now" was J.'s prediction.

"Wait a minute," I said. "A straight guy is going to turn gay
and be your boy friend just because you want a keeper?"

"There are no straight guys," J. observed, "when a cute boy
such as me is there."

This was churlish of me to say, but: "For all your genetic gifts
and uncanny ability to maintain fitness through the years with no
apparent effort, you are not a boy any more. You and Vince are
coevals."

" 'Boy' is just a word. It means that he's a big ol' hold-you guy
and I'm a little sugarcake."

"What happened two nights ago, J.?" Cosgrove asked.

"Well, you know, I generally go nude when Vince takes his night shower, and I show off when he comes out. He's really looking, too. Or, like, I model the new black mesh shorts I got. I asked him, 'Will the chicks go for it?'"

"But what did he make of that dinner with us?" I said. "Doesn't he know we're all gay?"

"He doesn't know anything. He never *notices*, the way we do. A couple of times I watched movies on TV with him, and he can't follow the story. And those girls he's always talking about don't appreciate him, but he doesn't get it. This one called Shona, when she comes over she mocks his attire and says why can't he have a snappy haircut like me. She deep-dished me right in front of him, too."

"Want to translate that term?" I said.

"Heavy kissing. And when they went into Vince's room, she said, 'Can't the cute one come along?' But then I heard her sighing out all these lovey things. I have told Vince not to see her if she's so cruel, but he just smiles and says, 'She's really stacked.' Did you notice how nice it is when he smiles?"

"I liked him," said Cosgrove, gathering the soup plates. "I think he is sad but secretly doesn't know it."

"Well, now he is completely going around naked like me. I said he should try on my mesh shorts, and when he did I complimented him on what a big total guy he is. And like a joke I said he could daddy-fuck me anytime, and suddenly right there his cock started to unpack and he had to duck into his room. So I was on to something."

From the kitchen, Cosgrove said, "I thought you were always dissing him."

"Well, he isn't cute. I maybe like his sincerity and such. Anyway, two nights ago, I went to bed before his shower with my door open. It was hot, and I was on top of the covers, on my stomach, pretending to sleep. He couldn't not see me. And it took a while, but finally he came in. I could tell by the way the light changed on the wall. He stood there for a nice long time, and I murmured as if in my drowsy happiness and moved my legs apart."

Cosgrove had outdone himself on the entrée, an entirely homemade *steak frites*, well-done as we all like it. J. embalmed his portion in salt and ketchup and cut into it without as much as an Oh, look.

"What tense moments as I waited in the dark on my bed," J. continued, scarfing up the beef. "I could hear him breathing as he turned me over, stroking me all about, and I pretended I'd had a nightmare. I should have an Oscar for that moment, where I'm saying disconnected things and not quite awake. It's a moment where I could be fucked, but he only asked if I wanted him to stay with me. I took his hand so tenderly and grateful, and I touched him in all strange places, so he wouldn't know what it means. And I made him go back to his room."

"It's Hungry Love," I said.

"Are we screening a video tonight?" Cosgrove asked J. over coffee. "Or listening to my exclusive underground tape of *Titanic*?"

"Didn't that already sink?"

"No, the great new show about it."

"I should get back to tend to Vince. He was threatening to make rice the hard way, where you have to keep stirring it, so who knows, there could be an explosion all over the kitchen."

At the door, J. said, "I like this kind of food. Remember before, how it was always that stupid tuna fish and hot dogs?"

Door closed, Cosgrove said, "J. doesn't love me any more. He likes me, but the deepness is gone, and once I would cry to say this, but now I see it as destiny."

"Really?" I asked, leading him to the kitchen for a cleanup.

"Some relationships are very important forever, but some for only so long. That's why straights have marriages—they have to force themselves to be together. With us, it's more realistic. We don't have marriage, because we know that people change their minds sometimes. Don't you agree?—and also I'm very sorry I was rude to you yesterday about Dennis Savage and being a tyke. I was cranky. I was Cosgrove."

I accepted the apology, resisting an impulse to pet him like a puppy. I don't want to spoil him.

It was nearly summer now, and Peter kept urging a Pines weekend upon us. Dennis Savage and I have retired from that youthful scene, but someone did press upon us the use of his house in his absence, and Cosgrove wistfully remarked upon the Magic of the Island, and Dennis Savage expressed the desire to expose himself one last time at the Meat Rack. So off we all went at noon on the Friday after Memorial Day. We took one of the jitneys that load up at Fifty-third and Second, Peter and Lars Erich splendid and subdued and Cosgrove blissfully crossing over on *Titanic* for the millionth time, on his headphones. Who was the Greek who said, "Everything in moderation"? My family motto is "Everything to excess."

Dennis Savage and I Talked Quietly Among Ourselves as we rode out of the city. He was interested in news of J., and when I commented upon the absurdity of J.'s setting out to seduce a straight man, he observed, "You know that boy never goes after what he can't get."

What Dennis Savage mainly wanted to discuss, however, was

the gay chat rooms he'd been wandering in and out of on his computer—cruising them, in fact, for a new buddy.

"I'm tired of living alone," he said. "I so miss having some cute guy do some mystifying and troubling thing, then suddenly turn to me with that Peter Pan bewilderment where they hold on for dear life."

"You can have Cosgrove on alternate Thursdays."

"What is it about those big domineering numbers that I never understood? Doesn't everyone want young, cute, and hold-on-to-you?"

A bit of Long Island Expressway rolled past as we considered that.

"Well," I finally said, "some see *themselves* as hold-on-to-you, so they need the domineering numbers." Looking over at Peter and Lars Erich, I added, "Which of those is—"

"Oh, Lars Erich has Peter on a string. He'll crush him in time. But Peter will rebound. I greatly admire him, you know. The way he fit right into gay life and started trying all its knobs. He makes the system work for him."

"Tell me more about the guys you meet on your chat lines."

There were fifteen guys in rotation, of whom six were special and three, he thought, extremely potential.

"Do they ask for a photo?" I wondered.

"Others did, not these. I would just say I had a bad experience letting my image loose in the interzone. Many people then said sayonara, and that's fair enough. I suppose I would have myself, once. No, of *course* I would have. But my fifteen—I think—didn't want a photo, even if they asked for one. They were afraid to have their concept of me compromised."

"It's a blind date without the date."

"Without the anxiety," he corrected.

"But, surely, someday you must meet, no?"

" 'I have danced with the first class, Edgar,' " Cosgrove quietly sang.

"Define 'someday.' "

I FELT BAD FOR my friend. He had been sage: got all the appetite out of his system in his twenties and then sought love. He found it, lost it, and now had a right to more. But how can anyone over a certain age fill out a chat-room profile? There's nothing wrong with being over a certain age, mind you: but I'm the only one who thinks so.

The Pines house, a bit to the west between the boardwalk and the ocean, was pleasant and roomy but no showplace. It took us forever to get there, with Lars Erich gleaming and exhibiting himself to every beauty who passed; in the Pines, one passes plenty. His shirt and Lederhosen had come off on the ferry, leaving him ultra-ready in a Speedo, and though Cosgrove countered this gambit by donning his paper-bag head, nothing distracted the passing gaze from Lars Erich. He was grinning at his fans, winking and flexing, all but signing his phone number to them in guide-dog training speak. When we passed one bright-eyed little number walking his white Lab off the leash, the dog leaped joyfully at Lars Erich as if he were one of those puppies raised by the Blüchers.

"These certain dogs will always love me," Lars Erich observed, kneeling to rub the gamboling animal's neck. Cosgrove took the opportunity to let Fleabiscuit out of his so-called (at least by Cosgrove) "executive" travel box, but still no one paid attention to anyone but Lars Erich.

"Does one not love these dogs?" Lars Erich asked, smiling at the dog's owner. "See what energy and love is here."

Perhaps taking that for a come-on, the owner ran his hand up Lars Erich's arm and called him "hot stuff."

"I have these friends, as you see," Lars Erich told him. "Perhaps later."

"See you at tea," said the dog walker.

It was like that all the way along: beauty approaches, Lars Erich flirts, nothing happens...yet.

"How is one to come to this place of the hübsche Dinge and not acknowledge?" Lars Erich said, quite softly, to me in the middle of all this.

"Peter is your boy friend," I replied. "What's he supposed to think while you pick up—"

"I were his love slave?" he asked, menacingly. "As *if*?"

"Okay, one half of you is smart and fascinating," I said. "You know what the other half is?"

"Were you looking for this?" Cosgrove asked, bustling up with the Signet Classics *Pickwick Papers* I've owned for decades and had planned, this weekend, to read.

"I wasn't."

"There it is, anyway."

That made a space, and Lars Erich occupied it by moving on. I suddenly realized what Cosgrove had done. He smiled and said, "He will never like it when you defy him."

"You're getting wise," I said.

"I have these coaches, you know."

THE HOUSE BROKE UP into diverse entities that first evening. Cosgrove and I went to dinner with old friends of mine while Fleabiscuit enjoyed a play date with Old Boy, the cocker spaniel next door. Peter and Lars Erich went to tea, ate out, and then went dancing. Dennis Savage saw to the groceries and went off on his own as mysteriously as possible.

Came then the morning, and "What am I doing here?" I asked Dennis Savage as he lazily started breakfast and I glopped up coffee in one of the house mugs, a commemoration of the marriage of Prince Charles and Princess Di. "This place is all for youth. Beyond that, it's nothing but sand and poison ivy."

"How about a bracing swim in the surf?"

"What are you cooking?"

"Raspberry-peach whole-wheat pancakes and Swiss sausage, paper garlic toast, and—"

"That really thin bread with the ... How come some cute guy hasn't moved in with you just for the food?"

"Sounds good to me," said one of the most beautiful naked young men you have ever seen. Dennis Savage and I just gaped.

"Hi!" he said, smiling through unforgivably big even white teeth and thrusting his dark hair out of his eyes. "Jim Burmeister."

He and I shook hands; Dennis Savage excused himself because of Cook's Palm.

Pulling on a Speedo and sitting on the stool next to mine, Jim asked, "Is there any—," but Dennis Savage was already setting down a mug of coffee before him (this one a souvenir of Iowa, with a map and an ear of corn) complete with honey pot and creamer.

"Many thanks," said Jim.

He's six five, by the way, just like Lars Erich.

It was Jim's plan, he said, to poison his coffee with three spoonfuls of honey and then a lake of cream. Yet one taste and he treated us to a great corny "Wow!," followed by "What's the secret ingredient here?"

"Chicory," said Dennis Savage.

Whereupon a second naked titan joined us, kissing Jim, shak-

ing my hand, pulling on a pair of Everlast boxing shorts, and giving the coffee its second Wow. His name was Sean.

Spiritedly empty palaver about anything at all followed, till I
tried to ascertain how Jim and Sean came to be here.

"We came back with . . ." Jim gestured at Lars Erich and Peter's
room. "Last night. I hope we didn't—"

"Not at all," I said.

Dennis Savage set before us one of the greatest breakfasts
since the convening of the Congress of Vienna, to another Wow!
from Sean and a Say! from Jim. Once we tasted, silence reigned as
we three got into some serious eating I want this known, boys and
girls: if Dennis Savage ever opened a restaurant Zagat would be
forced to bestow the first 31.

We were on our seconds when Cosgrove banged in through
the back door, wet from the ocean, also in a Speedo (and a *Steel
Pier* baseball cap), followed by Fleabiscuit in the world's tiniest
straw sun hat.

"Where'd that come from?" I asked about Fleabiscuit's headgear.

"Someone I know went to a fancy ball and saved one of the
party favors, including this dainty sombrero from an iced mar-
garita that brings Fleabiscuit into the height of fashion."

Fleabiscuit posed, so we could admire the hat, while Cosgrove
met the guests.

"It was the Harvest Moon Ball," Cosgrove then went on,
scooting onto a stool and accepting a plate with a look at Dennis
Savage that read as . . . well, accepting. Dennis Savage accepted it.
He even created a dish of tiny pancakes and sausage cuttings,
lightly cooled in the fridge first, when Cosgrove requested a "children's platter" for Fleabiscuit, who inhaled the whole thing in a
millisecond.

❨   ❨   ❨

"BUT I DON'T WANT to do foursomes," Peter told me at the same kitchen bar much later that day. He and Lars Erich not only missed breakfast; they almost missed Christmas.

"It must have been a high quality of foursome," I said. "Jim and—"

"When I was cruising, yes," Peter said, a please-hear-me hand on my arm. "But I'm in love now. I want to concentrate. I know it sounds strange from me, after . . . I just don't really see other men's skins at this point."

"Even when they're six five?"

"Lars Erich picked them up. I was just dancing."

"Why is everyone tall with you? You're tall, Lars Erich is tall, those two are . . . The whole thing is big, isn't it? I rule the world with *size*."

"It's not his looks," Peter protested. "I mean, it's why you notice him, date him. But then . . ."

"No, it's power, that simple. As in the animal world. It's antlers and fetlocks, markings, the killer's leap upon the prey—"

"I swear *no* to you," he insisted, another hand on my arm.

"I will never understand you," I said, "because I know what tricking is and I know what romance is, but you have the idea that you can—"

"What a splendid thing it is, a sunny day at the beach!" Lars Erich shouted as he stormed in shining-wet, trailed by Cosgrove and Fleabiscuit.

"These great waves!" Cosgrove agreed. "You're bigger than them, so you stand against them, but they come slapping you down, dousing you with their whole what-they-are."

He made the sounds and mimed the effects of the ocean's tugging power.

"You are swept away," Cosgrove concluded, going to the fridge.

"Yet one orange juice pick-me-up and everyone's as good as new."

Lars Erich was taking Peter in with one of those meaty smiles that made our German friend so interesting and disturbing at once, a world's fair during a world war.

"Peter is not liking last night," Lars Erich said, peeling off his swimsuit and grabbing a towel from wherever. "That Jim and Sean! What a worst thing to happen!" He had stopped smiling. "How much I love you," he whispered to Peter.

"Prove it," Peter replied, like a second-grader. "How much power do I have?" He got up and added, "What if No more sex with anyone else or we'll break up?"

"Bravado," said Lars Erich as Peter approached. Moving around Peter, Lars Erich took hold of him quite gently from behind as if to create peace between them, but he suddenly tightened his grip into a stranglehold.

"Let me go," said Peter, actually rather blandly.

"One sees what comes of defiance," Lars Erich told him; and Peter started to struggle.

" 'Klaatu barada nikto,' " said Cosgrove, coming over to them.

"Peter must calm down befirst."

"Let me go!"

"Let him go, damn you!" I shouted, and a startled Lars Erich released Peter so abruptly that Peter staggered before steadying himself at the breakfast bar.

"Wie Sie befehlen," Lars Erich told me, ever so courteously: As you command.

"This is conduct unsuitable to gay life," I said.

"It is not pleasing, his defiance," Lars Erich replied. "I warned him from the start how it is with me. I am in charge of him, and he loves me like that."

"I hate you like that," said Peter.

"'Ach, nun wird mir immer bänger! Welche Miene! welche Blicke!'" said Lars Erich, quoting mockingly at Peter: Now it's getting really scary! What a face! What evil eyes!

Peter just looked at him.

"Ja, smart Americans," Lars Erich whispered. "What is this poetic highlight?"

"Goethe," I said. "*The Sorcerer's Apprentice.* And you're the sorcerer, right? Peter's learning fast and hard."

"Peter teaches also," said Lars Erich, taking hold of him again, but nicely now. Peter did not resist; he had the look of a prisoner in love with the headsman. "Peter teaches me that I feel now as I have never before so felt. It is a cure for all woes."

"You guys have a problem, and you better resolve it," I said.

"No, it's true," said Peter as Lars Erich started to ... well, deep-dish him. "No, Lars ... yes, but stop ... okay ..."

"Lars Erich Blücher," said Cosgrove, "are you respecting the tone of the house?"

Eventually, Lars Erich took a time-out to say, "In the next life, when I become a cute little shorty, I will respect the tone of the house. In this life, I am in control, and all learn from me." Performing one of those penetrating looks at his lover, Lars Erich asked, "It is good like this? Nice, this taste? You will give me all your American kisses, ja?"

"Ja," said Peter, ready for the block.

YOU HAVE TO HAVE a best friend who knows all your secrets anyway and thus might as well be confided in. You need enjoyable friends, and you also need sexy friends. But what if they are combined into one figure, coming after you like your favorite nightmare?

I don't mean Lars Erich; I mean J., stalking the ever more enchanted Vince Choclo.

"Now he took Polaroids of me," J. told us one Thursday night. "And he got down my measurements, with his fingers playing along my skin, taking a little extra for himself. He even measured my mouth, and when he said, 'You got the lips of a pretty chick,' I knew I had him. He's so helplessly in need of someone who likes him, he don't care who."

"He 'don't'?" Cosgrove echoed, with consternation.

J. shrugged. "He talks funny and it's catching."

The dinner was spinach-and-potato soup, scallops over wild rice, salad, and tiramisù

"Here are the pictures," said J., spreading them upon the table as Cosgrove and I leaned over to see. "Those are my mesh sexpants. I told you about them. Vince likes to see how he looks in them."

"Sexpants?" said Cosgrove.

"Here's a few of the babes Vince dates," said J. "I snuck them out of Vince's box because he lets me get away with anything. That's the secret of how to love me, you know."

" 'Serena,' " I read off the back of one snapshot. " 'Jonquil,' " said another. Hot tamales, looking merrily wanton for Vince's memory box.

"And here's Red Backhaus," J. went on, pushing some more Polaroids at us.

"Gosh" was Cosgrove's report.

Unlike the amiably natural Vince, Red was Built for Contest. He had one of those uncanny physiques that is at once pumped and pulled tight. It was not a modest shot: the pants were open to the knees to display Red's manly pride. Yet the hero took no joy of it; his empty face seemed about to blush. One feature in particular set him apart—a close haircut of brown, blond, and red, the kind of visual that aroused commentary in a medieval village.

"I want Red in my porn stories," said Cosgrove. "I see him as a pie man going to the fair."

"He's more like Simple Simon," said J. as he gathered up his photographs. "Vince is pretty clueless, but Red is so dumb that people laugh at what he says. Then he cries right in front of you. He's short, too, and he's always saying what a problem that is with the chicks. He's the night manager of a gym near Prospect Park, so he can talk to the chicks in his job capacity. But when they put him down, he stays on alone after closing and uses up all the machines to work off his frustrations."

"How does he treat you?"

"I just ignore him."

"J., you should be nice to him," said Cosgrove, who only now gave up Red's photo. "When a guy feels unliked and someone is kind—"

"No, because I finally had zero hour with Vince, which I entirely came to talk about tonight. Is there more salad?"

Cosgrove took J.'s plate to the kitchen.

"How come the food here is so good?" J. asked.

"Cosgrove and Dennis Savage have decided to share an interest in cooking. Dennis Savage has been taking Cosgrove stage by stage through some of his dishes, and Cosgrove has been picking up secrets of the trade. Unexploited spices. The temperature of sauces. The application of sweetmeats."

"How come they suddenly like each other?" J. asked, a bit suspiciously.

"Beats me."

Six seconds, then: "How is he?"

"He's fine."

J. nodded. "It won't be as interesting to know Vince, because he doesn't have these amazing friends or go to *A Chorus Line* or a snazzy Oscar party where you vote for who will win and someone gets a prize. But it will be good for me not to have to be Little Boy Blue doing a party turn. This time I'll be more in charge. And it has its exciting side, to live with someone you hardly know and see their strange secrets come out all the time."

Cosgrove brought in J.'s salad refill and a pepper mill. Standing at J.'s left, Cosgrove asked, "Pepper, sir?," and J. nodded. Looking down at his plate after Cosgrove finished, J. went on, "I know I'll miss out on all the lively doings here," as Cosgrove went back to the kitchen. "I'm making the best of it, but probably I shouldn't have done what I did to Dennis Savage.... I thought having adventures was what we're all supposed to do."

He choked and looked up at last, his face hot with tears, and I called out, "Cosgrove, come quickly," and Cosgrove came,* salad and all, and went right to J. and pulled him up to hold him close, stroking J.'s hair and rubbing his neck as if this happened all the time; and then kissing him, and I mean deep-dish, with the racy pull that marks the connoisseur.

J. at length recovered himself and sat as Cosgrove pulled his own chair close for support. I was trying to imagine what their lovemaking was like—if indeed they ever did get it on—when J. quietly said, "I do still love you. I'm just in a different place now."

"What is that place?" I asked.

Ignoring me, J. went on, "This new part of the story started when Red got a crush on a girl in his gym. A real babe who flirts

---

*Have you noticed how important it is to have a live-in who is alert and listening and does not, in a crisis, call out a "What?" as vaguely as possible? An alarm is a *summons*. I have known couples of whom one half could accidentally burn himself while cooking spaghetti sauce and scream his building down till neighbors break into the apartment, douse him in cold water, phone 911, and see him off in the ambulance, whereupon the other half would wander out of the bedroom and say, "You want something?" To deserve love, one must *listen* to it.

away at everyone. She asked Red for help with some machine, and she sucked on one of his nipples through his T-shirt right in front of the whole place. Red told Vince, and Vince said, What if he and Red fucked her together? Listen to how he says it: 'I sure do like a triple.' And his eyes do that thing."

"Time," I said. "Place. Costume."

"It was before bedtime, in the kitchen, where Vince was cleaning up his usual mess."

Conceiving a desire for J.'s salad, which he was toying with but not eating, I tried to pull it over. But J. pulled it right back. "I was in my mesh shorts and going along real innocent. I even changed my voice a little, to be all moist and young. I said, How come Vince hasn't taken me on a triple? I would really like to see him daddy-fucking the chicks.

"Well, he was real interested in that. He said, 'Why would you?'

"I said, 'Because you're so big a man.' I said, 'I believe that if you kissed a chick and I kissed her, I would taste of you on her kissful lips.' No, that's *my* salad"—because I'd made another grab for it.

"I'll fix you an encore," Cosgrove told me.

"I want his," I said.

Retaining his salad, J. continued his tale: "Vince was finished in the kitchen, so I followed him into his room, where he started to undress for bed. 'I want to do a triple with you, Vince.' He says, 'Okay.' 'No, really,' and I took hold of his sides. I made myself as open as can be to him, saying he's my favorite daddy-fucker of them all, but what if he would daddy-fuck me and then tell Red? How could I hold my head high then?

"Now he's completely nude, and toweling off as always, even if he doesn't shower first. Everything's a little nutty about him. But he heard his cue well enough. He says, 'I would never tell Red, I swear. That would be our secret.'

"He had his hands on me by then, when I— Why do you keep taking my salad?"

"You're not eating it."

"That's not the point."

"I want you back in the family," I said. "I don't want you in a different place. I understand Vince's appeal, those slow, silent containers upon whom one projects all his needs. Nevertheless—"

"He is my savior, because he heard my plea. He pulled me onto his bed to sit in front of him and he took off my shorts. I said, 'Vince! Vince!,' and he kept saying, 'We won't tell Red.' He was all over me with hands and I still pretended that I didn't know what it would be, so I begged him, 'Don't daddy-fuck me, Vince!,' with my hands all on his neck and arms and that stupid shaggy hair which now I sort of don't mind, so of course he will fuck me. He says, 'You'll sure go over easy now.' He says, 'You'll like it like this, J. boy. You're a piece of J. cake for me to feast on.'"

"He said those words?" Cosgrove asked. "It's like a play."

"And guess who wrote it," I put in.

"I admit I arranged it," said J., finally passing me his salad. "But I didn't see anyone holding a gun to his head. And he was even feeding *me* lines, like 'It's okay for a fine young boy to struggle when he's got to be daddy-fucked.' So I knew he wanted me to fight him, and he was so hot when I did that his eyes went all sky-like. I whipped out from under him and backed away with 'You wouldn't fuck me against my will, would you, Vince?' And he came and got me so gentle and loving, saying, 'That's the best pussy of all.'"

THAT'S BUDDY LOVE. HUNGRY love is frustrating; buddy love is efficient, and there is never enough of it, though it is possible that most of the lifelong gay partnerships are built on buddy love.

On the other hand, if you want a lively story, you'll go with hungry love: so of course we have Peter and Lars Erich coming for dinner, which by now is like saying the Phantom of the Opera wants to check out your chandelier.

"Have I Julia Child for a roommate?" I asked Dennis Savage in our kitchen, as he and Cosgrove worked on the dinner: crudités vinaigrées, five-alarm chicken stew, garlic French bread, and silver cake.

"No, mince the green peppers unevenly," Dennis Savage advised Cosgrove, with a friendly hand on his shoulder and a warning eye for my attention only, "and the red peppers quite coarsely, with jutting edges . . ." Miming "Have to talk" to me, he took me into the living room.

On the couch, he told me, "Don't let this get around, but that chat-room stuff is not only addictive but evilly effective. There's so much of it. Men, men, every last Jack of them your type, and they're all, like, how smart and funny you are, and when do we meet. Well, you know I got around the photo thing, and my profile is a bald lie—"

" 'Thirty-four and rich'?"

"Thirty-three, in fact. Oh"—after a glance at his watch—"it's my time to chat with that boy in Hartford. He sent his picture, of course—slim, with shoulders. You know I love that look."

He got up. "Remind Cosgrove that the couscous has to be firm, and I'll be back soon for dinner."

He left and I went into the kitchen, tailed by a suspicious Fleabiscuit.

"I invited an extra friend," said Cosgrove, chopping away at whatever. "He is Nesto, and very Latin, so please be nice."

"Where's he from?"

"Tower Records, downtown. You always end up meeting guys there, but he was especially friendly, in these cute overalls with no top. I had to follow him downstairs into World Music just to get a look, and we started talking. He was fascinated that I have no day job, because he's out of work and his family is putting all this pressure on. He wants to learn about cooking from me, because a friend of his has a good job as sous-chef in a jazzy restaurant. He doesn't say a lot, but he's good ka. Could you please start the music? It's the *Capitol Sings* series, with perhaps Cole Porter first, ideally at a volume setting of, say, five and a half."

Musing on the irony of being directed by my, uh, employee, I set up the music just before Peter arrived, early, with a look of purpose in his eyes.

"A see-through embroidered shirt and Spandex bike shorts," I said, assessing him. "Doesn't that theatre of yours ever close?"

He dropped heavily into the armchair. "We just had a fight on the phone."

"Gee, what a shock."

Fleabiscuit, cheated of Peter's shoelaces, came out from under the couch, growling, and went into the kitchen.

"It started," Peter began, "when—"

"Oh, I have been here before," said I from my desk chair. "With Bill and Jake, it was Bill wanted to kiss in the street and Jake wouldn't even hold hands in secret passageways."

Fleabiscuit trotted out of the kitchen with a stalk of celery in his mouth, the bitty one from deep inside the bunch. He settled on the floor with it and stared at Peter.

"With you and Lars Erich, it's you're too wild but he's even wilder. Brinkmanship as lifestyle."

"I'm not that wild."

"Are you kidding? Chi Chi LaRue dreads to be seen with you in public. Donnie Russo's mother told him not to play with you.

Joan Crawford is afraid you'll die and come to hell. Why must I be a seer in this country of the blind, constantly explaining life to the people who actually live it?"

"It's not as easy as—"

"You have a problem and you need to solve it. If you don't, it will destroy you."

"What if we can't solve it, and why is the little dog staring at me with celery in his mouth?"

"If you can't, you should part company, and the little dog is staring reproachfully because in the armchair you are safe from his shoelace rape."

"Did you see what Jill did for Bobby last night?" said Cosgrove, coming out of the kitchen as he wiped his hands on a towel. He was referring to *NYPD Blue*. "What a babe, yet so loyal above all. She will do anything for a friend, even have sex with a nerd, which is what she did, though the nerd was kind of nice, actually." Then he went back into the kitchen.

"And you think *I'm* crazy," said Peter.

"Mind you, I'm not talking about compromise, because then neither of you will be happy. You're going to have to talk it out honestly and calmly: which parts work, which parts don't."

Fleabiscuit bit down on his celery and started eating it. He's the only canine I've known who likes crudités, but then Cosgrove did want a gay dog. When Fleabiscuit is cranky, Bette Midler's "Do You Want To Dance?" soothes him, and he has been known to attend brunches with that did-everything-last-night hungover look so trendy in the 1970s.

"The relationship," I continued, "must then emphasize the parts that work and utterly delete the parts that don't. Or you're going to have a big crash."

Peter sadly watched Fleabiscuit crunching up the last of the celery. "I know you think this is about Lars Erich's biting kiss that takes you out of day itself, or the way he towers over everyone. The physical, you think." He shook his head. "It's who he *is*. It's the ... person *inside* that build, and I can't save myself from him, or negotiate a relationship as if it were a book contract. Oh, I can see you not liking what I'm—"

"I'm not anything, just talk!"

"Yes, in this crazy house with shoelaces and Jill and—"

"Paraphernalia!" I cried. "Tell what it *is*! You're not just fucking, you're in *love*! That's why it's so impossible. Fucking's always about *you*—what you want, how you come, why you feel. But love's always about the *other* guy—how he affects you and what he does for you and what he'll do to you. No, you're right, this is not about skin. But if he weren't in that skin, *none of this* would *ever* have *happened*! How do you explain that?"

"The dog went away."

Silence.

"I have begged him, I have socked him, I have slamfucked him while screaming at him for his sins."

Silence.

"He just laughs. He says, 'We're going to whether you're happy or not, so let us amuse ourselves, my Peter junge.'"

"Hungry love," I said.

Fleabiscuit erupted out of the kitchen with his little water dish in his mouth, heading for the bedroom, with Cosgrove right behind.

"What's that about?" cried Peter, almost desperately.

"He's irritated," said Cosgrove, carrying the dog—dish and all—back to the kitchen, "because I gave him zwieback with the wrong flavor of jelly. He goes on strike."

Having gained the kitchen, Cosgrove added, "Everyone should realize that I wash my hands after carrying the puppy."

Down in the dumps, Peter muttered, "That's good to know."

The buzzer sounded; Cosgrove got it. "It's my new friend Nesto."

"Is he gay, by the bye?" I asked.

"I never asked. Latin boys have a powerful sense of privacy."

Nesto turned out to be about twenty and was much too spiffily dressed for our ham-and-egging cohort.

"Perfect," said Peter. "Enter a spice boy in his high-school graduation suit while my life is falling apart." Jumping up, he clasped Nesto's hand with "I'm Peter, and please don't be shocked at all the real life that is about to explode before your—"

"Nesto!" cried Cosgrove, running out with Fleabiscuit, who lightly yipped and frolicked. Broadly grinning, the two boys hugged; when Cosgrove turned back to us, his right hand gesturing proudly at Nesto, it suddenly struck me that I know very, very little of Cosgrove's relationships outside the family. It struck me as odd, in fact.

Then the buzzer sounded again.

"Uh-oh," said Peter. "Twenty miles of bad road."

"Come and see what I'm making!" said Cosgrove, taking Nesto into the kitchen.

Lars Erich came in like Richard III breaking into "the winter of our discontent." "Peter," he said, pointing. "So you downclose the phone on me, yet it is not finished. You will see that now, Liebling."

"Gosh, you look terrific," I said. "As if you were getting bigger every day."

"I give you a private show later, ja? First, I kill Peter."

"I'll be taking drink orders," said Cosgrove, coming out with Nesto and Fleabiscuit. Nesto had one of Cosgrove's pretzels. "There's red wine, sparkly water, vodka—"

"Yet who is this lovely chap?" said Lars Erich, moving up to Nesto. "A young businessfellow?"

Cosgrove introduced them as Lars Erich ran his hands over Nesto, feeling his contours under the coat. "Distinguished," Lars Erich called him. Nesto just smiled.

Then Lars Erich turned to Peter, his eyes a goblin's. But all he said was "I hear Sondheim, yes? The gay Mozart."

"It's Cole Porter," Cosgrove replied.

"I thought I was hearing lines of great wisdom on the impossibilities of love, the rich problems, the trickery of the self. I will to hear some of the great Sondheim lines." He smiled at Cosgrove. "Tell some!"

Cosgrove obliged with a mangled strain of *Sunday in the Park with George*—"The soldiers wiped their snot on us!"—before heading back to the kitchen. Lars Erich, just a bit thrown, lost his momentum, and Peter jumped in to seize control.

"In Sondheim," said Peter, "love is two opposing forces, like football." His hands mimed the urgent tango of the playing field, moving now toward this goal, now toward that one. "But love is not a game, a contest. Love must be an alliance." He was almost pleading, as he turned to Nesto for the outsider's disinterested affidavit. "Am I right?"

Nesto was about to reply when Lars Erich cut in with "It is not correct to want an alliance of men. That is not serious love, when hormones and instincts make an excitement. It is beautiful to fight. Fighting is sex."

Still trying to figure out where Peter got such an arrestingly expert take on Sondheim's theatre, I said, "But not in my apartment. Maybe not anywhere."

"Ja, I apologize for that, at least," said Lars Erich, circling the room, circling Peter. "It is such disgrace. Why must I do this? Then I look at Peter, and all I wish... When I see him, I can only... I want..."

"... to hurt him?" I asked.

After a long while of the two of them staring at each other, Lars Erich nodded.

"But why?"

Lars Erich said nothing.

"Oh, Lord," Peter muttered, seeing it coming, and then, indeed, Lars Erich charged at Peter, going around me and pushing Peter down—I mean, onto the floor—and getting on him to steal ferocious kisses from his mouth while Peter struggled and shouted. Lars Erich slapped Peter a few times, and though I tried to pull Lars Erich off, he was just too big for me. He was lashing Peter in German, dense with slang, and so run together that I couldn't follow it all. It was not, I think, abusive. If anything, Lars Erich was berating himself.

He wound down rather quickly, panting and still on top of Peter, now stroking his hair and licking his face. Peter had gone limp. Nesto was still sitting with the pretzel. Cosgrove, at the kitchen entry, was shaking his head, as was Fleabiscuit.

Then Lars Erich got up and shook hands with all of us very formally as if not all that much had happened, a little set-to rather than a riot. Nesto handed him the pretzel, and Lars Erich left with it.

"It's the drugs, you know," said Peter, from the floor. "He's been stacking like crazy. I keep telling him, don't I?, about the hazards…"

"Drugs?" I asked, mystified. I'm always mystified when gay men get into pharmacopoeia. If you aren't clearheaded, you'll miss all the cute guys.

"Aren't you going to get up?" Cosgrove asked Peter.

"I don't deserve to get up."

"What drugs do you mean?" I asked.

He waited a moment. "Steroids, of course. For the gym thing."

I was stunned.

"No. No, no, wait," I finally got out. "That intensely busy mind, that quoter of Hölderlin...is on *steroids*? I thought they were for those dreary huge guys in the competitions."

"Lars Erich is huge now," said Peter, very, very sadly and still on the floor. "Haven't you noticed?"

"But he trains guide dogs. He tells captivating stories about his little brother hiding a puppy's toys so that...and then he comforts his brother, who cries and cries in Lars Erich's redemptive embrace. Where...where would a middle-class boy like Lars Erich even get access to steroids?"

"From me."

We all let that sink in for a bit.

"But...*why*?" I insisted. "You don't need those drugs. Stonewall has always been filled with the big pumped-up guys who never—"

"You don't know what you're talking about," said Peter, sadder than ever.

"Would you kindly get up from the floor?"

"You don't realize how competitive it is now. In your day, it was big, and that was simple. Now it's big and tight, all chiseled, and you *can't get that* without the hard stuff. Please *hear* me, will you?"

He sat up.

"You *don't* understand about Lars Erich, the way his head gets into your head. I know that it used to be just looks and fucking when *you* were young, but times have—"

"How dare you?" I said, but mildly. "You think we didn't have feelings then?"

"You had poppers then. Isn't that why I ruined your dinner party and sit so humiliated with all this bod on me but I can't even defend myself? Your system was better, because I'm in love now..." He was raining helpless tears. "Want a look at love? No one fell in love in your day and got his whole insides, yes, quite

ripped out of him. There was only pot then, and everyone would
giggle on a high. Now you see me crying like a woman. Now, isn't
that the final bitch?"

Very worried, Cosgrove came up to him, trying to get Peter to
stand.

"Why don't I have someone like your friend here?" Peter
asked. He reached for Cosgrove, and Cosgrove backed away, but I
steadied Cosgrove with a hand on his shoulder.

"Let him," I said. "I need the scene."

"One of these easygoing kids," Peter went on, holding Cosgrove's hand and looking up at him, "who does what you want."

"He's as easygoing as *Finnegans Wake*," I replied. "Besides, you
don't want a kid. You want the whole nine yards of man, that
stinging clarity of a dream coming true. And now you know why
they say Be careful what you wish for."

That's when Dennis Savage joined us. He took in the room—
lingering just the slightest bit upon Nesto—and said, "So where's
Ernst Stavro Blowjob?"

"Nesto," said Cosgrove, "this doesn't always happen around
here." Released, Cosgrove went into the bedroom, followed by a
mildly growling Fleabiscuit.

"Why is Peter on the floor?" asked Dennis Savage, sitting on
the couch and urbanely miming the smoking of a cigarette. "No,
I'll guess. Lars Erich went ballistic on muscle-drugs and threw
Peter down and I *hope* Cosgrove is not letting the dinner overcook."

The little chef came in with the paper-bag mask, which he put
on Peter, saying, "He has to, for making a mess in my dinner."

"Who's the head of this family," I asked Dennis Savage, "you
or Carlo?"

"Both, but he isn't here, so me."

"Okay. *You* tell: now what?"

"Peter has to wear the punishment hat for two minutes. Somebody introduce me to this splendid young— Fleabiscuit, *no!*" (For
the dog was under Nesto's chair, his teeth a half-inch from a
shoelace.) "Then we eat. Over coffee and a sweet, we will discuss
possible solutions and arrive at the most practical one. Peter will
then solve his romantic problem and we can all get back into life."
Turning to Nesto, he extended a hand, saying, "By the way, I'm
the incredibly rich and successful Dennis Savage."

AFTER THAT, IT'S PERHAPS anticlimactic to return to
J.'s Thursday dinners, but we still have the third kind of love to consider. J. was more changed than ever, quiet and self-absorbed but at
least not moody and suspicious. He actually brought Cosgrove a
house present, an antique Pez dispenser with the head of Dracula.

With the hot days already upon us, it was salad night: tomato surprise built around a chicken-curry-walnut-apple medley, coleslaw,
and Cheese Selection Platter Deluxe served with Carr's wheat-
meal biscuits, a J. favorite. There was a time when he could go
through two boxes of them, neat, leading Dennis Savage to crab
in on that *Why am I the only sane one here?* theme. It's a fond
nostalgia of mine: to recall when we were all young and silly and
had nothing to worry about.

The conversation that Thursday was desultory, feebly trot-
ting down unfamiliar paths because all our basic subjects had
become taboo or at least awkward. That's when you know a relationship has shot its bolt: real friends never run out of things to
say. J. and Cosgrove even tried discussing fashion trends, a
bizarre expansion for two men whose notion of couture is *Open
a drawer and wear what you see, if possible with inappropriate
socks.*

Then J. said, "Has anyone wondered why I left Dennis Savage?"
Cosgrove replied, "Some are wondering."

"Now it can be told. It was almost entirely because he made
me have a day job, while you got to sleep late and goof around. I
wanted to show him how people would prize me."

"I sort of have a job," Cosgrove said. "I do the chores for two
apartments. Dennis Savage pays me forty dollars a week."

"You don't have to go out if it's wet. You don't have to take orders from crazy people."

Cosgrove seemed about to say that that was exactly what he
did, so I broke in with "Dennis Savage didn't make the money to
support a joy boy, and anyway that's not why you left."

"Oh?"

"It's like eighteen reasons, and we don't have all week."

"Vince doesn't make me have a day job. Now I can sleep late
and— Well, I have to get up with him and make his breakfast
while he showers. But after he goes I can louze around—"

"*Laze* around," said Cosgrove.

"—and as long as the place is clean and the clothes are washed
and folded in those neat ways like his stupid mother always did it
and the steak and baked potato is served on Monday, and the
chicken and noodles are served on Tuesday, and such like that, he
accepts me as I am."

"He accepts you," I said, "as a housewife."

"No, because Vince is my own sweet friend now, and I fill his
life. I take him on walks where he never was. Can you believe he
didn't know about Chelsea? I pack a guidebook and show him the
sites of history. Theodore Roosevelt. An Astor Place Riot. He has
become very appreciative of the old movies we rent, and guess
who he likes the most? Fred Astaire. I even took him to the theatre. Well, *he* had to pay. He was amazed it was so expensive. That
show you liked so much, Cosgrove. *Titanic.*"

"Did he enjoy it?" I asked.

J. was thoughtful. "He didn't say at first. But then he was always talking about it, I notice. Like, he kept asking why that couple had to quarrel so badly just before tragedy separated them
forever. Or why was the guy who built the ship redesigning the
blueprint after it was sinking? You can't change history with a
pencil, Vince says. So if he enjoyed it I don't know, but he sure got
into it somehow. And he's not pretty or smart but he says I'm his
daddyboy now, and he's going to daddy-fuck me every time. Is
this why women fall in love with guys who aren't cute, that they're
so dependable and intent on you? Dennis Savage always had other
things on his mind, because he's smart. Vince doesn't have so
much to think about, so he concentrates on me. Now I'm trying
to be real instead of amusing. Except I've been amusing for so
long, I'm not sure what a real J. would be. Vince asked me to pick
up a *Titanic* soundtrack. Is there one?"

"Not 'soundtrack,' " I told him. "That's the audio portion of a
film or, by extension, a recording made from it. Only movies have
soundtracks. Shows have cast albums, and, yes, Victor has
recorded *Titanic*, though it may not come out for—"

"I have a tape," Cosgrove put in while passing Fleabiscuit a
choice scrap. Fastidious at table, the dog will transport the morsel
to his dish in the kitchen, and only then eat it. "Someone I know
could copy the tape for you."

J. turned at that "Someone I know." But he made no remark beyond "That would be great." He went on to "Vince liked that chorus when they said goodbye at the lifeboats. He goes, 'Think what's
in their heads then!' And he loved the ending. We were so inspired
that he had me read to him from the Bible when we got—"

"What?" I said. "The excuse me *what*?"

"His mother always wanted him to read it," J. went on, unper-
turbed, "so finally he is. His mother is thrilled and calls it 'Bible

Group.' She imagines a load of us in bow ties saying, Does the Red Sea really part? He has a Bible she gave him, which closes with a zipper that has a tiny cross at the end. And the words of Jesus are printed in red. Imagine if we all had such a book, and our own words are highlighted. Sometimes I make up stuff instead of reading it. It's easy—'And lo, the sons of Gad went *out* forth to the baths *and* multiplied, for *in* this way *would* they know the hard-on that *is* God.' See how the noises are always in the wrong place in the Bible? It's so easy to fool Vince, he thinks no one would dare make up the Bible. Try to see me getting away with that with Dennis Savage. He's too clever for me, and of course he can't be impressed."

"He was impressed with you, all right," I said.

"Big deal," J. replied, still very calm. "I already know I'm cute."

"I didn't mean your looks," I said.

"When I moved in with Dennis Savage, he didn't break off with all his friends. They were always coming over and judging me."

He stared at me; I don't know what he was thinking.

"But Vince has dropped all his chicks for me. Except for Red Backhaus, his childhood friend, he has made me the center of his activities on earth. When we have video movie night, he has me lie against him on the couch, so we can hardly reach the dip with our chips."

"Chips and dip?" Cosgrove echoed with horror. Our galloping gourmet.

"That's what I'm telling you," J. continued, quite conclusively. "It's not about smart food or Broadway or times when you wear a suit. It is a thing you people don't know about, where he was sudden and panicky but is now slow and dreamy. He says the trick is not to try for a marathon, but to do it and shower and have dinner, then do it again and watch a VCR, and so on. He never runs out. We have figured out this way for him to smooch me up so thorough and for me to blow him so long that by the time he balls my fairy ass with his heavy fuck I will shoot my cream right over his head with a big noise. We fall on each other and hold on so rightly and out of breath that we only know the one fact that we are together. And he goes his mouth right against my ear to say, 'J. boy, if you ever try to leave me, I swear I will kill you.' "

"Well, that's true love at last," I said.

"Yes, isn't it?"

3

THE
ROCK
PEOPLE

I T IS A STATEMENT beyond contention that a young gay guy with Looks Control will be in possession of an etiquette, a lingo, and a major haircut: this is called a subculture. But only devotees of the most elect parish will know of such practices as birthday sex (in which your buddy's present is your current boy friend), "stacking" multiple rendezvous, and How To Go Steady With Three Men At Once Without Actually Cheating. This is called life in Chelsea.

My cousin Ken is my authority, as the captain of a clique of preppy linebackers who talked of nothing but *Ally McBeal*, which was still current then. When Ken first arrived in New York, he paid me an at first no more than dutiful call, to catch me up on family doings and to trade "when I figured out that you were gay" confessions. He also asked me for advice in stocking "classy novels" for a new bookshelf he had bought.

"They should be the most correct ones possible," he said, though he couldn't articulate further.

"Describe your apartment," I suggested, as if literature might match; but he was enchanted by that notion. He saw one's living space as definitive, and would often invoke people not by physical data but rather the interior decoration of their quarters: "smart," "sturdy," "effective," or "an erroneous bath mat." Ken's own apartment, on West Twenty-first Street, was spare and colorful, "a beautiful use of the space," as Ken's second-best buddy, Tom-Tom Hughes, put it. But then, so were Ken, and Tom-Tom, and all their friends. They were so in accord on what beauty is that they had contrived to resemble one another. The entire congregation ran to five foot eleven at about one hundred ninety-five pounds, with various shades of brown floppy hair and scenic teeth, and they were all twenty-eight years old.

I distinguished them by eccentricity. Ken's first-best buddy, Davey-Boy Carhart, was their recognized arbiter of visual style; it was he who decided which of the gang should carry the football they used as a group fashion accessory. Others decided where to go on Movie Night or negotiated the summer rentals in the Pines. Or Roland, happening upon Ken and me in front of Bed Bath & Beyond, would grab Ken to maul him in rough love till Ken cried out a password of surrender. Or Crispin would materialize from behind a prop tree to play gunfighter with Ken in the Chelsea dusk, where any act performed by lavish men instantly becomes good form.

They were a tight unit, all ex–boy friends. This created some tension in those glossy apartments. Harlan, in a brief era as the arbiter of style (till everyone realized that his right foot had only four toes), laid it down as law that no two former partners could date again unless a third ex completed a trio. Somehow, this was equity. But then Ken visited me for a "coffee meet" (one hour's socializing, no meal) to complain that while speaking to Tom-Tom on the phone, he heard Davey-Boy wickedly giggling in the background.

"I'm quite cross with them both," Ken told me. "Because they should have invited me over for a threesome. I expressed my displeasure by doubling my gym program."

"Does that work?" I asked, delivering the steaming mugs.

"Davey-Boy saw how angry my triceps got, and he was respectful for days. But Tom-Tom sulked at me. He said, 'Tu es vache avec nous.' He thinks French gives him the cultural advantage."

"Still, wouldn't you have been cheating on *your* boy friend?" I asked. "Royal?"

"Royston, and it's not cheating if you trick with an ex. Cheating? Cheating is when *you* call a new trick for a second date." He gently churned his coffee to stir up the honey, then asked, "What do I do about Davey-Boy and Tom-Tom?"

"What you always do," I said. "Restore the ethical balance."

Though none of them would articulate it thus, Ken is his gang's moral authority, like Pacey of *Dawson's Creek* or, for you others, Thackeray's Dobbin. When a wily devastato tried to infiltrate the group with a doctrine of bareback sex, Ken placed a ban on him, and his friends complied.

Well, mostly. Ellroy, Wilkie, and the irrepressible Davey-Boy eventually conferred to entertaining the newcomer at covert orgies for two, albeit with condoms. Ken ruled with severity, arranging for them to be tickle-tortured in blue plastic handcuffs, Ellroy by Anders, Wilkie by Morgan, and Davey-Boy by tender Ken himself. He wouldn't tell me where all this occurred or whether the culprits took their justice like men, except to remark that "Davey-Boy always struggles."

So my cousin really was the commander of them all, and dauntingly likable: buoyant, reliable, supportive, generous, and even smart. He had none of the Knowledge, however: my generation made that unnecessary by effecting the historical transition between national homophobia and *Will & Grace*. At dinner once, Tom-Tom proposed an around-the-table on the question "What do you like least about gay men?," and on my turn I cited the moribund but not yet terminated tendency by a few individuals to act like Auntie Mame. Ken, Tom-Tom, Davey-Boy, Bart, and James just looked at me. They don't know who Auntie Mame is.

Worse, Ken is the only gay I've ever met with absolutely no sense of humor. As he loved describing apartments, I asked him how he'd describe mine.

"I wouldn't," he said, in a tone of blameless honesty. Everyone laughs when I tell it. But he wasn't jesting: simply refusing to criticize.

Looks Control creates enthusiasts but also resentful fans. Davey-Boy treats Ken with idolatry, but there are also times when Davey-Boy might be the schoolmaster in an unusually brutal Victorian novel.

And it just goes on and on, like Peter and Lars Erich: hungry love, everywhere I look. Ken chatters endlessly about Davey-Boy. I hear "Davey-Boy should have been an international spy." Or "Davey-Boy is such a mystic. He gives you lectures on The One."

"What One?" I asked Ken. He had come over to my place to complain about yet more of the relentless tiny mischief in which his comrades lived and loved.

"Davey-Boy never says. But he is always making pronouncements. Did you hear that he will not have sex with ... well, this is what he *claims* ... he will not have sex with anyone who doesn't get along with children."

"That's an odd take," I said.

"But that's Davey-Boy. He says guys who don't appreciate kids are missing an all-important chip. See, you can't hit up little kids for a job or money or a rent-stabilized place someone just moved out of. So those guys are selfish and clueless and would not be good sex, anyway. And they will never meet The One."

I think Ken's buddies have met The One, at any rate, but I'm shy of saying so.

"Listen, I have this problem to tell," he went on. "That week when I went to the Greek Isles for a springtime pick-me-up? While I was gone, some new guy turned up at the gym and they started a sign-up sheet without me."

"A sign-up sheet?"

"Like, who gets him first, who second...and but the thing is, by the time I got back it was up to like twenty names. And so why did Davey-Boy and Tom-Tom think they had the nerve to play this kind of off-Broadway trick on me? Because I went right up to that new guy, list or no list."

"A sign-up sheet? The gym allows you to reserve men for sex in the order of—"

"Not the *gym.*" *The West Wing* isn't about a *plane.* "My friends."

"Tell me about the new guy."

"Oh, he's just endless. He walks..." No. "His back..." Wait. "He's got this boy-smile."

"That could be anybody. Brad Pitt, Aunt Laura..."

"Well, how would you describe the most excellent man in sight?"

"Is he The One?"

Ken considered, then shrugged. "Who knows about that concept? It may be something way corny that even Davey-Boy doesn't understand. But I'm going to collect this new guy, to rebuke Davey-Boy and Tom-Tom in their latest treachery, which *they* think I don't even know is because they love me so much they terrorize me to express their passion."

"The penalty of leadership," I explain.

He gets pensive. "It's simpler to be loved for yourself, isn't it? You know, your looks and your dick. The things you have. Then you just enjoy yourself. You don't have to worry about what to say at the right time. Or are you classy enough, with the usual nuances. You never can tell what someone likes for personality, but everyone knows what's cute."

"But you can't just walk up to a stranger in the gym and... can you?"

"I'm telling you, I already did. He couldn't speak because of a medical thing. He mimed for me. Something in his mouth. But they were all watching."

"The whole gym?"

"My so-called friends." He hefted the football a bit, rose, and drew it back as if for a pass at the diamond as big as the Ritz. "I am not prepared to accept their limits," he said, sitting again as he petted the football's lacings. "Linton got huffy with me in the showers about not following the sign-up order. I told him, 'Every man for himself.'"

These were fighting words, given Ken's gang's Morlocks-Eloi worldview, and Ken meant them.

"He can't speak because of a medical thing?" Ken went on. "As *if*. I followed him out of the gym, and after a subway ride and so on, I watched him meet some people for drinks. It was one of those high-tech places with all glass around, so—"

"What people?" I asked. "Like him?"

"Various people."

"No, I mean did those people give you some idea about whether the guy is gay?"

That stopped him, briefly. "It's different nowadays," he told me. "Everybody's completely mixed together."

"You aren't. Everyone you know lives and dates alike. You're a closed system, an all-boy flesh-and-cream."

"Oh, yes?" he replies in a cool and even wondering tone: but his eyes are blazing at me. "We live alike but they spied on me? Followed me, like hunters? Yes, you didn't know this"—because I looked puzzled—"but Davey-Boy and Tom-Tom and that dimwit Devon with the blond streak across the hairline that is so not in style yet shamelessly watched me across the street from the new guy's drink place. Well, I went right up to them, and Tom-Tom asked for the football back in that stupid French of his.

'Rendez-nous le football.' I had to fight him for it. Aren't you listening to me?"

"Of course, I'm—"

"Right there on the street, you understand? So people could see my best pals and me brawling! And who won, I ask you? As if I couldn't take Tom-Tom on any street in this world! I threw it at him to bounce off that big little-boy build he's so proud of. Like, I need his fucking football? And I'll date that new guy. They can *eat* that sign-up sheet, which you notice I wasn't even here when they started it. And that was no accident, was it? They believe I need a takedown, that all-boy system you think is so neat! And no, I am not crying, so just get back with your sympathy while I am hard as stone."

I froze.

A pause.

"And so," he finally said. "I still have the football. I have Bar Credibility. I have a wonderful power. I have a better job than most of them put together, even if I'm bored with it. You can be hot and educated at the same time. Tom-Tom? He gets his reading in with the Undergear catalog. He couldn't place a comma correctly if it meant sex with Matt LeBlanc."

Another pause.

"My best pals. But who kept the football? Who beat Tom-Tom right there? That's a good system, isn't it?"

He broke this pause almost immediately.

"Would you please stop looking at me as if I were crying?" he said. "I'm going to show them what a good system is. I don't have to cry when my feelings are hurt, or ever."

So he shrugged again and seemed quite calm about it; but life in Chelsea erupted in total war. All birthday sex and movie nights were canceled without notice, and everyone was miserable but determined.

"What a posse of misfits," said Dennis Savage. At first, he had been amused by my Tales of the Chelsea Boys. But now their boundless religion of hot had become as tiresome as Madonna's cone bra. "They're so picturesque and unified," he noted. "Like when when explorers went too deep into Africa and stumbled upon isolated tribes with unfathomable customs."

Assuming the voice of a sycophantic guide out of some old movie, he said, " 'We must tread carefully, oh bwana, for it is the Valley of the Rock People. If by some evil mischance they should surprise us here, be certain to copy their every mannerism, no matter how quaint or unseemly, or they will surely annihilate our entire party. But come, oh bwana, let us pass swiftly on our way.' "

Meanwhile, Ken's gang was doing no better with the new guy at the gym than Ken had done. The cynosure never shot anyone down exactly, but then he never did *anything* exactly. He remained unavailable and inscrutable.

Or not inscrutable: Russian. That's what Ken told me, on the phone, urgently inviting me to his gym on a guest pass to Speak for Him.

"It's so weird how he's been wiggling out of reach, always," Ken was telling me. "I watch them taking their turn with him, with the others all glaring at me. What a war in the gym! But I'm over it now."

"Over it?"

"Caring . . . about how they treat me." A silence follows, in which we both try to decide if that could be true. "Anyway, I saw it all come down at the bench press. Dickinson approached him, but he started dealing in an alien tongue, and he has this friend there, who pipes up that he only speaks Russian. And you do, too, right? At last I'll show those jokers who is in fashion."

My college Russian is about as vital as Stalin, but I was curious to see this show. It's so reminiscent of early Stonewall culture— of its appetites and styles—yet so smoothly coordinated and homogenized that it recalls Lincoln Steffens' remark that he had been "over into the future, and it works." Yet Soviet Russia didn't work, did it? It didn't even deserve to.

"Sure, I'll come," I told him. "Maybe I'll luck into a spin class."

"That's what?"

"Aerobics on bicycles."

It sounds extremely questionable to him. "Like bumper cars?"

"The bikes are stationary."

"We don't have that California stuff. This is a serious gym. Your free weights, your machines."

"You are a serious people," I said; but as usual he didn't get it.

That night, Davey-Boy telephoned me. He said he wanted peace among his kind, and he wondered what my role might be in this, the next day at the gym.

Watch me be careful. I like him, but I have a loyalty issue.

"How did you know?" I asked.

"We are the kids in the code," he said, "and we understand each other so well."

"You have too much code, and you hurt my cousin's feelings. I shouldn't be talking to you."

"Let us harmonize, cousin."

"Yes, you're smooth—but Ken ranked you out about the football, didn't he?" A little exasperated with the whole thing, I told him, "You're like pubescent orphanage kids eating extra candy at a late-night spanking party."

"Your cousin is the superior being among us. I have gotten high on his truth many the time. No drugs, just Ken raw. My mouth all on him so, and the way—"

"I forbid you to share this with me."

"Just tell us your terms."

"I don't negotiate with terrorists," I said, ringing off.

BY THE TIME I met Ken in front of his gym, I was keyed up with curiosity even as I dreaded being part of it. What, approach a stranger in a place as judgmental as a body house? Ken was so anxious that he could have been an ancient Greek box-office treasurer waiting for Aeschylus to introduce the second actor.

We both calmed down somewhat after observing the solemnities at the front desk, suiting up, and hitting the main weight room, a vast contract in the boilerplate of vanity. Men pulled, thrust, mirrored themselves, chatted, admired one another, ballooned and tightened. A few women were irrelevantly scattered about, as if fronting for a conspiracy of some kind. I caught sight of a few of Ken's former comrades as he pointed out the new guy patiently racking up a heavy score on the quad machine. The Kens clustered and broke apart and reclustered at the edge of my vision while Ken concentrated on what really mattered: revolt. Reaching some sort of climax, the new guy grew still, heaved up out of the metal, and examined himself in the glass.

"See?" Ken whispered.

The new guy: iconographically apt, a physique as crowded as opening day of the Olympics topped off by a glacially benign handsomeness. The Norwegian water polo team's version of a naughty French postcard, I thought; with Brazilian ears, or something. Your basic devastato, yet raised to the highest possible level. Far out of the ordinary, even for Ken's demanding taste. Theatrical, conservative, fantastic. A midsummer night's dream. Still: how good-looking does one have to be now? I don't mean Is it fair—I mean Is it possible?

"No one should have that," I muttered. *No,* I meant No one *can* have that. And of course even that's incorrect.

Then we saw Davey-Boy fraudulently idling past the new guy, whistling and flexing and showing off his veins.

"Go!" Ken told me. "Stop that showboater!"

I hesitated, but it was one of those moments when You're going to do it right now or You're never going to do it. So I went up to the new guy and said, "Ya slishal shto vy govoritye pa-russki." I hear you speak Russian.

Turning from the eternal mirror, he looked at me and said, "What's that, Somali?"

"Russian."

He shrugged, started toward yet another hotness machine, stopped short, and looked back at me with a grin.

"*You're* one of them?" he asked.

"I'm . . . ambassador."

"Yeah, huh. For which one?"

"My cousin Ken."

"But who is he, is what. I get so many in each different place. Turn them *all* down, sure. You have to. Or the whole world would spin off crazy."

He looked closely at me, then went into some lazily exhibitionistic gym thing, pulling up his tank top while pushing down the waistband of his shorts. When Davey-Boy does it, it's cute. When this man does it, it's an outrage, something essential that you're not permitted to know about.

"See, I feel them all around," he went on. "Trying to control me. 'S'why I always say no. No is control. No is me. Are they looking?"

I just kept watching him.

"Sure they are. Now you look inside."

He indicated the mirror, wherein I saw the reflection of Ken's entire gang, assembled in disapproval.

"How I see it," he said, "they could be cruising themselves like so."

I turned around to seek out the real Ken, to signal to him that I was as close as I would get and that he must step forward. But I couldn't find him.

"They should look deeper than the mirror," the new guy went on, shuddering at the cool of the place and to emphasize the lovable bounce of his hair. "I turn from the mirror."

He abruptly did, and so did I. Before us stood the Kens—Ken now among them—all gazing upon the new guy with resentment. Ken even handed the football to Tom-Tom. Solemnly!

"They make a *great* set," the new guy observed. "How do they tell each other apart?"

"Harlan has nine toes."

"So which is your cousin, now?"

"Fifth from the left."

The new guy took note. "Impressive, you *have* to say so. Yet who isn't, today? Look how the others never stop watching him." He waved at them, but they just stood there passing the football around. "They seem so impatient. A habit of youth. A failing, perhaps an energy. I was impatient once."

"You're no older than they are," I pointed out.

"No, I've been here forever," and he stepped forward to say to them, "I'm the one you can never have."

All together, Ken's play group glanced inquiringly at me. I shrugged. They looked back at the new guy, and he now took a step toward Ken, modulating his voice so the two of them might have been in the confessional. "They'll always struggle," he said, as if making the most obvious of remarks. "Suck it up and deal, guy."

And off he went.

"You're free now," I told Ken, and his pals dispersed to various machines. On the way, some of them gave him love pats or neck rubs, and Crispin drew his gun and let Ken shoot him dead to fall with spectacular and I have to say even joyful abandon into Ken's forgiving arms.

"I may be free," Ken told me when we were alone, "but I'm very cross with you. Did he at least tell his name?"

"Odysseus."

"Yeah, right," he said, weighting up the bench press.

"He is called 'No Man.'" Seized by a thought, I added, "The Rock People came out of their valley and caught sight of the world."

Ken sighed, slamming on a forty-five-pound plate with the familiar metal slap. "Do you know what you would be so much more present-day trendy without?" he asked me. "Those fucking gay riddles."

4

We've Been Waiting for You for a Long Time

WHO WAS YOUR HIGH-SCHOOL crush? Mine was Evan McNeary, whose realtor father was the wealthiest parent among my classmates' families. The McNearys owned twenty-five acres on Long Island Sound, with not only the customary pool and tennis court but an equestrian stable as well. Evan tended the horses, and all those hours with the brush gave him a heavy upper torso unheard of in a twelve-year-old. With his darkish skin tone and black hair he seemed absurdly masculine for seventh grade, especially because of a classic grand endowment, fat as can be, with a heavy-lidded mushroom cap.

On the first day of soccer practice, as I was dressing at my locker, Evan came back from the showers, startling not only me but Russell Livermore, who had the next locker over. The next day, Russell came sidling up to me in the lunchroom to murmur, "Did you see that Evan McNeary? He must beat off every night!"

No, I was thinking. *You* beat off every night. Evan beats off three times a night—that is, if the quaint notion that size and appetite are linked has validity. Had he been a defenseless kid of the uprooted class, perhaps a graduate of foster homes, Evan might have attracted the attention of many an opportunist and become as erotically educated as Joe Dallesandro was when he stepped off that Greyhound in Los Angeles. But the moneyed middle class raises its offspring delicately. Anyway, Evan was one of the least outgoing guys in all of Friends Academy. The voluptuous physique and the primly pompous persona made an odd blend, as if a Classics professor specializing in Dubious Sources in Herodotus spent secret weekends emceeing vaudevilles at Scheherazade's.

Evan and I palled up for some reason, and we could have been called best friends if one didn't apply the concept too nicely. It wasn't because I had a case of hungry love, because Evan lost the Debauched Scooter look almost as soon as he had attained it. Besides, I had discovered the appeal of the older male in that same locker room, when I passed Senior Danny Eider-Ainsley telling Junior Garrett Williams that they had the two best bodies in the school. Garrett's was one of those naturally expansive layouts, and he took Danny's praise with an uninterested shrug. But Danny himself, one of the few seventeen-year-olds of that era to maintain a home weight-lifting program, was clearly sending out a sincere, not to say passionate, message, and that moment remains my most consequential high-school experience.

So Danny Eider-Ainsley was gay, too: straight boys have no need to share thoughts about who is more beautifully made than who else. But Evan was less readable, because he was going to be one of those homosexuals who aren't gay. Do you know the type? It's not simply that they lack the Knowledge or that their idea of a pop singer is Vic Damone. They seem to not get what the rest of us do for fun. All they see in gay is a rococo charade, and they often end up married to a woman and treating everyone to a sermonette on how alienated they once felt.

Dennis Savage has no patience with Evan; for a while, he banned me from mentioning him. Until Pennsylvania. It seems that somehow or other Evan fell in with a group of gays who had all moved out to York County, not all that far from Harrisburg. They were bachelors in an enclave, in a time capsule: for fashion never visits the country. Evan still lived mostly in New York, but he kept talking about leaving, and finally he took a place in Dillsburg, among his new friends. And then he learned something about the enclave he had not known before: they juiced up their sex life by paying local men sums of money to perform sexual acts at parties.

And now Dennis Savage was interested.

"Your friend is bringing back the fifties," he said. "He's befriending fear. It's that pre-Stonewall thing, Athletic Model Guild meets the Phantom of the Opera. Sulky trade, beseeching queen. Is he dangerous? Is it better that way? 'Slash me, my fool!'"

He, Carlo, and I were kicking it around at my place; this must be twenty years ago by now.

"I believe it's fair to know about this other kind of gay life," said Carlo quietly. "Where guys don't have it all laid out in front of them like rides at Disneyland. The bars and the dancing. Magazines to tell you what everything is, clothes and such. Out in the most part of the world there, they don't know how gay is supposed to go. They don't even know what to call it. Meet a guy in a bar, he says his girl friend kicked him out just now, where's he going to bunk tonight. Like his looks? You say, I got room."

Carlo showed us how this is done, shrugging off a kind of smile.

He goes, Well, thanks. So you get there. It's nervous, right? 'Cause if you're gay hotshots hooking up at the Ramrod, you know what's going to happen. These other guys, now, they're not sure what they want, 'cause the way they grew up, nothing's allowed. 'Course, you get boozed up first. Even then, sometimes, it's nothing doing. Other times, the whole place starts to get real focused. He says, I sure would like to cockadoodle you. He says, Know what that means?"

"'Cockadoodle'?" I echoed.

Carlo grinned. "Crazy lingo, yeah. It's not 'cause they're dumb. It's 'cause they're alone."

He jumped up, went into the kitchen, and came back with an

apple. "There can be some nice stories in it. Big Mike Peterson back on leave from the Navy rows his high-school English teacher across the lake to a deserted shack to share a joint. Let's strip down, says Mike. Or young exec and the boss on a business weekend travel three states away from their real lives, ordering steaks from room service. Do I get the promotion, Mr. Carstairs? Well, Gridley, I'd say that depends on you. Or truly just Coach and Roddy."

"Tell that one," Dennis Savage suggested.

A horsebite of apple. "Well, you know Coach. He's a big number, with deep intentions. They say he was married once, in prison once, in the Foreign Legion once. You name it, it's got a Coach story. Roddy's the captain of the baseball team, and all he wants is to climb inside of Coach and never come out."

"Photo and phone get prompt reply," said Dennis Savage. "Visuals, please."

"What for I need to describe to a pair of experts like you, who've had their personal vision of Coach and Roddy on file since Pokey was a pup?"

"Clint Walker," I offered.

"Wesley Morgan," said Dennis Savage.

"The story can be anything," said Carlo between apple bites. "'Cause opening up the opportunity's easy enough. The real story starts with how these guys deal with what they're doing. They can hide their feelings—but what *are* their feelings? Nothing's allowed, right? Sure, if it's for money, they can pretend that there aren't any feelings in it. There's no them in it. The trouble starts when they meet up with Coach and there's no money to protect them from their feelings."

"Was there a Coach for you, Carlo?" I asked.

After thinking it over, he said, "I'll pass on that one. Story's a little spooky."

"They're all spooky," said Dennis Savage.

"I never wanted to be a part of those corruption parties, or whatever you might call them," Evan had told me. "They take turns giving . . . 'head,' I believe, is the phrasing. As if lining up for a bus. Each has a limit of one minute, and the one who . . . fires the cannon, as one might say, wins the betting pot. I was very disquieted to hear about this, but I suppose you're familiar with such sport. From your roguish experience in the Manhattan gay world."

"I see Roddy as anxious," I announced. "Confessional. 'I always liked you, Coach. Do you like me?'"

"Coach is gruff," said Dennis Savage, joining in. "His words seem to reject the young athlete even as his hands rove—"

"Coach is silent."

"Coach is kissing."

"No," I said. "He goes, 'Can I whisper in your ear, young fellow?' The world turns so utterly still that a rotting fence falls over in Norway and they hear it in a church bingo basement in Boca Raton. Roddy holds on to Coach's massive shoulders and Coach inclines his head . . ."

"His tongue moistens the boy's shell like ear as he says . . ."

"He says . . ."

We were looking at Carlo to conclude our tale.

"You got it too romantic," he told us, rising to line up a shot of apple core at the kitchen sink and send it home. "Kid swings on Coach's dick till Coach pulls him up and says, Let's do this right. And he takes him to the bed and cockadoodles him."

The three of us contemplated that for a bit. Then I said, "Well, there'll be no Coach for Evan. He's romantic. Flowers pressed in a book the day they pledged their love."

"In the life that we're talking of," said Carlo, "they don't do love. Love is for women, so they can raise children or teach school or be Nurse Laura Barton."

"I was going to leave this party," Evan had told me. "It had the taste of the New York homosexual, setting his traps and covering up with his West Side witticisms. But this night the ... guest, as they term it, was a fellow called Slim. He had a handlebar mustache and a way of looking right at you after you had finished your sentence, so you would say more, to keep him there. You quite babble your heart away. His name is Henry Muller, but Slim is so much more appropriate. He needed the money to make the mortgage payment on his farm, and I found that so sympathetic. He's no drifter, none of your gay-bar riffraff. I offered him all the money he needed, and he didn't have to do anything for it. They had him undressed down to a rustic cache-sex, just a flap of white linen tied at the waist, and he looked so genuine that way. His eyes were misted at the humiliation, and I wanted to save him. The other ... yes, *guests*, wouldn't you know it, were just local ruffians. They lacked every quality except availability. They couldn't be degraded, try as you might. Ask them to masturbate themselves while riding a tricycle in a lady's wig, and they'd simply say, 'That's twenty bucks extra.' But Slim seemed so noble even in his shame that he inspired me! I turned to look at the rest of the party—how gleeful they were at breaking down this beautiful being's pride. They *feast* on man!"

"But, Carlo, isn't it easier our way?" I asked.

"Surely. But you'll always know what you're getting, like opening a box of cornflakes. What happened to discovering?"

"He came away with me without even putting his clothes on," Evan recalled. "A bold stroke for a fine cowboy, certainly. He was grateful for his rescue, and so he endeavored to share his male warmth with me, despite his shyness." Evan smiled here. "You'll think me excessively fond, calling him a cowboy. But York County farmland is virtually in the Midwest."

"The Midwest starts at Tenth Avenue," I told him.

"Carlo, which is more fun," Dennis Savage asked, "that other world or ours?"

"Depends on what you want out of life."

"I knew I couldn't compete with the gay cognoscenti of the city," Evan told me. "Those practitioners of the art of being gay, with their drugs of pleasure and sinful circus."

"You know, it really isn't all like that," I said. "Gays choose their lives just as straights do. There's nothing about drugs and circuses in the contract."

"But do you know," Evan asked me, "in your wonderful city, anyone so genuine that he is wistful in his cache-sex, yet so wide-shouldered from farm labor?"

Was I talking to Stonewall's Emily Dickinson? I said, "Don't forget that you're somewhat substantial yourself. I never told you how amazing you looked in seventh grade."

"Doing what?"

I gave up with a sigh.

Evan went on, "You were the only one who was kind to me then. You're not like the others, and we must always be friends."

AND SO WE WERE, at intervals when he came to New York for some family do, and in his homemade Christmas cards—always views of Slim's farm—and occasionally a letter. The birth of a calf, the trouble with some machine, intrigues of the local homosexual enclave. Over the years, the tale of Evan and Slim grew into a wonder saga, especially as the Stonewall ideal of braggy promiscuity gave way to the post-AIDS ideal of loving monogamy. No one else in my family had as much as met Evan, yet we all referred to "Evan and Slim," always as the control in an experiment whose other participants were by comparison fly-by-nights lacking in vision. Together these two stood, windswept in

Pendleton shirts and Timberlands, resolute yet playful, a Jefferson-
ian icon of independence: the yeoman farmers.

So when Evan suddenly invited us out for a weekend, my first
thought was How can we possibly stand the scrutiny? And isn't
the ideal best appreciated from afar?

I didn't tell the others till one evening in my place. It was right
after dinnertime; they're less wary then. Dennis Savage was in the
kitchen, preparing freeze-boxes of the leftovers of a Wiener
schnitzel with horseradish cabbage he had cooked for us. Carlo
and Cosgrove were watching *Survivor*, that show in which Americans are dumped into a jungle and left to fend for themselves.
This one was *Survivor: Thailand*, and our two television critics, filling me in on the show's format, explained that the series had lost
much of its dramatic validity now that the cute blond guy had got
voted off for letting his tribe's boat float away.

"Cosgrove," said Carlo, struck by the brilliance of a new notion, "why don't you send in a tape to the producers for next season? They surely like a gay character nowadays."

"I'm waiting for *Survivor: The 104 Bus.*"

"How about *Survivor: Dillsburg, Pennsylvania?*" I asked.

My tone got their attention. Even Dennis Savage came out,
dish towel in hand.

"That's Evan and Slim," he said. "A trip?"

"All of us?" asked Cosgrove.

"All who want to," I replied.

"Would Cosgrove be happy there?" Cosgrove went on. "On
the farm?"

"Ask Carlo. He was a farmboy once."

"You, Mr. Smith?"

Carlo, who had been stretched out to full on the couch,
slowly pulled himself around and rose to loom over us with his
bigness, his implausible realism. The truest man may grow a bit

soft with time, but he never loses power: because he has seen
what the rest of us only dream of. He has been—as he himself
put it—discovering.

"Did you milk a cow?" Cosgrove asked Carlo. "On your farm?"

"I did when they could find me."

"How farm *is* this place?" Dennis Savage asked. "Is it, like,
crops and a one-hoss shay? Do they herd sheep?"

"Do they *hear* sheep," Cosgrove corrected, quoting from *A
Damsel in Distress*. "And what would sheep even say?"

"It is so farm," I said, "that it has been in Slim's family for
three generations. It's that land thing, where everyone in the place
loses his identity to become one with his dynastic fate. It's the op
posite of gay life, in a way: no one is allowed any choices. Any liberty. You live for one thing only: the land."

"Did you like the farm, Mr. Smith?"

"Smells bad and it's filled with people giving you orders."
Carlo moved close to Cosgrove and ran his hand through Cosgrove's hair so exactly on the center parting that he got a shiver
out of him. "And you have to get up early for the rest of your
life."

"How early? Nine-thirty?"

"Five."

"Oh, I will not be on the farm."

Everyone sat down for Discussion Group.

"What's Slim like, again?" Dennis Savage asked.

"I've told, a thousand times."

"Just once more."

"He's your destiny, wearing nothing but a piece of white linen
tied around the waist, with his patch roughing out at the top and
his manhood hanging out below. His eyes are sad, but if you love
his land, he will love you."

Carlo said, "Do what?," Cosgrove made a low noise by way of

sarcastic rebuke, and Dennis Savage waved the nonsense away with "And where does Evan fit into that?"

"Evan pays for it," I said. "His money has no content. No myth. The *land* gives a guy content, makes him complete. Yes. So Evan found completion with Slim."

"I always said he was a puffcake," said Dennis Savage.

"A 'puffcake'?" Cosgrove echoed, feeling the new word as a tempting little rebus.

"A scatterbrain."

Fleabiscuit, who had been on a play date with the corgi in 5L, was now brought back to us. Apparently he had been up to some serious frolicking, for he scarcely got onto the couch next to Cosgrove before dwindling into deep nap.

"So who's going?" I said.

Dennis Savage immediately signed on, but Carlo said he'd wait to hear it as dish and Cosgrove worried it for a bit. "Would there be legendary farm recipes for me to learn?" he wondered.

"I know about the food," said Carlo. "Let's tuck into macaroni and cheese olé."

"What's that?"

"Macaroni without the cheese, because it's been another hard month. That's all a farm is, I recall, eight hard ways from Sunday for the rest of your life. Unless you light out for a place where they like you."

After Dennis Savage returned to the kitchen to finish with his freeze-boxes and take them upstairs to his place, Carlo said, "It's fine seeing young Cosgrove getting along so well with Dennis Savage. Time was, he'd come in and Cosgrove'd spray him with the mustard squeezo thing."

"Couldn't that have been an accident?" said Cosgrove, blushing.

"Not twenty-three times. Bud, what do you make of this invi-

tation from your buddy out of the blue like so? Think it means
something?"

I was rummaging through some notes in preparation for the
evening writing session, and it took me a bit to switch from one
concentration to the other. "Means something . . . No. Or maybe.
Evan's a lifestyle snob, so perhaps he wants to show off the . . . pu-
rity, I guess . . . of the country. As opposed to us city sybarites
with our nugatory little pastimes."

" 'Nugatory'?" said Cosgrove.

"Useless."

" 'Nugatory,' " he repeated, saving this one, too, for later.

Carlo absently put his arm around Cosgrove's shoulder. "It's
nice to know friends from so far back," he said.

"It's fun revisiting my innocence, I guess. The trouble with
Evan is, he's so virtuous about his virtue. There's something un-
natural about it. It's too aggressive to be genuine."

"I'm bored with genuine," said Cosgrove; and Carlo nodded.
"What I like's a good act," Carlo said, "like some guy practices
tightening his eyes down to slits, checks it in the mirror. Yeah,
you'd date that guy. You recall Jim Krokis, pumped-up darkhair,
big on the scene some years back?"

"One of Dennis Savage's tricks," I noted.

"Ever hear of Jim's Latin-guy act?"

I shook my head.

"Well, Jim's no Latin guy, *but*. If he says he is, you could believe it. 'Cause he's dark and . . . something. And our Jim here falls
in the B group, but he has such taste as would please him to go
with the handsomest guys. So there's cruising tension. But Jim is
smart and artistic, you might say. And he goes out nights as a
Latin guy who can barely speak English."

"Why?" Cosgrove asked.

Carlo shrugged. "It's hotter."

"Why is it hotter?"

Carlo thought briefly; no explanation. "It just is," he said. "So when Jim likes a guy, he turns into Tomás. Puts on the straight foreign guy's dignity and shyness. See how well he thought it over? And he chooses his words to sound like they come from someplace gay guys haven't been to yet. You know, like, 'You is Ryan? You sure is nice. Ryan like Tomás?' He lowers his voice as if the whole bar is listening to them on personal-issue walkie-talkies. He's shy and Latin, see? Catholic, guilty. 'You like mambo, Ryan? You like Tomás mambo you *por completo* for a secret?' "

I asked, "What if he was talking to someone who really was Hispanic?"

"Jim knew Spanish from school, so he's ready. Says his accent's from Canada."

"Someone I know is Hispanic," said Cosgrove. "But he doesn't think he's hotter just because."

"It's only hotter if you have to work for it. We don't believe in the hot we were born to. And who knows if Jim's score improved after all? Maybe some guys played along and laughed at him underneath. But he did say that fuck-talk was hotter his way. At that point of no return, mouth to mouth as he pumps away big-time? 'Oh, Ryan, sure be brothers now with mambo, sí, Ryan? Sí, mambo? Sí, Tomás?' He's going on like that, and some of his partners would shoot just hearing it."

"But why was that hot?" Cosgrove asked.

"Because he loved them so."

After a silence, I said, laughing, "What does that *mean*, Carlo?"

He looked at me for a bit, then lightly brushed Cosgrove's hair again. "Okay, chief," he said. "You going down on the farm, or what?"

"I *shall* go," Cosgrove replied, "though I fear that Evan is a nugatory puffcake."

"Yeah, I figured you'd have something like that for us."

DENNIS SAVAGE RENTED A car, and I rode map, though Evan's directions had less to do with towns and turnpikes than with "Go fifteen minutes after the red barn with the green door to an unmarked dirt road."

"When can we have a rest stop?" Cosgrove asked.

"A rest stop?" said Dennis Savage. "We haven't crossed Fifth Avenue yet."

Well, it took forever, and once we had passed New Jersey and entered Pennsylvania I had to put up with teasing from Dennis Savage, who kept asking if various ghoulish creatures were relatives of mine.

"I'm not from this part of the state," I said, "you quaint little . . . Wasn't that our turn just now? At Bigelow's Egg and Scrapple House?"

Dennis Savage slowed and made a U-turn, saying, "Do you suppose being hidden away like this is part of Evan's identification? We have to seek him out like a genie in the forest."

But we finally got there, pulling up a long drive to a big clearing behind the main house, where a bunch of guys were working on what appeared to be a stalled tractor. Animals were everywhere, including those chickens we liberals buy our eggs in support of, freely ranging all about us.

"It *is* a farm," said Cosgrove in wonder, staring out the car window. "There may be a tire swing in the hay mow."

One of the tractor guys detached himself to walk toward us with a tiny businesslike smile. He was in overalls and a flannel shirt, suitable for the October chill. The others paid us no heed.

"That's Evan," I said.

We got out, and I handled the intros.

"We've been waiting for you for a long time," said Evan; but we weren't all that late.

Then Slim came out of the farmhouse. I'm not going to describe him, boys and girls; you've all seen a Slim or two. He moved up behind Evan, put his left hand on Evan's shoulder, and shook his right hand with ours, just like that. Look at us: the gay farmers. Love our land and we'll love you.

"Slim'll take you upstairs and then we can show you around," said Evan.

We slipped in a rest stop and then did the tour. It was a farm, all right, with a few surprises. A rescued burro had a stall of his own in the barn with the horses and cows, and an old floor-model Victrola stood next to the stall.

"Put on a record and see," Slim suggested.

Cosgrove slipped on a disc, wound up the machine, and set the needle down. Some old dance band started whacking away on Rodgers and Hart's "My Man Is On the Make," and the burro's ears shot straight up.

"What's his name?" Cosgrove asked.

"Bix," said Evan, making one of those mock-resigned gestures at his partner: he insisted, so I humored him. The secret of staying together is not compromise but giving in.

"Could I pet him?" Cosgrove asked.

"I don't want you in a pen with a donkey," I said.

"What are you, a parent?"

"No, a crossing guard."

Slim chuckled as he led us out of the barn and along various byways. At one point, he went off to oversee the repairs on the whatever it was in the driveway and Evan took over. It was Slim's style simply to point out things; Evan extolled. Everything was wonderful on the land. It was drug-free, smoke-free, sin-free. More than once, Evan squeezed my arm and told me how happy he was to share with me the sights of his marvelous life.

"I need you to understand," he said, pausing as if to make this moment as awkward and bewildering as possible.

Dennis Savage got me out of it by asking about crop rotation and other agricultural devotions, and we finally swung around back to the house and into a huge cyclone cellar sort of place, finished as a rec room with pool table, jukebox, and, way in the corner, a full-scale puppet theatre with antique homemade marionettes hanging on a display rack nearby. The characters were somewhat oddly chosen, presumably by one of Slim's ancestors and for the production of a work of some personal relevance. There was a lumberjack. There was a guy in black with a turned-around collar who I assumed was a cleric, unless it was supposed to be David Belasco. And there was a fairy princess. Cosgove immediately grabbed the two males and started up an act.

"We were very poor when I grew up," said the lumberjack. Both puppets then turned to look at Dennis Savage.

Thus cued, Dennis Savage asked, "How poor were you?"

"So poor the mice had to order out."

Everyone laughed except Evan, who went on to tell of the rollicking yet intimate gatherings the basement routinely hosted.

"There is a holiness to friendships we maintain over the course of life," said Evan.

Exasperated, I asked him, "Were you like this in high school?"

"Come quickly, everyone!" cried the fairy princess. "They just shot a dog in the street!"

Dennis Savage again played straight man. "Was the dog mad, Fairy Princess?"

"Well, he wasn't very happy about it."

After extracting Cosgrove from his comedy, we went to our rooms to dish and complain.

"Slim's a picture, all right," said Dennis Savage. "Even after all this time. But Evan's such a...I think 'stick-in-the-mud' does nicely here."

"Why don't *we* have a puppet theatre?" asked Cosgrove while sorting through the CDs in his carrying case. "I could put on shows."

"Why don't you start a catering service for gays who give dinner parties but don't want to cook and clean?" said Dennis Savage. He seemed confident of the notion, as if he'd been thinking it over for a while. "Carlo could bartend, and you could run the kitchen, cook the meal, and take home a check."

It was such a good idea, after all of Cosgrove and J.'s crazy schemes to make money, that Cosgrove got engrossed in the concept and didn't say anything at first.

A knock at the door, and Slim came in. He made the hostly gestures, and Cosgrove bubbled over with a consideration of the "lifechoice resources" of rural life. Or something like that. I kept thinking back to Evan's tale of the night he and Slim met, of queens getting Slim stripped for an exhibition as if at one of Tiberius' orgies in his notorious retirement on Capri, of how Evan saved him for a private exhibition and a lifetime of clean, manly devotion—so much more admirable than our sordid urban carnival. As Evan never tired of telling me.

"The main thing," Cosgrove was saying, "is that Cosgrove may soon have his own cooking show on cable. Each week, I prepare a dinner for a gourmet guest, and then my co-host, Nesto, has sex with the guest. What do you think, Slim?"

Slim sat on the edge of one of the beds with an expectant look, and after two beats Dennis Savage accommodatingly spirited Cosgrove out of the room. I sat opposite Slim.

We were just two now, and Slim nodded. Then he began. "I've heard cuckoo things about New York cable television," he said. "So they really have sex on it?"

"They show porn clips. Cosgrove's cooking show is rather ahead of the curve."

He nodded. "But there are many pleasures available in a place like New York. Right? They say that men can find quite what they want."

"Have you ever seen New York?"

"I'd like to, but there's always something that needs tending to around here. I wish I had someone to talk to about it. I heard there's a place like a hotel where men walk down halls with just a towel over their shoulder, and they haven't a care in the world as they go into a quiet bedroom for two."

Pause.

"Is there such a place?" he asked. "In fact?"

Pause.

"I heard that one man can stand behind another, and slowly run his hands over the other man's skin, feeling sure of each part before he moves on to the rest. You have your forearms and fingers to touch. The upper torso is next, isn't it? You can take your time, they say. He won't run away. He has a bottom like a peach, and when you part the globes to gaze upon the eternal ring, you sample the tightness with a slow, circulating tug. He says, 'To fuck me?' and you answer, 'Why not?' It's easier if they take happiness pills."

If I had a line here, I didn't utter it.

"I also heard about a place where men sit around a large poker table on stools, completely stripped. One man is under the table, giving a blowjob to one of the players. The others have to guess who it is by how dim he gets in the card playing. Have you played cards that way?"

I just looked at him.

"Businessmen travel to New York for the purpose of ordering Brazilian cocktails which make them woozy and open to suggestion. And when a football team visits, it is likely that two of the teammates shower together, get all soaped up, then take it to a lie-down. The big guy does the honors. Then the trainer bursts in, and do they look embarrassed. They say they were just wrestling, to keep in shape."

More pause.

"We don't get a lot of news out here," Slim then announced, as if he had been no more than discoursing on local peasant folk-ways rather than giving me his confession. And "It's getting late," he added. "The friends are coming over."

"The friends?" I asked.

"The Enclave. Yeah, that's ... It's how they like to see them-selves. As if they had something special to protect in this part of the world."

He suddenly got to his feet.

"I'd better go help Evan set up," he said, and I was alone. So I took a stroll and found my other two in the barn, playing records for the burro. Of course, I promptly told Dennis Savage about that scene with Slim. He didn't find it all that odd.

"This is a different place," he reminded me. "It's bound to have different people in it."

"Different from what?" I asked.

"This little guy prefers Cole Porter to the rest," said Cosgrove. "His ears go higher for the hot stuff."

I let it drop, and just enjoyed the music; finally it was time to go to the party. We had been hearing the guests arriving, in fact, and when we, too, went into the basement I thought of that moment in *The Roman Spring of Mrs. Stone* when Vivien Leigh walks into her own party and some woman cries out, "Trust you to know *that*, Rollie!": queens of both sexes, aging boys, and cousins of the parish. The queens were vapidly abrasive little snitches, the aging boys were as narrow as their crew cuts, and the cousins were good sports, always looking to be helpful. They bustled about with paper plates and cups as Evan conducted the buffet like Stokowski. Slim, looking guilty, assisted Cosgrove in the performance of another variety show in the puppet playhouse.

"They're straight, they're guilty, he's ready to rule!" Cosgrove was declaring. "Judge Cosgrove!"

Slim was endearingly clumsy at it—real men have no art, have you heard?—and there may have been some displeasure, at least from the queens, at Cosgrove's lack of shyness. Contrary to proverb, when in Rome one does absolutely nothing, hanging back with respectful timidity: or the Romans will resent one's self-assurance.

It was a long party. After the eats, the jukebox came on and there was dancing to old hits recalled from proms. "Teenager in Love." "I Just Saw an Angel." Slim and Evan slow-danced like the designated couple at a wedding as the queens managed to applaud and sneer at once, the aging boys got lost in thought, and the cousins doted. Then Dennis Savage cut his finger on some broken glass.

"Where on earth did you find any glass down there?" I grumbled as we headed up to our rooms for a medical interlude. "With all Evan's millions, you'd think he'd do better than paper plates and—"

"That's the club style, informal and easy-go. Gosh, this thing is bleeding."

"Hold it under the cold water, that'll discourage the flow of blood. I'm going to wash my hands separately."

Hauling out the first-aid kit, a steel box of heavy content, I then scrubbed my hands at the bathtub faucet.

"What is that," said Dennis Savage, eyeing the metal rectangle, "the cabinet of Dr. Caligari?"

Fishing out a tube, I told him to wave his finger in the air to lose the excess water. "This is a common household antibiotic, and you will notice that the salve does not come into contact with my fingers. Okay. Band-Aids"—as I undressed one—"are now packaged with a useful peeling gadget instead of the old red string that always failed to work."

Still considering the big steel box with worry, he said, "Are you going to operate or something?"

"Let me see the wound."

He extended his finger and I fastened the bandage. "Firm, you see? Neither loose nor tight."

"Neither Slim nor Evan. Why do you talk so while you do it?"

"To put the subject at ease."

"I am about as at ease as Trotsky was when Stalin's friends came for trick or treat." He inspected his finger. "It's very professional, though."

"I got a merit badge in First Aid."

Sitting on one of the beds and admiring his Band-Aid, he said, "A Boy Scout merit badge? Not a merit badge from some underground theatrical organization for beginning the beguine more times than . . . What?"

Packing up the first-aid kit, I asked him, "What do you think of Slim, by the way?"

"He's very sexy and confusing. One of my least favorite types."

"What's your favorite? When you were recruited, what special person did you name?"

"Ty Hardin."

A rustling in the hall warned of approach, and a queen and an aging boy appeared. The latter said, "Evan wondered . . . you know...," and the queen put in, "If you can tear yourself away from your thrilling coffee-klatsch, that is."

Dennis Savage held up his bandaged finger. "We had a medical emergency."

"Poor puss," said the queen, in the combination of sympathy and assault that serves as the type's defining tone.

Dennis Savage looked at him for a bit, then asked the aging boy, "Why do you pal around with that?"

Probably joking, the aging boy replied, "You don't get a lot of choices in a small town," and the queen let off the customary enraged comebacks. We just pushed past them and returned to the party.

THE NEXT DAY WAS unprogrammed, so we kind of hung around and assisted at the more colorful agrarian activities—yes, they work on weekends—while Cosgrove played 78s for the burro and improvised in the puppet playhouse. We had promised our hosts a gourmet dinner from scratch: Cosgrove's latest masterpiece, spaghetti and meatballs. This is not the standard plate of noodles. The meatballs, a blend of beef, pork, and lamb, are exquisitely tiny; the spaghetti sauce is really some melted "fresh grated"; discreet tablespoons of tomato sauce are no more than distributed here and there.

It never fails to delight, and Cosgrove was eager to show it off, so he, Dennis Savage, and I decided to spend the afternoon in town, picking up the makings. "Town" was no more than a crossroads civilized by commercial establishments; we walked there, partly to pass the time and partly to try the rural atmosphere on a lovely rural day.

That turned out to be a mistake, but without bad decisions life writes us no stories. In the grocery, Cosgrove was rounding up his "ingredients," as he puts it, when one of the aging boys from the night before came in with a queen we hadn't met.

"No," the queen told us immediately after the intros, "they keep me away on the important occasions." Leaning in too close, he added, "Afraid I might *blab.*"

Dennis Savage decided to help Cosgrove—immediately—and I used my trusty escape line, "Oh, there's Evita, I must say hello."* But the two of them caught up with us at the checkout, where the queen offered us a ride back. I knew to say no; but I hadn't planned on Cosgrove's having to tote quite so much in the way of raw fixings. So we piled into the queen's old Ford—the aging boy went off somewhere—and by the first stoplight the queen was ripping into Evan and Slim and their love affair of the ages.

"It's all such a fraud, isn't it?, for all those high notes Evan loves to sing. Doesn't tell you about all the times he had to go chasing after Henry in some bathhouse. Yes, we have them. You New Yorkers didn't invent sex."

In the back, Cosgrove pretended he had suddenly noticed Dennis Savage's bandage, presumably to interrupt the flow of slander pouring out of the queen.

"Did Bud do first aid at you?" Cosgrove asked. "When I see that metal box come out, I take the first bus to Indianapolis."

"Thank you for noticing," said Dennis Savage. "He's going for another merit badge."

"I long to know what merit badges *you* won," replied Cosgrove, to prompt a new line of discussion.

---

*I coined this exit bit years ago, at a party, when conversing with someone who turned out to be bad company. I had meant to say, "Oh, there's Patti LuPone, I must say hello." However, I couldn't remember her name. Her most famous role at that point was Evita, and that's what came out. I still use it, because it has an unexpected quality that gives the subject pause, allowing me to slip off into the crowd, or at least behind a prop tree. Also effective is Dennis Savage's variant, "Oh, there's Evita, I must call the embalmer."

"They should give Evan a merit badge for lost causes," the queen put in. And then he burst into song, to the tune of Edith Piaf's old standby "La Vie en Rose":

> *Don't you know we love the land,*
> *Our Pennsylvania land?*
> *It's in the Muller bloodlines. . . .*

He went on, "Yes, we call that 'the Evan cabaret,' don't you know."

"That's your idea of a song spoof?" I said. " 'Our Pennsylvania land'? What kind of queen are you? You've got the meanness and the anger, but you're completely missing the zippy fun. If I gave Lypsinka thirty seconds and any Piaf solo of his choice, he'd come up with something zany. Sidesplitting. *Gay.* Didn't you hear we're not in Kansas any more?"

Determined to spin out his tale, the queen raced back in with "You're so right, my dear, except every Muller male has died young and crazy trying to make a living out of nothing. Henry hates the farm. He's only there because Evan keeps it going. He's not like us, you know. Evan. He's a spoiled rich kid."

"Bud's a spoiled rich kid, too," said Dennis Savage. "He and Evan were the last to free their slaves, and even then they forced them to tour in a bus-and-truck *Porgy and Bess.*"

"Would you please?" I told Dennis Savage.

"Maybe we should walk this last section," said Cosgrove.

The queen went right on with "Everyone thinks Henry is the man of it, but Evan likes to play boss, doesn't he? His money gets into everything. He bought Muller Farm and Henry Muller right the way with it, didn't he? Then he tells Henry who can come to their parties, and who of us Henry can have sex with. Henry does anything for money, I bet Evan didn't tell you that. Yes, till Henry runs away again. We have a cabaret about that, too."

"Don't sing, please," said Cosgrove.

"But Evan always finds him. He hires detectives."

We swung into the driveway of Evan and Slim's place, and the queen was silent till we got to the house. Evan was standing there, and not, surely, by chance. He seemed to know that his legend had just been elaborated upon. The queen got out and slammed the door defiantly, but then he just stopped where he was, gloating for certain. Cosgrove went off to the kitchen. Evan glanced at the queen, then left him where he was and guided Dennis Savage and me indoors.

Let me say this: I demand Live and Let Live from others, and I obviously, then, spend heavily of it myself on their behalf. I don't care what some queen, or anyone, says. It's none of my business what Evan is or isn't.

Dinner was uneventful, despite that wonderful pasta. Cosgrove troubled to keep the conversation humming, but he got scarcely a drone out of Evan; and Slim was, as Dennis Savage said, confusing. And these are our poster boys, children—this the alternative to the alleged drugasexo turpitude of Stonewall.

Suddenly, Dennis Savage got on a jag questioning the validity of the queen as a type. My best friend is normally anything but controversial among people he doesn't know, but this night he was unstoppably off on a thinkpiece about the behavior and purpose and meaning of the queen.

"Why, for instance," he asked, "do they use that catty little bleat for everything they say? They're like those jackasses who pull on your cheek making nauseating koochy noises who get offensively surprised when you shove them away in disgust. Or wait—are they some show-biz invention? A blend of Oscar Wilde and Auntie Mame? They're playing a role that doesn't exist. There never was an Auntie Mame, and I wonder, after what

I've come to know as a gay man, if there even was an Oscar Wilde."

Cosgrove, who is very close to a queen called Miss Faye, ran off to toss the salad.

"Bud complains that his cousin's Chelsea Boy coterie lack every sort of intellectual curiosity. Every time he sees them, they're exactly the people they were before. They won't learn, so they don't grow—and such tales of their exploits as have been detailed to me reveal the usual testosterone competitiveness. They quarrel. They fight. But they never try to degrade each other with whiny cawings. They don't strike poses. They're men and they act like men. And you know what? People who meet them don't think they're picturesque or difficult or loathsome. People who meet them like them."

Silence.

"I have spoken," Dennis Savage finally said, taking up his fork again and adding, "Cosgrove, this is your finest dish of all."

Well. That was good for me; how was it for you? Slim and Evan were by now completely silent. I've never seen the salad go so fast. Then Evan got up with "Come with me for a talk" on his face and I followed.

We went outside in the snappy cool of an October that isn't doing fall quite yet, and Evan began, "I haven't lived a lie, despite what you may have been told this afternoon. I lived an ideal. It's a work in progress. All ideals are."

"You don't owe me an explanation," I told him as we walked his pathways, lanes running between great places where things grow, where matter is created. The farm is life.

"What did he say to you?" Evan insisted.

"That which all queens tell of—love is our doom, not our blessing. We are beyond even His redemption at last. That's what he said."

That hint of religious consideration can throw people off, but as we walked I could tell Evan was rebounding. Of course: we share a background, and he knows what I know.

"If you understood our struggles," he said. "How he wrestles with his demons. Such as those lost weekends in Harrisburg. I guess you heard of *those*."

"Lost weekends in Harrisburg?" I echoed, murmuring in the tone one takes for "Snow White used her strap-on on Dopey?"

He came to a stop and said, "Look around you. Yes, look."

We had reached the horses' corral, empty in the evening. It was, informally, the center of the front part of the farm—the façade of the place, so to say—with the farmhouse and outbuildings to one side, the barn off to the left, and fields stretching away to the right.

"Isn't it fine to live in a place that belongs to you?" Evan asked me. "A place with meaning? With *liberty*? Who owns a city? An apartment building? Who owns your life?"

I had nothing to say to that, so I turned a page of text to "Do you know that all my life I've had a crush on you?"

He looked puzzled. "Why?" he asked.

Why? Because—if younger readers will pardon a reference valid only to their elders—every generation has its Letch Feeley, but every individual of us has an Evan McNeary. Letch stuns us into knowing who we are; Evan tells us where to go with it. You might see the one as the ideal and the other as the work in progress.

We had stopped. Now we started moving again, not talking any more. Well, I did indulge myself in a repetition of "Lost weekends in Harrisburg," for echo texture. Otherwise, we were silent all along our walk, around the corral and among the fields and at length back into the house through the rear door leading to the basement rec room.

"I wish you could have seen Slim and me years ago," Evan told me, locking the door behind us as we got inside. "We were so sure of each other, and so much alike."

I did see you years ago, you alone. And of course we were unalike, you and I; and have remained so. I admire what you admire, Evan: I simply don't believe it can be found. Rather, I imagine, it finds you.

Moony in his nostalgic haze, Evan approached the puppet theatre. "Yes," he said. "Yes, Slim and I used to put on shows with his sister back then. She was the perfect fairy princess."

"Is that when you went chasing through the bathhouse?" the lumberjack puppet asked, leaning forward to peer at Evan.

Startled as if by a shaking of the earth, Evan took a step back and looked sharply at me. I heard running footsteps somewhere as the fairy princess flew down to the stage with "Evan pays for it, and all is revealed in the exciting conclusion."

The steps must have been Slim's, because now he came roaring down at us to throw himself at the little playhouse, ripping away the curtain and breaking off the top and sides with his hands. "Were we waiting for *this*?" he shouted, grabbing at the very walls of the house of stories with a determination one sees only in the devotees of disreputable gods. "For *this*, I ask you?" he added, with a frustrated wrenching that finally flung everything everywhere to reveal Cosgrove, still holding the puppets as he backed away. Panting, Slim lifted the stage itself and threw it across the room to cartwheel along the floor and fall at the wall. And so Slim tore his theatre down.

No one moved or spoke.

Still panting, Slim went over to the couch and sat. Evan, gazing upon his man with faith unshaken—faith, even, dismissive of more enjoyable religions—joined Slim. Slim took Evan's hand, and Cosgrove laid the two puppets on the couch with them.

Dennis Savage was standing in the doorway; I don't know how much he had seen. The three of us went upstairs, packed, and drove off without saying anything to our hosts. I suppose we'd already said it.

The ride was silent till we got back to the highway, when Cosgrove suddenly piped up with "If I would have a puppet show of my own, I will present 'Little Red Ridinghood,' based on a cartoon I once saw. The cops will release the wolf if he leaves Little Red and Grandma alone and goes straight. So the wolf agrees. Then he gets to the door, and just before he runs out, he says, "I'll go straight—straight to Grandma's house!"

I laughed involuntarily: a reflective chuckle.

"What's so funny?" said Cosgrove. "Because I know you're laughing at something else."

"I'm laughing at the alarmed expression on your face when Slim wrecked the theatre. And what did it mean that 'all is revealed in the exciting conclusion'?"

"It doesn't mean anything. It's art."

We drove on in silence till Cosgrove asked if we could have the interior lights on so he could practice alarmed expressions in the rearview mirror. Dennis Savage and I got into a refreshing dispute about how many exits we had to count off till the next turning, and about who had more fun in high school, and about the appeal of the handlebar mustache.

And Cosgrove, celebrating with a resplendent yawn, said, "Isn't it time for the first rest stop?"

5

A
DEATH THREAT
FROM
MY FATHER

KEN NO LONGER BUYS classical CDs; he likes to come over and listen to mine. Short bursts work best—tone poems, overtures, the occasional aria. At first, Cosgrove joined us, to feed Ken historical background and critiques of the available performances. But Ken was mystified by all those words about music. Music is music. One doesn't talk about it. One listens to it.

Cosgrove threw up his hands and withdrew from the concerts. "That cousin of yours lacks collecto," he told me.

"He doesn't lack collecto in Chelsea," I said. "They call his dick 'Titanic' because thousands went down on it."

"Dennis Savage is right. You like anybody cute."

"One has to be nice to gay relations."

This last remark was so patently hypocritical that Cosgrove enacted that sarcastic old mime of feeling my forehead for a sign of fever to explain my deranged condition. With a mid-October Indian summer working, he went off for what he calls a "look-see walk" with Nesto; and Ken enters.

"The problem with family," Ken says, "is that they can drive you crazy yet you have to go on knowing them. Can't live with them, can't live without them."

"I can live without them," I said, raking through a pile of CDs I had set aside for Ken's visits.

"I sort of have similar troubles with the guys."

Meaning his Chelsea coterie.

"Do I love them and all? Of course. But the focus is that I'm very tired of that little apartment and extremely bored with my work." Ken has one of those sophisticated computer jobs that people like me can't remember the name for and can barely describe. It treats the situation of a small business going into expansion mode and requiring more infrastructure on the screens. Ken talks to senior staff, designs a new program, then teaches it to the company. It pays well, at least.

"So," he goes on, looking over my shoulder at the discs, "I reach that place where I need different, and it makes my friends tiresome, because they're just more of . . . who carries the football this week. Whereas I might want to be in Wonderland, where you meet a guy you have to start from scratch with and you can be surprised. My friends so far? I knew them before I met them. And the guys you pick up are the Undergear catalog, only talking. Sebastian's ambition is to make some guy's wildest dreams come true. I need a guy who doesn't have dreams. Play some music, okay?"

I put on Richard Strauss' *Don Juan*.

"Which is this?" Ken asks.

"It's about a search for the ideal partner."

He nods and, after the music ends, tells me, "He was seeing The One, but he gave up and died. I heard that."

I nod.

"But couldn't *I* find him," he goes on, "in the world today? I know exactly what I want." He warns me with a look: "Yes, I've given you his measurements. The colors of him. But I don't want him knowing he's hot, you know? Bartholomew's set himself up as a cruising teacher on the Net. Like those guys coaching chess fiends, only about tricking. Even shy Tom-Tom goes up to guys on the street without knowing if they're gay. Guess what his line is?"

" 'Hi, fullback. Live with your folks?' "

"No. He says, 'Were you in that Brad Pitt movie? The scene where . . .' Come again?"

I repeat the fullback bit.

"That's a tricking line?" he says, going deadpan. "A *real* one?"

"A spoof one."

"What's the point of a spoof tricking line?" he asks in a tone mixed of grief and incredulity. "That's like spoof underpants. Spoof orange juice." Going into the kitchen for some sparkling water, he concludes, "Isn't that the problem with you Stonewalls—that everything has to be a riff? Some things should be real."

"The bigots think nothing about us is real. Absolutely nothing at all."

Ice plopping into bubbles. "What do they think we are, then?"

"Bad children. They want the English Nanny to shake and bake us into cookies."

"It is so way not enjoyable when you get abstract on me." He returns with his glass and one for me. As I take it, he gets even more serious, as if he'd been planning something for a while and just now decided it's time.

"I have confided a lot in you," he says. "Because if I tell one of the guys, then they *all* hear it. Do you confide in return?"

I shrug. "My blameless life."

"It would be best if you shared something dangerous with me. Something personal and . . . What?"

"Ken, you grew up seeing me in the family context. That's as unprotected as—"

"That's *company*. Like Davey-Boy and Sebastian and the guys. I want you to show yourself alone."

I could have said no. But Dennis Savage is right: I like anybody cute. Including relatives.

"Want to see the last letter my father wrote me?"

"Hand it over, cousin."

I've a cache of Special Mail: Ayn Rand's refusal, when I was at *Opera News*, to discuss Wagner's idea of heroism; Tommy Tune's note after a newspaper piece on *Grand Hotel*; poison-pen sends; and so on. This particular letter came to me ten years after I terminated my relationship with my parents.

As Ken reads, let me explain, boys and girls. When I started this series, I wanted to concentrate on gay men doing gay things. I presumed that a difficult family background would distract from this drive-line, and I decided to demote my parents to walk-on parts. Okay; though this does omit a lot of drama and thus cuts holes in one's story. And now Ken looks up from my father's letter.

"Uncle Edgar wrote this?"

I nod.

"To you, right? Because there's no salutation."

"He wasn't in a saluting mood."

"It's outstandingly barfy where he says he's 'willing to meet you anywhere anytime.' He underlines that as if making some great concession. And where he says you won't meet him because you're not a man. Is that how he'll win your heart and mind?"

"He's trying to manipulate me by threatening me with a low opinion. But you know what I think is the first manly virtue? Independence. Real men aren't afraid of other people's opinions."

"He must be crazy," says Ken. "He begs you and threatens you. He's on his knees to kill you."

Ken takes a swig of water. He's thoughtful now, a man of business and science.

"You have to destroy this letter," he tells me. "You can't let anyone find this after your death. It would be a very bad career move."

So we burned it alive in the kitchen sink.

"Okay. And now there's this other thing," says Ken. "We're going to make porn movies, and Davey-Boy wants your input on the plots. It's a sandwich brunch. Is Sunday good for you?"

A SANDWICH BRUNCH IS typical of Ken's group; they rarely cook in any real sense. There is a huge ice bucket of bottled beer, usually Beck's or Tsingtao, and a platter of cold cuts on fancy bread in quarters. Turkey with Russian dressing, Boar's Head chicken, and cheese combo are most common: for those of you who want to keep up with the younger generation.

We met at Roland's, though Davey-Boy presided. He delayed his talk till the very end, however, after we'd done the usual round-the-table on a pertinent question of the day—which was, this evening, Which gets you further socially, a very long but skinny dick or a beer can?

Finally, Davey-Boy outlined the project: a cooperative venture into porn videomaking, with the Kens as stock company and back-of-camera staff. There were two partners outside the group who were supplying the start-up capital and equipment. Some strategic factors had yet to be considered, such as where exactly they would be taping—in various apartments? On the Island? And what kind of porn was this to be? Pure Eros, or story lines? The balletic kind of sex, on the hood of a coupé, or moving up a staircase, propelled by abandon?

Then I piped up: "You have to decide whether the sex should be stage-managed around kiss panels and come shots and so on, or whether you simply fix your lens on two guys who know the ropes and tie them true in real time. High-tech porn directors can spend two days getting down one little date. It can seem surgical in its precision, like Kristen Bjorn designer sex. Shouldn't sex be raw and messy?"

Wilkie said, "I'd like to hear some red-hot talk instead of—"

"But what stories?" Crispin put in. "The Shoemaker and His Apprentice? Or—"

"It should be about our lives," Wilkie told him.

I asked, "Isn't porn a mad excursion? It's wish fulfillment."

Everyone answered at once, and Davey-Boy, clearly relishing the activity, quieted them down for "We must emphasize a trademark and sell an entire line of product, not just a title here and there. They must hit our dot.com and long to follow the careers of our showcase personalities."

Well, the room just glowed at that, even when I mildly said, "This isn't Shakespearean rep, now. What career do you mean? Fucking?"

Davey-Boy would only smile.

"Yes, an established top finally makes his debut as a bottom," I went on. "It's hardly Laurence Olivier playing Oedipus and Mr. Puff in the same evening."

"I have vintage titles for us to screen," said Davey-Boy, with the seductive yet reassuring tone of the con man who never gets home from his day job. "Here is where we start, gentlemen."

Roland's apartment consists of one long room, so we had to reimpose the furnishing arrangements for home theatre. Ken went off to the belasco, and when he emerged—just when two mechanics had turned from a Chrysler to work on each other—I went up for a chat.

"Is this serious?" I asked him.

"You don't approve, I guess."

"Am I a puritan?" I asked, truly wondering.

He touched my arm. "It's okay. Your generation is pretentious. It's lovable."

I took refuge in an old joke. "Pretentious? *Moi?*"

"Well, like you aren't tattooed or pierced."

"Nor are you."

"I will be."

That shocked me, and I forgot to hide it.

He smiled. "I like you best when you don't know what's happening."

A quick look at the television revealed a change in program, to vanilla prancing by the Athletic Model Guild: an Ancient Roman theme. Ellroy called to us to join in the screening, while Davey-Boy paused to expatiate on some nicety of porn etiquette. But Ken just said he could see from where he was and, turning back to me, went on with "You're old-fashioned, and it's your best quality. Drugs? Never touch them. Unsafe? I'm the Scarlet Letter on. Booze? Never before midnight. Cruising pose?" Here he heroically extended his arms in what he felt was an old-fashioned come-on, though it looked more like Marivaux rehearsing at the Comédie-Française. Or no: Mr. Puff.

I said, "I'm just asking if you want to take such an irrevocable step."

Glancing at the video screen over my shoulder, Ken said, "Being gay is irrevocable, so what's the difference? Isn't that your friend, though? The one in your building?"

I turned to the TV screen to find yet another film, this one in color. Dennis Savage, a cleric in a book-lined study, was apparently about to discipline an altar boy. Rehabilitation, in the form of a dramatic reading from Saint Thomas Aquinas, preceded punishment. As the good father bent over an impossibly vast volume sitting on a lectern, the younger man—one of those skinny kids who could be anywhere from eighteen to thirty—undressed him. This was performed ritualistically, in a series of sly, subtle, and very smooth maneuvers. I got it: the clergyman doesn't realize that he's losing his three-piece suit button by button. Accompanied by the almost inaudible droning of his lecture, the kid's movements became hypnotic, as when he stood behind the older man to rub the lapels of his jacket before grasping the collar to gentle it off; or when he methodically edged the belt through its loops with a soothing pull before winding it up and setting it lovingly on the desk.

Dennis Savage seemed to be about twenty-five and at the height of his gym period. He looked wonderful. His stripping procedure was more direct, but of an occult nature, a worshiping in stages laid down by clan elders. He unbuttoned the kid's shirt but did not remove it, pulled the kid's pants down to the thighs, then pushed his shirt back off his shoulders. Junior immediately fell to his knees to shop the top man's upturned dick, and after a short while the latter pulled the kid up, sat on a couch, and set the kid athwart the theocratic knee with his pants still around his ankles while reaching for a heavy wooden paddle with a long handle.

Our audience, given to hoots and commentary minutes before, was absolutely silent. Everyone knows that porn will comprehend the occasional paddling scene, but few of us have actually seen one and probably assume that it is faked or softened in some way. Not here. The *crack!* of wood on flesh was barbaric, and several times the camera stole close to catch the older man's quiet rhapsody and the ambivalence of the kid, who hadn't been careful what he wished for. When it was over, the top turned the bottom over and began inching down his trousers, got them off at last, saw to the socks and the shoes, and then took a questing little tour of the student's skin. The older man's face bore no expression throughout this operation, even when he pulled the boy close to cradle him.

They posed thus, as the lights faded. When the picture came back on, the performers were already on a doggy date. It was a violent one, reaching a high point when the kid shouted, "You're going too hard" and his master yanked the kid's head back with a handful of hair to shout, in turn, *"More! More! More! More!"* They came right after, it appeared, their faces aligned in a mien beyond even the customary gasp of the divine. One last thing: the camera closed in on the kid for a head shot, and, moist and spent as he was, he lazily curled out a "Thank you, sir." There the film ended.

After a short silence, Davey-Boy got up to retrieve the tape. He looked thoughtful, and didn't cue anything else up.

"The top is a friend of yours?" Harlan asked, as stirring filled the room. Crispin went to the fridge for beer refills.

"Would you call that," said Tom-Tom, "a representative sample of your friend's tricking style?"

"In his wild youth, perhaps," I said, examining the tape's packaging to learn the title of that arresting little sketch. Oh, of course. "He's quite reformed today, I believe."

"That's another thing," said Wilkie. "Do we include the rough stuff?"

"Fetish is trendy," said Davey-Boy.

" 'Thank you, sir,' " Tom-Tom echoed, infusing it with fear and wonder. He has the sweetest heart of all the Kens, and arouses protective instincts on his behalf in a surprising variety of types. His feelings are almost as big as his arms.

"No, Tom-Tom," I said.

"What no?"

"That's not how he said it, Tom-Tom." I like to use his name a lot; it's like stealing kisses.

"How did he say it?"

"Like a pro."

"We should include a lot of scenes with guys in authority like that," said Crispin. "Commanding officers and cops, you know? Or even diplomats on a trip. You're sharing a room, far from your wives." He turned to Tom-Tom, who was still going over his recent exchange with me and wasn't ready for Crispin's hand when it touched the back of his neck. Tom-Tom jumped; and Crispin, getting into his part, calmed him with caresses. "No one has to know," he purred to Tom-Tom. "And you want that peace treaty, don't you?"

Tom-Tom suddenly started weeping, and Crispin held him. The Kens all get hard when Tom-Tom weeps, and they take turns holding him and stroking his hair. He'll go home with one of them tonight.

I walked Ken the three blocks to his place, and at his door he asked, "Did you know that about your friend?"

Answering a different question, I said, "I'm not sure how I react to Davey-Boy's idea."

"You think it's immoral."

"It's not immoral. But it's worrisome."

"I like that you're looking out for me," he said. We shook hands and I went home. I had a lot to think about, so I walked the whole way.

THE IMPLAUSIBLY WARM WEATHER suggested to Lars Erich a ride in the Park; but I know he really wanted to talk about Peter.

"Of course, we must be breaking up at this moment," Lars Erich told me as we pedaled over the rise of the big hill leading to the museum. "I will always love him, but we are not matched. He looked extremely handsome pleading with me not to part at last. But he is relieved in a secret way. He was thinking I would perhaps stalk him and create commotions."

Lars Erich had showed up shirtless in Lederhosen, sneaks, and an Alpine hat, and what he was creating was accidents as gaping bikers lost control of their rides and narrowly missed crashing. Like a number of terribly effective physical specimens of my experience, Lars Erich takes no notice of his charisma. It's all someone else's problem.

"You're too crazy to be a boy friend," I said. "You're fascinating company, and I bet you'd be a triumph in a lifeboat. But you're too *very* for the everyday."

"Yes," he answered. "Yes, it is true as you say it." We held off speaking as we rode up to the water fountains that guard the Fifth Avenue exit, Lars Erich naturally zooming up to brake at the last possible second, daring inertia to throw him. He pulled off his hat and thrust his head under the water, then shook his hair like a dog. As we started riding again, he said, "Even so, I am certain that I want excitement only. I am not interested in your everyday."

"Would you ever appear in a porn movie?" I impulsively asked.

"It is a most unexpected question," he answered, smiling.

"I mean, if an offer came your way, would you consider it, or do you think of letting strangers in on your action to be crossing a line of some kind?"

Thinking it over, he said, "What is the reason for porn? One is short of money. Or one feels somehow unrewarded in the world and must expose his best features to admiration. These are not my needs. So I have no reason for porn."

"You wouldn't do it for a kick?"

"Why is it a kick?" he countered, riding along no-hands like a circus stuntman.

"What I mean is," I went on, trying to formulate the question that would yield Final Answer, "is there some moral position in this, or do you just not care?"

"It is not something I think about."

We rode in silence again, cutting through the Transverse to

the West Side, gaining the hill after, then sloping down to the next water stop. We said very little till we got to the benches outside Sheep Meadow, where we banked our bikes and rested.

"It's sad about Peter," Lars Erich more or less sighed. "The breakup is always sad. But he is not fun to fight with. He doesn't need power over others. You are like him, too."

"Live and let live," I said.

The mild weather had brought out the runners, and we revered a few as they passed. One was notable, I thought: not so much handsome as very well made with interesting parts and a curious appeal in his almost ordinary face. In sneaks and navy blue running shorts, he was someone you almost dismiss in the first few seconds but before much longer prefer to Mark Dalton. And watch this: while the other runners ignored us with those thousand-yard stares as fixed as bayonets, this one slowed down and veered off the asphalt in our direction. He was still in motion, shifting his weight from leg to leg, as he planted himself before us to state that he lived nearby and Lars Erich was welcome to visit his apartment.

"I am with my companion," said Lars Erich, indicating me. "It is also possible that I am too crazy to be a boy friend."

"I already have a boy friend," said the runner, still oozing from side to side, holding focus. "I just want a date. I'm here every weekday, if you feel differently tomorrow."

And with that, he started off on his laps again.

"You have astonishing self-control," I said as we watched the runner recede southward.

"Why have you asked me about this making of porn? Have you asked Peter? Or your amusing young friend in masks? Why is this a question for me?"

"It's just that some guys of my acquaintance have decided to incorporate as a porn studio, and for some reason I am disquieted. Of course, there are hidden difficulties that may deter them.

They might easily tape a scene or two, then drop the whole thing. But you might know something. I mean, because you're so wild. I hope you're not offended."

He didn't appear to be. "Is it a classic form or romantic?" he replied. "Classic is about knowledge. Romantic is about emotion. I always ask this first."

"I don't think porn is either."

"Everything is either. Say this—what do you see in these visions of men having sex?"

"I see freedom from straights."

He considered this.

"Because," I went on, "all the characters are available men. Even if we're supposed to think of any of them as hetero—cops, or whatever—or even if the actors themselves are marketed as hetero, they're still having sex with other men. So straight is in effect expunged from the world."

"What is such an English word, 'expunged'?"

"It means No More Fathers, and boys just get to have fun."

"It is wonderfully alarming. Maybe I make some porn after all, for this political statement. I am called Eberhard Kokk, and everyone rumors that I am a video star to get over my sad romance. It is said that I make classic porn, a sexual instruction. But my heart knows it is romantic porn, about the sorrow of love. And yet we see that man before, running, and then he comes up. So there is always more love."

"That's the message of porn, isn't it?" I said. "It's the ideal gay condition—no one gets turned down."

"I think I have been turned down," he told me. He let out one of those little exhalations of bemused resignation. "Because I am too crazy," he said.

☾ ☾ ☾

KEN LIKES TO CONTEMPLATE Beethoven now, usu-
ally an overture but sometimes an entire symphony. "It's like
Meeting," he pointed out, "because you just sit there wondering
for forty minutes."

One day, after Wilhelm Furtwängler's reading of the "Pas-
toral," he said, "Tom-Tom likes you. He says he comes to visit
here. What does he do?"

"Listens to music and talks about you."

Ken nodded.

"Well," I went on, "and his family. His new job downtown. You
know what's funny about your gang? You're all very, very close,
but it's sex close and style close and sandwich-brunch close. And
now it's to be porn close. But at least some of you are looking for
someone to be honest with. Don't you . . . like, trust each other?"

"He's closeted, you know. Tom-Tom. Perhaps it bothers you,
being so defiant yourself. That Stonewall thing. Down with
straights."

"I'm too lazy to be closeted. It takes so much energy."

"Tom-Tom hopes you'll get political on him and coach him in
how to . . ." He performed this little act he has invented: he mimes
pressing a button on a remote and makes a fast-forward *zzzt*
noise. He skips the boilerplate.

"It's really none of my business," I said.

Ken slowly shook his head. "You're so . . . pure. So way what
you are." He wasn't admiring me, just trying to find the word that
means Maria. So I gave it to him:

"'Independent.' I trust in Beethoven and liberty and not making excuses. I trust in the West and its belief systems, which gave
us a civilization known by art so abundant that it breaks into vast
groupings of elitist, bourgeois, and pop. I trust in music and theatre. I trust in gays, who have their own vast groupings yet to be

charted. I trust in the holy Western trinity of Dante, Goethe, Streisand. I trust in myself."

"I can see why Uncle Edgar and Aunt Beatrix can't handle you," he said, amused.

"Can't control me, rather. Because gays are as independent of fathers as art is independent of the state."

So that put a button on it, and we paused to start the next topic. "Tom-Tom talks about me?" he asked.

"You're his Beethoven."

He got up, crossed the room, and examined the jewel box of the CD we'd just heard "'Wilhelm Furtwängler,'" he read out, pronouncing it so badly it rhymed with "Beetlejuice." He fingered the booklet as if looking for a visual, his key into everything. What does music look like? Was Beethoven tall? Laying the pages down, he said, "My friends? Why do they . . ."

"Look up to you?"

"Yes."

"I think it's because you are paying no price, and they want to learn from you how it's done."

"No price?"

"No cross to bear. No problems."

"So I'm carefree?"

"Aren't you?"

After saying nothing for a long time, he told me, "I want my friends to like each other, but not too much."

In no time at all, it seemed, it was another Thursday dinner with J. To make it interesting, we asked him to bring Vince along, and I decided to add in Ken for that piquant mix of types that makes a party all the go. And, on a hunch, I asked Dennis Savage if he'd like to socialize with his ex after all this time and get a load of the boy friend.

I did it on impulse only minutes before the dinner, upstairs at Dennis Savage's place while Cosgrove coolly prepared his twenty-four-condiment lamb curry in our kitchen. It was still curiously warm for fall, and horribly dark out, almost black, with a promise of weather capable of anything. One thinks of people killed by a stroke of lightning, such as the twenties drag queen Bert Savoy, whose act Mae West adopted and made famous. Bert Savoy's catchline was "You mussst come over," and that's what I said to Dennis Savage.

"Tonight?" he said. "For the weekly dinner with ... him?"

"His roommate, Vince, will be there, too. I think you will find him congenial."

"I will come. And, pardon me, but I've been meaning to tell you that I envy and respect your relationship with a fine young fellow named Cosgrove." Looking outside at the strange gathering of clouds and anger, he added, "I musn't envy, I know that."

"You've had everyone," I said. "You took cruising seriously, de-voted yourself to the gym and mastered approach technique, and I admire that. You scored at your choice, conquering and plun-dering ... I mean ... Sorry, that didn't come out right."

He smiled.

"It's the great gay democracy," I explained, "in which anyone can become president. Only the president doesn't rule, he scores. We defy rulers. We seduce their sons. We are their sons."

A great thunderclap was heard outside.

"We defy each other," I went on. "No—we amaze each other, so that Dr. Scott can pose for Colt under a mythopoetic working-class pseudonym and become the Man of the Age. It doesn't mat-ter if he's gay or straight. What matters is the revolutionary act of being naked and stupendous. But this is a gay act in effect, because isn't homophobia really a fear of nonconformity? Yes, it's a fear that our independence rebukes their lack of imagination."

Dennis Savage looked out the window again. Or, rather, gazed, taking it in.

"I spit at conformity," I said, and there was a flash of thunder.

"The fathers are angry," said Dennis Savage.

"Porn spits at conformity, doesn't it? And it's the great democratizer, because in porn everyone is a man and every man wants all the other men. There's no real life in it. It's utopia."

"You don't ever get intellectual about porn with me," Dennis Savage observed. "You hardly ever mention it at all. Just today, suddenly."

"In the future," I told him, mistakenly trying to say nothing by waxing garrulous, "everyone will be a porn star for fifteen minutes." I was afraid my silence would talk, so I was filling it with words, which can be disguises. "Do I dispute man's inalienable right to live porn? Nay, I enthuse over it!"

"What's got into you?" he asked. Then he almost jumped at a gigantic whack of thunder.

"They're coming for us," I announced. "We don't have much time left."

"You're in too serious a mood to be joking," he said. "You've gone too far and you're trying to get back. Tell me what's wrong. Is it romantic, social, or professional?"

"It's cinematic."

He went quite, quite still, then said, "You saw it, didn't you?"

Boys and girls, I was not going down without a stall: "Saw what?"

"That porn thing I did. *Please, Sir, I Want Some More*, or something?"

"You made porn, did you?" I replied, trying to get a joke up. "*Academics Unleashed*, co-starring . . ." I trailed off.

"Is that what's got you twisted up with speeches and the blurting out of innermost thoughts? Yes, I like it rough sometimes. So what?"

"That's not why I'm upset," I told him, though I was still haunted by the shameless expertise of that *"More! More!"* refrain. "And it's called *Thank You, Sir.*"

"So you did see it."

"Shouldn't I have been already aware that under the bourgeois façade hides an alarming wild man?"

Outside, the weather gods let off the thunder as big as Moloch.

"One more of those," he said, "and the dinosaurs will be extinct all over again."

"I like you so much," I told him.

Two beats. He reached out a hand and rubbed my forearm a bit, which meant, I guess, Yes, okay, don't worry. Then, without changing expression, he said, "If you don't stop acting like someone in a David Mamet play, I am going to turn you in to the gay stylemasters and..." Thus he, too, trailed off.

"The very jests evaporate on the tongue," I helpfully put in, and he laughed.

"Actually, no one gets everyone he wants," he said then, "which is how I ended up making that movie. The kid was straight, so that video was the only way I could get to know him. And he liked it rough, so don't blame me."

"How can he be straight and like it rough? He shouldn't like it at all."

Putting a hand on my shoulder, he asked, "Are you all right now?"

"No."

"Good," he said, moving toward the bedroom. "Help me pick out a..." He stopped and turned back to me. "You're *still* not all right?"

"I'm all right, but I'm confused. And Mamet isn't correct. It was more like Chekhov played in the style of Pixérécourt. And don't bother changing. It's just my cousin and Vince Choclo."

Dennis Savage nevertheless decided to put on a more adventurous shirt, and I followed him into the other room, to further sound effects in the heavens.

"Whatever happened to Cosgrove's mildly arresting Hispanic friend?" he asked.

"Nesto. He's still around."

"Could he possibly be asked to the next party?" Pulling on a thin cotton turtleneck in navy blue, he tacked on "I'd love to have a second look at him."

"I'll speak to the chef. You might as well score Nesto and complete the set."

"Of what?"

"Men on the planet earth."

THE THUNDER HAD GROWN so intense by the time we got downstairs that Fleabiscuit was shivering under the couch. Dennis Savage went right to the kitchen, there to spend freely of advices and queries, and when he finally got around to the taste test he was like the Curies discovering radium.

He also discovered Cosgrove's new abs, for when I joined them he had the front of Cosgrove's shirt pulled up and was admiring the emerging outline of muscle.

"When did this happen?" Dennis Savage asked.

"Bud's cousin inspired me to try a lifting program all my very own."

"With what?"

"You've seen those weights in the bedroom a thousand times," I said, helping myself to the curry taste test. Well, actually, all I did was scarf up one of the twenty-four condiments, shredded coconut.

"Hey!" said Cosgrove.

"Those are working weights?" Dennis Savage asked me. "I thought that was a stabile."

"He's made me his love-slave muscleboy," Cosgrove went on rather chattily. "I have to bulk up or face life on the street."

"I expect someone or other would take you in," Dennis Savage observed. "Someone to teach you the meaning of the word 'Daddy.' "

And the heavens gave way with a wallop, my friends. You have never heard a storm crack open with such . . . I almost wrote "finality." Fleabiscuit yipped and ran into the bedroom to find his security blanket, and Dennis Savage once more raised Cosgrove's shirt to feel the proud divisions.

"My," he said.

"No, *my*," I told him.

"Now I *know* you're all right."

"J. has a family emergency," said Cosgrove, shredding more coconut. "He's back in Cleveland. So it's just Vince." To Dennis Savage, he added, in meaningful tone, "Vince *Choclo*."

Dennis Savage was disappointed to miss J.; but there are Thursdays to come.

Back at the window, I said, "I hope the two guests don't get caught in the wet. That downpour would cut right through an umbrella."

The buzzer rang from downstairs, and the doorman announced Vince Choclo just as Fleabiscuit returned, clasping in his teeth the red blanket he takes naps on and sometimes just carries around as a conversation piece. Cosgrove says that Fleabiscuit especially likes the snazzy green racing stripe that runs along one edge.

"You'll enjoy Vince," I told Dennis Savage. "He's a real character."

" 'Enjoy' in what sense? As in 'think he's hot,' perhaps?"

"He's more the jerko galoot sort, I'm afraid. But he's rather endearing in his own strange way. Like a bear riding a tricycle in a Russian circus."

The doorbell rang.

"Come and see," I said; but when I opened the door we saw a stranger: about five foot eight with a redhead's coloring and a clownish smile and the most astonishing physique ever stared at. And we did stare, right through the white T and cotton drawstring-sweatpants, drenched to see-through.

"I'm not really Vince," he said, dripping away in the sixth-floor hall. "He had to take his mother to the clinic."

And there he stopped, smiling broadly, as if that explained it.

Dennis Savage and I just stood there, so he added something. "Your guy at the door was like a general. I shoulda saluted, huh? I give it to him that I'm Vince 'cause that's how you're expecting me."

"Who are you?" I asked.

"Like I said, Vince couldn't make it, so he asked me to come in his place and be neighborly. He don't—"

"Red," I said. "Backhaus, right?"

"That's me," he smiled out. But he was starting to seem nervous and uncertain. So Dennis Savage and I got him inside and did the intros and Cosgrove came out to wave and Fleabiscuit did a little rolling dance with his blanket, subtly contrived to put guests at their ease.

Red Backhaus—Vince's lifelong buddy whom he loves and teases, you'll recall—was taking in the apartment. Dennis Savage and I were so busy reading each other's signals that I don't remember whether Red actually said, "Gawrsh." It may have been "Nice place you got here."

We steered him to the bathroom to get dry with the promise of fresh clothes to hop into. Believe it or not, we keep a drawer of old throw-me-outs (because of course you never see them again) for just this purpose, in an old suitcase way in the back of the bedroom closet. It took me a bit of a while to find them, and as I pulled out a set of sweats, Dennis Savage walked in with a grin on his face.

"What?" I said.

"Nothing. Except there's a little excitement in the apartment."

I heard the buzzer and called out to Cosgrove to pick it up. "What excitement?"

"Well . . . it's not in the style of Pixérécourt."

And just then Red came into view, completely naked and toweling himself off with gusto. He must have been extra thorough with his genitals, because he had wood on—and while I've seen this kind of mischief among old buddies out at the beach, I've never known it done before people you hardly know. And isn't Red straight? But wasn't Vince straight before he met J.?

"Good thing there's no girls around," said Red.

"That's the club motto," Dennis Savage replied, to a crash of thunder as punctuational as a *Tonight Show* rim shot.

I stepped forward to hand Red the dry clothes. Then I: one, heard the door slam; two, saw Cosgrove cross the living room toward the kitchen dragging the blanket with Fleabiscuit lying on it on his back, wurfing in ecstasy; three, took note of Ken efficiently pulling off the hooded sweatshirt that, with his vast plastic umbrella, had kept him dry; and, four, watched as Ken turned toward Red, Dennis Savage, and myself.

You need the visual, boy and girls: Red has one of those very hard-to-get layouts with no fat content or water retention. His is the body you see in medical charts: just muscles, really big ones in the arms and shoulders, with a long torso down to no waist and then operatic thighs and melodramatic calves. No hair except a blameless crew cut and a tiny patch at the place of sin. A shock right there in your apartment: who would have thought that dinner with your cousin starts with a view of The One?

Or so I read on Ken's face as he and Red looked at each other. Dennis Savage and I, behind Red, could not reckon what Red might be thinking, but I definitely heard the building shake to the pressing of organ pedals pitched too low for tone.

"Who are you?" Ken finally asked.

I said, "He's why fathers make death threats."

And Red, without moving in any direction, said to Ken, with a tone of appreciation, "You got muscles."

6

WILL ALL THE STRAIGHT GUYS PLEASE GET OUT OF THIS BOOK?

K EN AND I ARE listening to the only one
of Brahms' symphonies that is affable
rather than dramatic: like Ken himself.
It's the Second, in D Major, and we've reached the third
movement—the woodwinds whistling their docile melody over
the plucked cellos—and Ken is smiling because he knows I am
dying for the Red Backhaus story and he hasn't said a word about
it yet. He will, of course. He needs to go over it and learn more
about it with me. He needs to confide, and only in someone who,
like me, won't sell his secrets to Chelsea Boys for a flirty lunch.
He needs to stun the etiquette and just go on about himself for
hours. But he wants me hungry first.

I already know most of it, if in abstract terms: how Ken
started out as the champ of Chelsea with the run of the hall, and
then got tired of what was known and Sought Mystery. Others
join cults or get into radical politics; Ken wants to do something
with a drunken sailor on the morning after. He hopes to know
what else is gay besides gay.

The music ends, in that touch of Beethoven in the last brass
statement of the fourth movement's second theme. I button off
the CD. I sit back down and wait. It's time.

"Isn't it funny when guys look to you for approval?" he asks.
"As if they could pack on hit points with praise from you? Some
of them are very intimate about it, and I don't need that. But
some can be easygoing. It's a joke session to them. Tom-Tom, you
know. And Red. They don't snap at you if you're not giving them
the little attentions they want. They're patient. Or sometimes

they cry, it's true. Tom-Tom's such a little kid, despite his size. But Red? Can you see that bigster in tears? Is it amazing?"

"Have you fucked yet?"

Ken drew his head back slightly. He didn't exactly smirk, but I could see his teeth.

"Listen," he said. "Red is strange and interesting, and he flexes the tightest pump ever seen. He's the man to know. But is he one of us?"

"Does he call you?"

"Yes."

"To do what?"

"To talk, mostly."

"But do you date?"

"Just dinner in junkhouses, because he's afraid of fancy places. Like he's never had champagne or red snapper. All he wants is not to be criticized and laughed at. And I'm his pal, so I don't. If you treat him right, you can put your hands all over him, and he doesn't suspect anything. He's trusting. And he thinks it's this joke format we have, so he feels me up, too. Is he bold? Is he laughing all the time? Sure. Then he gets quiet the way heteros may at times do. And he rests his hand on my head and says, 'You're my pal, right, dude?'"

"We used to say, 'Man, that's heavy.'"

"It rocks. He's naïve and scared and he's in my power."

"You sound like Davey-Boy."

"Oh, this important thing, now—Tom-Tom's birthday party. He wants you to come, too."

"I'm flattered. Is it just your group, or—"

"Oh, no. Never. Birthdays? We don't do them, because every year after twenty-five you're less marketable. It's nothing to celebrate, is it?"

I said, "You don't really believe that, do you?"

There followed one of those silences during which you realize that you have been offensive. He rebuked me in mild tone: "It's rude to suggest," he said, "that I couldn't reasonably hold an opinion that doesn't accord with yours."

He was right, and as I apologized, he did the fast-forward thing, skipping on to "It's Tom-Tom's office friends. He likes them but they problem him. Or just one of them does but the others enable it. It's complicated, like everything with Tom-Tom."

A thought hit me. "Would Tom-Tom like Dennis Savage, do you suppose?"

"He liked him in that video, all right. But your friend is too old now."

Honest as ever.

TOM-TOM'S BIRTHDAY PARTY WAS one of those "meet at someone's apartment for drinks, gang goes out to dine, and the rest of us pick up the check" evenings. Ken forgot to warn me that Tom-Tom's co-workers were straight twentysomethings. Not one of my favorite groups. Also, for someone who is supposed to be closeted, Tom-Tom seemed to have no secrets from the males, who were doing that trendy nineties thing of flirting with the gay boy and making lewd tease jokes. There was only one woman, and she apparently hadn't heard the news about Tom-Tom. She, too, flirted with him, but quite sincerely, it appeared, and on the way to the restaurant she took his arm, which I'm quite sure he doesn't like. True, he never tried to discourage her. But when I walked him and Ken home after dinner, he did nothing but complain about the unwanted attention.

"And if I tell her to stop, she just does more," he said. "She wants to go steady. I won't even date her once—why should I? And it's not as though I could skip her calls. She's in the *office!*

She's at lunch, when we go, trying to feed me right at the table. Like a . . . pet doggy!"

"What does she feed you?" Ken asked. He was worried—I guess—at how distraught Tom-Tom sounded and trying to soothe him with a distraction.

"Guacamole chips," said Tom-Tom. "You know heteros can't go out without ordering chips and dip. And when I tell her to stop feeding me, she goes right on doing it, so I have to emphasize, and she says, 'Don't be so defensive!' She's pushing at me and accusing me and she's walking arm in arm with me and I *don't* want to *do* it any *more*!"

"Can't you take your arm away?" I asked.

"Yes, and I *told* you, then she *accuses* me. She's Bridezilla! Or it's that sarcastic tone of 'I won't bite you,' and other stupid things. Well, it's not about biting me, is it? I don't want her helping herself to my arm!"

After a bit, Tom-Tom added, in a quiet voice, "I'm never really happy except with my true friends, Kenry."

"That's a cute nickname, Tom-Tom," I said.

"What nickname?"

Ken laughed. "That's my *name*, cousin Bud."

"Kenry?"

They both nodded.

"How come I didn't know that?" I asked. "You've been family for . . . years."

"Well, you've always been sort of in your own family, haven't you, oh my cousin?"

Pensively, Tom-Tom put in, "It's funny that you two know each other"—which, translated from the Chelsea, meant "I never met a gay male over the age of thirty-five before."

⟨   ⟨   ⟨

TOM-TOM WAS SO UPSET about the girl in his office—Maureen by name—that he made an appointment to swing by on Saturday to talk Strategy and Feelings with me. But meanwhile something else had happened. A longtime friend named Stanley invited me to the opera on the spare half of his pair for the Friday night before. He had somehow ended up with two singles, so we were separated. At the last intermission, he set up a meeting after the opera's end at the usual place, and I agreed without thinking about it. But we weren't going out after, so why meet?—and in fact Stanley got delayed. He may have slipped on a pat of butter in the Grand Tier and was even now being seen to by the emergency medical team; or maybe he was just gabbing. In any case, I split, thinking nothing of it. Wouldn't you have done the same? But Stanley saw it differently; and Stanley was mad.

No, he is not an episode in my past—did you ever know a gay man named Stanley? He was just a music-and-theatre friend, and not one of the more engaging personalities, at that. But when I got home, Cosgrove told me that there was an "interesting" message for me on the tape, and he watched me as I played it. The words were simply "This is Stanley and I want to talk to you." The low, menacing tone, however, revealed that Stanley believed that he now held screaming rights to me.

"At last we know that someone's in trouble," said Cosgrove, barely restraining his glee.

"One is in trouble only with one's fate," I said. "Not with some jackass braying for attention you don't owe him."

"The terror," said Cosgrove. "The brandings."

"Go make cupcakes or something," I told him.

Okay. Now came Saturday and the meeting with Tom-Tom; but first we had Red Backhaus, who dropped in on some social pretext but who really wanted to talk about Ken. Do you wonder if you ever get to be the protagonist of your stories? I'm the best listener in the business, but why am I always the adviser when no one else is?

It's a living, I guess. Red's patter is like dodgeball: it keeps coming at you from all directions. He says things like "What I hate is when chicks say they want to fuck you when they really mean they want to *fuck* you. You know?"

Tom-Tom arrived almost immediately after Red, and the two of them got very curious about each other. It was engrossing to see Tom-Tom gradually accustom himself to Red's conversational gambits, which sound like the mad outbursts of one of the wilder characters on a cutting-edge cable-channel series.

"Are you a cousin, too, Tom?" Red asked. "There's plenty of cousins around."

Tom-Tom looked quizzically at me.

"A cousin of Ken's, he means," I explained. "No, Red, *Tom-Tom*"—a gentle emphasis for nomenclature correction—"is Ken's friend."

"My friend is Vince," said Red. "And is he a kidder! Says how a rooster's different from a faggot? 'Cause one says, 'Cock-a-doodle-doo' and the other says, 'Any cock'll do.'"

Silence.

"Okay," says Red. "I'll leave out that joke when I do the Comedy Club."

"You're very handsome, Red," said Tom-Tom.

"What, and me so goofy?"

Tom-Tom looked over at me again, as the phone rang. We let the tape take it, and heard the silence of someone who means to lurk and threaten. Soon enough, Stanley spoke, very angrily: "You better call me, you insincere bastard." Then he lurked some more, and then he hung up.

"Dude," said Red.

Tom-Tom now asked Red if he was Ken's new friend from

Brooklyn. Red said he was. Then Red asked me if I'd read all the books in the apartment. He rose as if to examine them from up close, but managed to get into a pose-and-flex session, showing off. I began to realize that Red was another of those men who are insecure socially but comfortable—eagerly confident, even—as a physical entity. It's how he keeps from worrying.

"I see you work out, Red," said Tom-Tom.

Red approached Tom-Tom. Silent and smiling, he offered Tom-Tom his right biceps to admire, tightening it up as Tom-Tom gave it a squeeze.

"Now you, cute dude," said Red.

Tom-Tom isn't used to this. Like all the Kens, he's very built, but his physique isn't something he does anything with. It's armor. Tom-Tom dutifully flexed his right biceps for Red, but without the flashy narcissism that Red affects when he exhibits. Red poses like someone who's been studying the pros. Tom-Tom poses like someone who would rather be the mustard boy at the preparation of a sandwich brunch.

Even so, Tom-Tom was game. "Have you tried this look?" he asked Red, pushing the short sleeves of Red's T-shirt up to the shoulders. First one. Then the other. It had the deliberate slo-mo effect of the stripping scene in Dennis Savage's porn film; I was seized with the feeling that I was watching a new reality show called *Fetish*.

"Great look, cute dude," said Red, in a completely happy mood. "What if I answered the door like this and a chick was there? Would she know how I feel about her?"

Tom-Tom was getting the rhythm of Red, and this time he didn't look at me before responding. Tom-Tom said, "She would dream of you day and night."

Red was so glad to hear it that he turned to me and gestured at Tom-Tom with an "Isn't he nifty?" pointing of the index finger.

Then he got almost mysteriously thoughtful as he rubbed his palm against his left arm just where the skin met the sleeve. He seemed to be actualizing a fantasy of some kind; Tom-Tom was hypnotized. How much, he must have been thinking, can one get away with now?

"It shows the real man," Red said, as if to himself. Then he smiled at Tom-Tom. "What's this look called, Tom?"

Think fast, Tom-Tom. "Bud, what's it called?" he asked me, the little sneak.

Red looked at me again. Tom-Tom was staring at Red.

"That's the Valentine's Day Superdate Look" was all I could muster.

"This girl at the gym where I work?" said Red. "She's always saying she'd like to come over, but when I mention a day she's suddenly busy. Could she be teasing me? 'Cause I got a case of the fucks for her."

"Would you two please sit down?" I said. "All that standing and touching and confiding is making me anxious."

They broke it up and parked themselves, Red on the "shoelace" couch, where Fleabiscuit was patiently awaiting a customer.

"Some of the girls today are very sinful in how they talk," said Red, addressing a new paragraph to Tom-Tom. "I was telling our host before how some of them like to haul out those strap-ons on a guy. One said to me . . . well, not to me but to my buddy, Vince Choclo? She said, 'I want to feel your tightness and see how you come.' I mean, *dude*."

Tom-Tom just sat there, falling in love; and I got tired of being the butler in a drawing-room comedy, so I grabbed a lead role by taking Red up on that line of conversation, and we batted it around for a while. He got so into expressing his viewpoint— really, into the novel experience of being listened to—that he followed me into the kitchen on the sparkling-water refills trip. And

Tom-Tom followed *Red*, and three bodies rather fill my little kitchen. Yet there was no sense of anyone's feeling crowded or needing to defend his patch. Even Red went with it, eager to talk sex with men who wouldn't keep challenging him the way his day-to-day chums probably do. As I outlined in the first piece in this volume, there's no feud like two straight men who think they're friends.

Now Red left the kitchen with a "Be right back" and headed into the bathroom: which I was hoping would happen.

"Tom-Tom," I said as he followed me and the seltzer into the living room, "you are, I trust, aware that Red is Ken's friend first?"

He shook his head. "Ken said No more sign-up sheets. It's every man for himself."

"You're going to risk your best friendship over some——"

"Do you *see* that guy? He's Fuck Daddy Supreme! And Ken told me that they aren't dating in the true sense. So how would I be cheating if they only have lunches? The thing is, Is Red straight or what?"

"He's . . . what."

Tom-Tom looked crafty, a face I'd never seen on him before. "I'm going to test and see, just watch."

"How, Tom-Tom?"

He put a finger to his lips. "J'ai mon plan," he said. He knows that he's at his cutest when he speaks French.

As soon as Red came back, Tom-Tom told him about Davey-Boy's plan to get into pornmaking, without defining the kind of porn it was.

"Davey-Boy?" echoed Red, burping after a swallow of seltzer bubbles. "Who's that, some gunslinger?"

"He's my closest pal after Ken. He wants us each to concept a porn story and then film it as the star."

"Oh, man," said Red. "Can I get in on that?" To me, he

added, "And don't tell Vince, okay? Because he always horns right in. Here's the deal—it's in my gym, where I'm helping Jennifer with her program. You don't know her, but she's got a pair of bamboulas...and...*and* her tops never reach her shorts, right, so there's always a real nice view there. This lady is a beautiful piece of real estate, and I'm just playing along real cool when, whaddaya say, her top gets caught on something, and the two lovely friends pop out so near my face that I can't help it if I suck from one to the other so deep and slow. Mmm, so tasty."

Pausing, he looked up as if at a screen, to check the footage. Then: "So she loses her balance and accidentally pulls on the string of my Wilsons and they fall to the floor. Out comes Thumper, and I say, 'Okay, give me ten.' That means ten minutes of blowjob."

While he was guffawing, I cut in with "Red, is this porn or a Marx Brothers sketch?"

"The who?" he asked.

"If everyone would please let me do my piece," said Tom-Tom. "Ahem." He didn't clear his throat, but rather uttered the word itself. "In my story, it seems that a rising young stockbroker's assistant is coming back from a party when he sees a guy sitting in the stairwell of his brownstone. It's someone who lives in the building. 'What are you doing out here in the hall?' 'My girl friend kicked me out for bad attitude.'"

Red was nodding vigorously. "He probably didn't get the flowers for her mother's fucking birthday or something."

" 'We can't let a handsome fellow like you spend all night in the hall.' So now they're in the stockbroker's assistant's apartment at bedtime. His name is Fred."

Tom-Tom paused, and Red asked, "When's the chick? You know?"

"Jennifer's not in this one, Red," I told him.

"Is Ken in it?" he asked, perhaps just starting to catch on.

"No, I am," Tom-Tom replied. "Did I mention that the other guy—his name is Darryl—is wearing nothing but overalls that show him off to a T?"

" 'Dude looks like a lady,' " Red quietly sang, recalling an old Aerosmith hit. He seemed rather calm, all things considered.

"Now, Fred is trim enough," Tom-Tom continues. "But Darryl takes his physical fitness very seriously." Tom-Tom dallied on the "very," drawing it out with the sound of something creaking as it is pried open.

"What kind of story is this?" Red asked Tom-Tom. "A suspenseful mystery?"

"A big surprise," said Tom-Tom, "is Darryl's dick, which is long and fat, with veins as big as snakes. At the sight of it, Fred faints. Luckily, Darryl catches him."

The phone rang.

"The tape'll get it," I said, as Fleabiscuit nosed out for a shoelace sortie.

"Look at the pooch," said Red in a dreamy voice; then we heard Stanley saying, "Listen, you fucking traitor, you call me back or I'll come and get you so help me Christ!"

"Du-hu-hude," said Red.

"When Fred comes to," said the dogged Tom-Tom, "he is under the covers with a wet hand towel on his forehead, and Darryl is sitting on the bed."

Tom-Tom paused again, either for dramatic effect or to check the weather in the listening room.

" 'All set now?' Darryl asks him, and Fred nods. Darryl just sits there, and finally he takes off the towel and says, 'Can I come in with you?' Fred says okay. They lie there for a while. Then Darryl says, 'It's lonely like this. Can I hold you for a bit?' Fred says okay."

There was a Luftpause as the three of us watched Fleabiscuit take out Red's other shoelace.

"After a while, Darryl says, 'I'm not getting too familiar, am I? You may not know about a husky guy like me getting on you like this.'"

"That's a lovely touch, Tom-Tom," I noted. "Dated but authentic. This is, what, 1958 or so?"

I might as well have been speaking in Urdu; Tom-Tom was concentrating on Red and would brook no interloping. His eyes said, Ken doesn't need the way I need; he is a perfect life-form and a little not human.

Going on with his tale, Tom-Tom said, "Darryl wraps his legs around Fred. He says, 'I've got a pretty hairy chest. That doesn't bother you, does it? That I'm holding you and you can feel the hair on my skin?'"

"Does it bother him?" Red asked.

"He doesn't answer. He's listening to Darryl's breathing. Then Darryl says, 'Did you ever fuck with a guy, Fred?'"

And Tom-Tom waits. A long, long time.

"Did he?" Red finally asked.

Tom-Tom looked at Red. Yes, of course, he had in fact been doing nothing *but* look at Red. But now he shared his look, giving as well as taking. "Allons-y, mon bleu," he said.

"Yes," said Red. "But what did it mean?"

"'Let's get started, new guy.'"

Red thought that over for a bit, then told Tom-Tom, "Dude, you got *issues!*"

Taking it in perspective, Tom-Tom had to admit that his scheme to "specify" Red (as he put it) had failed. But I did persuade Tom-Tom to confess his interest in Red to Ken, who I thought was being swindled. Oddly, Ken said it was better this way, because with two operatives trying to score Red, the project had what Ken called "outing security."

This I found exasperating, not to mention mission: impossible. But at least Ken offered a half-plausible explanation for bisexuality in men. He said, "These guys are very turned on. Their culture wants them to be, but also they just *are*. So there's all this something in them, and they don't know what to do with it. They're a waterfall of hunger—where does it land? And they have these nutty social needs egging them on to go wherever they'll be liked."

That was interesting. But if that's all it took for a straight man to experiment, how come we don't get a whole load of them crossing over?—and that's what I said to Ken.

"How do you know there *isn't* a whole load of them?" he countered. "They aren't likely to speak of it. Besides, are we talking of straights or of 60–40s?"

It's the one notion for which he has borrowed my terminology; they don't have an equivalent in Chelseaspeak.

"I still find it amazing that you let Tom-Tom have a go at your dream man."

He shrugged. "It's because he's getting such a bad time at his job, and we all have to . . ." Fast-forward. "It's not because I fear his competition, because I don't have any."

And you know he never jokes. O brave new world, that has such people in't!

TOM-TOM REALLY WAS getting a bad time at work; he had but to appear for Maureen to make a beeline for him, and none of his co-workers was helping him resist her sheer command of him. Indeed, according to Tom-Tom they delighted in creating ever more ludicrous excuses for her behavior.

I was serving Tom-Tom in my usual capacity as Good Listener while Dennis Savage reviewed the erotic fiction that J. and Cosgrove had been writing. None of the stories was finished; some were nearly complete and others fragments.

"Carlo's been helping us with ideas," said Cosgrove, giving the adoring Fleabiscuit a pat. "And those are the stories that are almost done."

"What am I supposed to do?" Tom-Tom asked me. "Give up my job?"

" 'Frankenstein Gets Randy,' " Dennis Savage read out, picking up one story from the pile. "Is 'Randy' an adjective or a character?"

"Both," said Cosgrove.

" 'The French Lieutenant's Punishment.' "

"That one has the popular military motif."

" 'It Happened in Bloomingdale's.' 'Lou Ferrigno's Excellent Adventure.' 'Geppetto's Kink.' "

Dennis Savage looked at Cosgrove.

"That last one goes a little over the top," said Cosgrove.

"Will somebody please help me?" said Tom-Tom.

I told him, "After that performance you gave the other day, recounting the adventures of Fred and Darryl, you don't need help. You're masterful, boy. You're in charge."

The phone rang.

"Yes, Stanley?" said Cosgrove into the air, as the phone continued to ring. "You want to do *what* to Bud?"

Dennis Savage laughed, and Tom-Tom made an irritated face; in fact, it was a business call. I took it, and when I got off, Dennis Savage, Cosgrove, and Fleabiscuit made leaving noises and began to disperse.

"Cool," said Tom-Tom. "Because I want to tell Bud about my first date with Red."

Dennis Savage, Cosgrove, and Fleabiscuit froze. Slowly they turned. After trading looks, they came back and arranged themselves in a pattern suitable for Listening To Major Dish.

My blurb was ready: I said, "He tells a good story, too."

"It was the first time we were alone," Tom-Tom began. "After all the music and socializing. It was at my place, and I was pouring out my heart to him about my troubles, when someone wants too much from you and won't leave you alone. And was he bored! He cut in, all of a sudden, with 'This one guy? He says, How much would I take to kiss another guy, smooch on the mouth. Me? Not for a thousand bucks. Says, Come on, you'd go for five hundred. Oh, would I? Five hundred! Well, maybe. Then he's, like, So what about two hundred and fifty? What about one hundred? Keeps working me down 'cause he's such a convincing dude, with his theories like a mad scientist.' "

"Where was this?" Dennis Savage asked.

"Can I use it in a porn story?" Cosgrove put in.

"Are you quoting him exactly?" was my entry. "Because it really does sound like Red. And I need to—"

"It was my place. We were sitting on the couch, listening to music. Ken lent me a CD to play because Red likes CDs. Ken says it's because Red doesn't ever know what to say, and with music on he doesn't have to."

"Ken advised you," I said, "on how to steal his boy friend?"

"I'm not stealing unless they're having sex, and Ken says they aren't."

"But did you?" Cosgrove asked.

"We were on the couch, very next to each other, and he will touch you as he talks. They do that. So Red goes on with his kiss bargaining: 'Guy gets me down to five dollars. You do it for a five? Kiss a guy for five?' "

" 'They do that'?" Dennis Savage said. "And who is 'they'?"

Hesitating, Tom-Tom finally decided on "The somethings. Like Red."

"No more questions, just do it," I ordered. "Guy gets him down to a five. Then what?"

"Red said, 'Okay, smack a dude for five. Whaddaya know, guy pulls out the five, holds it in front of me. Says, "Well, big guy?" Even if I'm not so tall.' And Red says that and waits, close to me, his hand on my shoulder moving the very tiniest bit. He waits and he waits."

So did we wait.

Enjoying the suspense he had created, Tom-Tom at length got to "So *I* said, 'I'll kiss you for free, Red.' Still he waited. It was almost comical, like an actor forgot his lines on opening night. But then he nodded and said, 'Let's kiss and see.' It was the whole kiss, too—deep tongue and holding me and saying things. 'That guy with the five has a chick who treats him right.' Running all the words out between his mouth on me again. He says, 'Dude shucks off his loafies and she fucks him with a strap-on, right on his back like a chick. Shoves his white tank top up to his shoulders and his pants down to his knees.' See how he has it all described in his mind? And kissing me still, this is. He says, 'But she don't get his clothes off, because they like to fuck dirty.' "

Cosgrove's mouth formed an appalled O at the failure of subject-verb agreement, and he covered the ears of Fleabiscuit.

I asked, "What are 'loafies,' for heaven's sake?"

"He means 'loafers,' " Tom-Tom replied. "That's what he calls anything that isn't boots or sneakers, even tie-shoes. He'll say, 'Tom-Tom, those are cute loafies you got on.' And we're pals now. He calls me 'Pipsqueak.' And my only dream is to fuck him. Of course, I want to fuck him dirty, though he'll never consent. I could doggy him at best, because getting doggied means you're just a guy who's getting creamed out. But if you're fucked dirty with your loafies shucked off, you might as well be a chick."

"Tom-Tom," I said, "I greatly fear we're losing you, because I don't know where you are going."

"To the shithouse, to fuck dirty with Red, of course."

"Tom-Tom, *stop!*"

"C'est cocasse."

But now he did stop. We all stopped.

"Are you happy?" I finally asked him.

He blazed at me a bit. "Are you?"

"I was, till about four minutes ago."

"Was Red by any chance..." Dennis Savage began. Then. "Was he talking about himself? Getting fucked?"

"I doubt it," Tom-Tom replied. "He just obsesses about women fucking guys with those wear-me dildos."

"Did you tell Ken about this?" he asked. "Shouldn't he have this information?"

"I'm guilty about Ken. I'm guilty pleasure today."

It was all a bit unhappy but also, as Tom-Tom noted, rather cocasse, which is to say "weird yet amusing." Anyway, now it was over, and Dennis Savage went off to write and Cosgrove took Fleabiscuit for a walk, leaving Tom-Tom and me alone.

"I wasn't making it up," he told me. "But I think he's straight, after all. He just likes to fool around and feel erotic and dangerous. That's why Ken doesn't really care that Red and I are friends. Ken doesn't like straights, you know. He's pure Chelsea. He's never had sex with a woman; we call that 'a thoroughbred.' He resents that I'm closeted."

"Tom-Tom, you are about as closeted as the plaster gnomes on Lane Fuller's patio."

"I mean to my family and at work."

"Speaking of work—"

"Let's don't speak of it," he quickly put in. "It just gets worse and worse."

Then the phone rang, and the tape took it, and Stanley screamed at me some more.

ON WHAT TURNED OUT to be the last day of the Indian summer, I went walking through Chelsea with Ken after a lunch at Davey-Boy's for more porn planning. Ken still hadn't agreed to take part; he was, he said, "pondering the variables." But I was ready to see that project collapse like a canasta table at a garage sale, because there's too much porn in our lives as it is. There was porn in the way that Ken stared at Red all through dinner on the day they met. What a waste of intensity, for they had drifted apart and Tom-Tom had taken over.

"Wasn't Red The One?" I asked Ken.

He shrugged. All about us on Eighth Avenue, local lads were voguing and fleshing, gazing and collecting.

"Did you ever meet The One, cousin Bud?"

"Yes. Beethoven."

And right out of nowhere there came looming up at us yet another Angry Man Who Regards Ken as a Piece of Unfinished Business. It's a genre. And let me tell you, boys and girls, it is not fun to be the impediment to their having an intimate conversation with the man they love to resent.

This one didn't even say anything as he pulled in at Ken's dock. He gave me a flick of a glance, then pointed at Ken in a meaningful way. Ken pointed back as he moved on around him. I braced myself for a scene, but the stranger merely fell into step with us and, in undertone, tried small talk.

"No," said Ken.

"No what?"

"No everything."

We lost him in the foot traffic for a bit, but he came ramrodding back with the threat of disorderly conduct in his body language. But ho!: just ahead of us were two cops with cop looks on their faces. They hate New York, they hate gay guys, and they're ready to arrest. Ken and I walked specifically toward them, and the Ken guy faded into the scenery.

"They get mad because I just drop them," Ken explained. "But why confront? They'll only argue with you. When it's over, goodbye."

After a half block or so he added, "I'm tired of needy guys. They punish you with stress if you don't give them every single thing they want. They argue when you thwart their will. That's why guys value you, cousin. You don't argue."

"I thought they value me because I'm smart and I explain their lives to them."

"That, too," he said, in the tone you use when Trent Lott asks if he's pretty and you reply, "Of course."

It was very Chelsea that day, very cruisy and competitive. With everyone young and cute and fit, what are the grounds for rejection? A hangnail? I suddenly put into words an idea that had been haunting me for a bit of time: "I wonder if it would be better if you could choose between having Looks Control but taking a chance on what fate selects for you, and—on the other hand—having ordinary looks and perfect health till you die in your sleep in your eighties. You know, my college roommate, Harry Anderson, is dead. The girl I dated at the time, Deborah Fahnestock, is dead. And my closest woman friend from just after college, Alice Williford, is dead. You can't help but notice that you aren't twenty-two any more. That you are in a kind of mysterious peril. Maybe they should put a new clause in the gay contract."

We walked in silence for a while. Then I asked him where he was recruited.

"In the Wilkes-Barre Kmart," he answered. "Some guy in housewares."

Which amazed me because, you know, he has no sense of humor and never cracks a joke. We continued to his building in more silence. As we shook hands, he smiled and said, "You dated a woman?"

MEANWHILE, BACK AT THE ranch, I found Cosgrove running a listening room for Red and Tom-Tom. The subject was *Till Eulenspiegel's Merry Pranks*, which Cosgrove regards as his biography, and the two guests were sitting opposite each other, their eyes locked. I got busy with various put-aways and such in the bedroom and did not come out till the music was over.

"You play host for a while," said Cosgrove, reboxing and shelving the CD with his usual collector's care.

"I hope you're in a sweetheart mood today, Tom-Tom," I said.

"We're all in a nice mood from the music," said Red, getting up to move around and show off, "and Tom's my great new buddy."

"That guy called some more," said Tom-Tom. "The one who's mad at you."

"Doesn't it make you jumpy, him doing that?" Red asked.

I replied by distributing refills of the sparkling water, and asked Red what's new. Before he could answer, we were distracted by the sight of Cosgrove setting on its end the big cardboard box that our new television had come in; he had been saving it for no apparent reason. Now he placed upon it three playing cards, moving them about in occult patterns with a sly expression. Then he paused as Fleabiscuit stretched up with his paws on the edge of the box and nosed one of the cards. Cosgrove picked it up; beneath where it had been lay a dime. Is that what they use on the street?

"And we have a winner," Cosgrove announced. Generally, he asked, "Try your luck?"

"You have your own three-card monte stand," said Red, genuinely impressed. "This place's got everything." He went over to watch the play of cards.

"Don't be appreciative," I warned. "It only encourages him."

"I always wondered how it works," said Red. "How much is a bet?"

"This is Shirley Temple monte," said Cosgrove. "We play for fun."

Red turned around to grin at us.

"All right, that's it," I said, getting up and quoting a line I'd been waiting years to use: 'Don't come around here with your vaudeville tricks!' "*

Cosgrove giggled, grabbed the cards and box, and ran off, Fleabiscuit scampering after him.

"Sometimes you kid around with friends," Red observed. "And sometimes you help their pain."

"Red's giving me advice on my work troubles," said Tom-Tom.

---

*Lee Strasberg said that to Robert Lewis during rehearsals for the Group Theatre's only musical, Kurt Weill and Paul Green's *Johnny Johnson*, in 1936. The Group were thespians of intense vocation, but they weren't singers, and Paula Miller—Mrs. Strasberg and, incidentally, Marilyn Monroe's future acting coach—was laying an egg with "Mon Ami, My Friend." The number left Miller alone on stage to make an exit to a humiliating silence, and actor Lewis suggested to director Strasberg that Miller leave during the music as a cover; Strasberg gave the response I quote. For some reason, Lewis' memoirs recall the incident yet stop short of the last line. It's a treasurable outburst, because Strasberg is exactly wrong. What does he mean by "vaudeville tricks"? Good stagecraft? We did not hear the anecdote in full true till Lewis shared it with an interviewer; it is quoted in Foster Hirsch's *Kurt Weill On Stage*.

"The kid here's got a wedding chick on his tail," Red told me. "The ring, the dress, deposit on the hall."

"Red," I asked, "did you ever consider becoming a firefighter?"

He had a habit, when surprised by a non sequitur question, of "opening up" his facial lines: his eyebrows would slide toward the hairline, his nostrils would take in air and expand, and his mouth would relax in a half-smile. I liked to see it happen.

"Why do you ask?"

"Because you'd look great in the clothes."

And then he just smiled. He isn't used to praise, which is why he sticks close to Tom-Tom, who flatters him as one pets a lovably clumsy dog rescued from abuse.

"Red says I have to get tough," said Tom-Tom. "So there's no confusion."

"You got to draw a line," Red added. "One way or the other, see? Or they create smokescreens."

Red demonstrated, imitating the antagonist disguised as a friend: " 'It was the anniversary of my divorce,' " with his head leaning to the right. Then: " 'Well, who wiped himself on the drapes?' " with his head to the left. "They make lying excuses," he concluded.

The phone rang.

I said, "Let that be Dennis Savage, any of several Michaels, Ken, cousin Ken, Erick, Matthew, the twins, Peter, Lionel, Clint, Scott, Jim, the other Jim, Kern, Ian, Gordon, or my agent."

It was Stanley, raising hell. The other two listened without looking at me, and before the taping ended I started in on what in classic French drama is known as *la tirade*.

"This is what happens when someone who gets no respect from anyone establishes a telephone relationship with me. Eleven o'clock of a weekday, news and views on theatre and music. No one else gives him that attention, but I'm lazy at that time, vulnerable to distraction. And hearing myself map out my positions means I don't have to take notes for the next book, see? I get work relief and the freak on the other end gets ego affirmation. Everyone else in that particular social loop just tolerates him. I give him welcome. He needs it, and then he needs more—and that's what's happening to you now, Tom-Tom. You *can't* draw a line, because they'll just argue with you. That's all a freak does—he hurls words at you till the end of time, the uncountable lies of the ego war. And mark me, Tom-Tom, they'll keep on coming at you, like that girl in your office, because they know how much you hate it. That... aggression is how they know they're alive. They don't fight with each other. They fight with you, crossing line after line. Draw a thousand of them, make it clear as Day of Judgment, carry a loaded pistol with the fanatic intention of blowing their fucking heads off if they cross the line, and by the gods and their gay little planet *they will cross the line!* And you know why, Tom-Tom? Because you give good hurt. When they impose their will on you, they want it harming you so much that they can lick it up for snacks. They can't do it to Ken, because he's blunt and fierce and powerful. You can't hurt Ken; Ken can hurt you. They can't do it to Davey-Boy, because he's tricksy. Yes, my precious. Everybody wants Davey-Boy, which means that everyone needs his respect. So they won't trouble Davey-Boy. Remember that brunch last summer? In honor of Sebastian's... or who cares what it was. Davey-Boy showed up in the pants and open vest of a suit with no shirt. I'd never seen that look except on a stage. And Davey-Boy has that insanely tight little waist and the oddly pumped yet flat chest with an absolutely horizontal line of definition along the bottom. At the sight of him, Colt models retire in despair. Ty Fox quit his gym. Yet nobody dares take Davey-Boy's hand, because what he'll do to them in response will not be an egosyntonic experience. But you, Tom-Tom, are tender. You are their meal. And all your life, or at least till you lose your looks, which I hope is never, they will be coming at you to play you and irritate you and——"

"Dude," said Red quietly, standing next to me in the middle of the room. When did I get here? I looked at Tom-Tom, whose face was awash with tears, and as he jumped up to hide in the bathroom, Red intercepted him and the two held each other. I backed away to sit on the couch. Tom-Tom was blatantly feeling the upper portions of Red's torso while Red murmured, "That's okay" and "Come on, now" and "Be righteous, dude."

Soon enough, Tom-Tom broke the embrace and said through his tears, "How much do you like me, dude? This much?" He held Red's hands about eight inches apart. "Or this much?" Fifteen inches.

Realizing that a lot depended on his answer but surely having no idea what penalty or reward was promised, Red temporized with "Well, how much do you want?"

Hesitating for perhaps two seconds, Tom-Tom yanked Red's pants open and got on his knees to pull them down, saying, "Don't be cruel or surprised, Red, because you are my favorite guy of all, even when I'm crying."

And with that, Tom-Tom started swinging on dick. And I sat there. And Red put his hands in his pockets—no, that won't work. So he crossed his arms, and felt funny that way, too. Then, obeying some primitive instinct, he held Tom-Tom's head and massaged his ears. Feeling he should say something, Red thought for a bit, turned to me, and came up with "Dude's pretty flirtatious, huh?"

Dude was also an excellent cocksucker, bold and nuanced. Tom-Tom's all set for Davey-Boy's porn company; that much we now know.

Cosgrove and Fleabiscuit came back in from whatever they were doing in the bedroom, and they, too, just stopped to watch.

Red obviously thought he should pass a remark to Cosgrove, if only to normalize the bizarre.

"This ever happen to you?" Red asked him.

7

THE
PORN
STORY

COSGROVE WAS SERIOUS ABOUT going into the catering business. Notably, for the first time in his many professional undertakings (which is another way of referring to the various loony schemes he has been involved with over the years), J. was not to be Cosgrove's partner. There were no partners this time. Cosgrove was the sole proprietor of Catering R Us, though Carlo and Nesto had signed on as waiters.

The concept was simple. If you wanted to give an Important Dinner Party without undergoing the grunt work, Cosgrove and company would prepare and cook the meal, serve it, then clean up after, for one hundred dollars a guest. Liquor of any kind was extra; Cosgrove figured that folks into serious entertaining are also serious about the table wine and the operation of the bar and would just as soon handle that themselves.

Bemused by Cosgrove's business acumen, I listened appreciatively as he fielded phone inquiries. ("We put word out on the street," Cosgrove informed me. He also dropped an ad into *HX*.) There was a choice of three menus—French, Italian, and one described as "decorating your table in designer shades of lightning, keyboard, and parade." Most of the inquiries were just that: one hundred dollars a setting is a major investment, even for one's fortieth birthday, say, or to celebrate you and your lover's first anniversary (that is: after one week). Finally, someone turned up who wanted the French dinner for six on New Year's Eve. Cosgrove was so joyful that he danced whenever he spoke of it, and Fleabiscuit dreamed of a golden collar to call his own.

Meanwhile, the Thursday meals with J. had dwindled into the occasional afternoon visit. Life with Vince meant no day job, yes. But according to the traditional working-class attitudes that Vince was raised in and adhered to as unquestioningly as a Carmelite, there was no such thing as the husband comes home from work and the spouse is not there.

J. didn't mind, he said. He liked the structure, he liked being depended on, and most of all he liked Vince. Love? "The love thing is for movies," said J. with a shrug. "I don't want to be in love," he explained. "I want to be happy."

Maybe he was, because he showed little curiosity about Catering R Us, and seemed unconcerned that Cosgrove was doing something interesting without him. Marriage can create that: some people simply cease to notice what occurs outside the nest. Besides, the now ever bustling Cosgrove persuaded J. to collaborate in finishing one of their porn stories, and I offered to buy and publish it if maybe.

"Which one is this?" I asked, as Cosgrove presented me with pages in a plastic Staples folder. J. was quietly sipping cocoa in his London Underground mug, which he has parked with us for these occasions.

"You haven't seen this one yet," Cosgrove told me.

"It was originally three stories," said J. "Cos thought they were..." He turned to Cosgrove.

"A unit," said Cosgrove.

I read out the title: " 'Pajammy and Corndogger Meet the Slutty Professor.' "

"It was going to be 'Dangerous Sexpigs of Psycho City,' " Cosgrove explained. "Followed by 'Escape from Psycho City,' then—"

" 'Return to Psycho City,' " I guessed.

J. said, "I wanted to call it 'Who's in the Pay Toilet?' Rather piquant, wouldn't you say?"

"Let's read," I suggested, and I did, aloud:

Pajammy and Corndogger were on the loose. Armed with only their faithful seltzer bottle, plus their mysterious secret weapon, the Acme Patented Cockalizer, they roamed the Old West from Bedmess Junction to the Big Junk Corral. But how could they know that Psycho City was where Sheriff Slade was at war with the Smooth Boys Gang? He swore to drive those rustlers out of the territory. The sheriff and his deputies were hairy-chested rufftuffs, so loving and brutal. When a stranger came to town, they would crowd around him in the saloon to find out if he was a Smooth Boy. How could they know? They would loosen the stranger's clothes, play doctor, taste his parts. The rumor was that you could get high on Smooth Boy shoot cream. It was the only way to get stoned in the Old West.

Sheriff Slade was addicted to cream. It happened like this: he and Lady Clairetta Boothroy were dating, but Lady Clairetta was so dainty she wouldn't give up her charms unless the sheriff brought some cute young dude along. They would all have tea and play strip poker till the boy had lost his pants. Then Lady Clairetta accidentally knocked over the jam pot and had to lick the mess off the boy's cock and balls.

"Goodness, how tasty," she would say, cleaning him up so thoroughly.

But this time the boy was Johnny Mambo, hero of

the seven seas. Sheriff Slade got suspicious as Lady Clairetta lapped away. Could she be getting high? He noticed her blissful state as she cooed, "It's sexlicious." That sheriff was so nosy. He pushed Lady Clairetta to the side just as Johnny Mambo let fly with jizz thick as cake frosting, all on the sheriff's face.

"Let me clean you up, darling," said Lady Clairetta, but the sheriff's tongue was going all about, and now he got high, too.

"Johnny Mambo feels good like that," said the sheriff.

And that's how he got hooked. All he cared about was getting high on Smooth Boy cream. What if a cowboy was new in town? Sheriff Slade would interview him.

"I'll ask the questions around here," he would snarl, feeling the cowboy's skin through his clothes. Sheriff Slade would say, "Where are you from?" while examining that cowpoke's tight little waist. "Hmm." Sheriff Slade would say, "What firm are you with?" while pressing that lad's shirt against the pec line. "Hmm." Sheriff Slade would say, "You better stop that rustling" while stroking the boy's soft hair and falling in love.

The boy would say, "I wish to rustle you, Sheriff. Yes, I do."

So they'd go to Fuckin' Tree Hill, and Sheriff Slade would get high. They would speak the forked tongue of love in the position known as "family style," so the sheriff could smooch the boy as he loved him to and fro.

"Take me home, rufftuff!" the boy would cry.

The sheriff could be strict at times. "I'll teach you to rustle cows!" he would husk out.

"You don't have to teach me," the boy would reply. "I already know." Then he would shoot cream, wailing, "Here goes nothing, Sheriff!"

It was a good life, except the sheriff wasn't doing his job. Anarchy was everywhere. But this was just the right atmosphere for Pajammy and Corndogger. Pajammy was a merry sort. He would make a party all the go when he said, "Let's have a gang bang. I'll be Little Frisky!" That meant he would serve as the guest of honor.

Corndogger had secret ways. When the sheriff's new deputy, Flex Dumhed, came to town, all the ladies started flirting under their parasols. They loved the way Flex would make the Friday evening sarsaparilla sociable memorable by dropping his pants and imitating a puppy. Then the ladies would take turns housebreaking him, and feeding him treats hidden in their quim. Flex would yip in delight.

So that's when Corndogger knew it was time to apply the Acme Patented Cockalizer. He and Pajammy laid a trap, painting a sign reading, "Undergear Sale, 95% off." Flex fell for it, following rickety stairs down to a deserted cellar where our heroes were waiting. When Flex came in, they jumped him and tied him up. Then they got his clothes off with a razor blade.

"No!" Flex Dumhed was heard to cry. "No!" For he had listened to the tales.

The Acme Patented Cockalizer looked like buckskin shorts with side-fastenings and a low waist. It was very sporty. Except once you turned it on, whoever was wearing it would be thingamajigged through his genitals to the very center of his experience. It was

joy and torture at once. But Corndogger did not hesi-
tate, so resolved was he to make an example of Flex
Dumhed.

Pajammy was setting the dials. "Medium?" he
asked Corndogger. "High?"

"Set it to Killbliss," said Corndogger, from the
depths of his cold heart.

They turned it on and watched Flex shouting and
flopping around. Were they touched by pity? No. For
this was the Wild West, where compassion is weakness.
Corndogger folded his arms, calmly watching Flex in
his luscious agony while Pajammy performed a samba.

Then Sheriff Slade and his deputies broke in.

"Turn it off!" Flex cried.

Corndogger and Pajammy drew their trusty seltzer
bottles and began the fight, but they were outnum-
bered and arrested. When the sheriff shut off the
Acme Patented Cockalizer, Flex cried, "Turn it on!"
He was so confused.

"This is what comes of playing the ladies' man and
becoming decadent in the Old West," said the sheriff.
In the hoosegow, Pajammy and Corndogger had only
one guard, an older cowboy named Pierce Mayplow.
He was stern but kindly. Oh, it was so lonely for him
in that jailhouse, he said. The sheriff and his deputies
were always out checking for dress-code violations in
the saloon or playing strip poker, and Pierce never got
to join in.

"We'll play strip poker with you, Pierce," said Pajammy in his most winning tone.

Pierce was wary. He said, "Wall, I guess you little
scapers is up to no good with ol' Pierce."

"We'll even give you a handicap, Pierce," said Corndogger, stripping off his shirt and string tie. And Pajammy removed his famous derby.

"Strip poker, eh?" said Pierce, moving a little closer to the cell with his iron ring of keys. "It shore is mighty temptin'." But then he stopped, unsure. So Pajammy said, "You were always my secret hero, Pierce."

Pierce came into the cell, and they played a few hands, till all three were naked. Pierce's dick was so heavy that the floor sagged under him. Pajammy was appreciative. "You're sure got a lot of love to give, Pierce," he said.

Corndogger held back as Pajammy showed respect for Pierce in the time-honored manner.

"Yeah, you like ol' Pierce, huh?" said Pierce.

"Can I feel your tightness, Pierce?" said Corndogger, coming around to stand behind the cowboy. Pierce was in a buckaroo's dreamland from Pajammy's sucking, so he didn't answer. Corndogger slipped a finger inside.

"What's that feeling in the rear?" gurgled Pierce in a faraway voice.

Pajammy was blowing Pierce, and Corndogger was rubbing his fingers together inside Pierce.

"Yar," said Pierce. "Yar. Yar."

"This is called 'the cricket,' Pierce," said Corndogger. "See how I cricket you?"

"Yar. Yar. Yar."

"Feel good, Pierce?" Corndogger asked. "Because I can tell that you're fuck-tight especially for me."

Pierce's voice went way high, and he came so big that it was an earthquake that wrecked the jailhouse. A bit later, Sheriff Slade and some of his deputies

came down the street to find Pierce sitting on the cell
bunk wearing Pajammy's derby and a look of vacant
thrill. The walls and roof of the jail were lying around
in pieces, and Pajammy and Corndogger were nowhere
to be seen.

Disgusted, Sheriff Slade yelled, "Call out the posse!
We'll hunt them vipers down!"

Pausing in my reading, I asked the authors, "Where did all this
invention come from? I thought you were going to write 'My Sister's Boy Friend' or something."

"Peter Keene helped us with ideas," Cosgrove replied. "Also
Lionel and Carlo."

"I made up the names," said J.

"Tom-Tom gave us pointers for the sequence with Pierce, who
is quite my favorite character. Tom-Tom is surprising, you know.
When you first meet him, you might think he was like I used to
be, all confused and without a proper place in the world. But I'm
surprising, too."

"There are a lot of misspellings," I told them. "And someone's
idea of punctuation is very curious."

"Every seven words," said Cosgrove, "in goes a comma."

"I'll spruce up the tech before publication," I said. "How much
do you want for this?"

"I will definitely need a CD trip," said Cosgrove. "I'm running
low on my French Romantics."

"I want bought for me a really nice sweater for Vince," said J.
"All he ever wears in the cold are sweatshirts. It's his birthday
soon, and he should have something classy, because he takes care
of his mom so thoughtfully."

"Have you met her?" I asked.

"No, but we're always on the phone, it seems. I fill her in on what happened on *Passions* when she has to miss it for Widows Anonymous."

"What's that?" Cosgrove asked.

J. shrugged. "Oh, I just call it that. It's one of those support groups."

Cosgrove gave me a cup of coffee, and I went on with the reading:

> Pajammy and Corndogger were busy escaping. They didn't have far to go, for right before them was The Quimby School for Young Gentlemen, Marmaduke Quimby, Headmaster. But the school was really run by Carboy. By day? A scholarly eleventh-grader. By night? A revolutionary who yearned to overthrow Marmaduke Quimby's regime with acts of secret defiance. These would be such as panty raids on the tenth-graders and making risqué improvements on the science projects set up for the Knowledge Fair.

"Risqué?" I echoed.

"Lionel," said Cosgrove.

> When Pajammy and Corndogger matriculated, headmaster Marmaduke Quimby gave them a personal inspection before they could be students.
>
> "Such fine specimens for The Quimby School!" cried that Marmaduke Quimby. "Strip, that I may weigh thee! Only the most excellent young boys may be set on my scale. Oh, but they mustn't be rash, or severe measures shall be taken. Yes, young boys need

plenty of birching. It's my way of expressing affection. Yes. Oh, such lovely specimens. Which one shall I eat out—uh, weigh first?"

"Oh," said Pajammy, "most worthy headmaster! Please do strike but that pose once again!"

"What pose?" asked Marmaduke. He tried a few to be helpful.

"Somehow he reminds us unconditionally of that model of rugged virtue for young and old, The Noble Boxer. Does he not, my lord Corndogger?"

"He does."

"I do?"

"That magnetic forehead! See how the chin juts!"

"Consider the superb fan," Pajammy added, feeling Marmaduke's bottom under his coat.

"You flatterbox!" Marmaduke cried. "But I tell you I love it."

"If you'd remove your things, sir," Corndogger smoothly intoned. "Yes, right down to the skin. Is he not a rare sample of manhood, Count Pajammy?"

"Rare, indeed," Pajammy replied, producing from his travel bag a set of Everlast boxer's shorts and gloves.

"And see," said Corndogger, beckoning to Pajammy to join him facing the naked Marmaduke. "The sex patch, as modest as a young girl's."

"Lionel?" I guessed.

"Peter Keene," said Cosgrove.

"I think his additions are dopey," said J. "They're like Shakespeare in a Three Stooges short."

"But it's nice when everyone wants to help you out," said Cosgrove. "That's how you know that people care about you."

J. shrugged. "I have Vince now," he said. "It's a different case."

Soon Marmaduke was suitably attired, and the gloves were secured very, very tightly on the fists. Corndogger coaxed him into the pose of The Noble Boxer, while Pajammy, unseen, dipped once more into his bag. In his secret way, he pulled out the Acme Patented Cockalizer, and stood ready behind Marmaduke.

"Like this?" Marmaduke asked, putting up his fists in an antique pose.

"Just like that," cried Corndogger, leaping forward to pull down the Everlast shorts as Pajammy attached the Acme Patented Cockalizer from behind.

"Don't forget the side-straps!" Corndogger shouted.

"The setting, Corndogger?" Pajammy asked.

"Set it to Valentine's Day Super-Climax!"

And Marmaduke Quimby went bouncing and quacking around the floor in tortured ecstasy as Pajammy and Corndogger made their escape. They met Carboy in the school chapel. He told them of the plot to take over the school, and they told him how they had neutralized the headmaster. Only one enemy stood in their way now—the Slutty Professor. He was engaged in performing drastic experiments of an erotic quality on the faculty and boys in the school.

The three new comrades must take him down. "He *shall* be overthrown!" they vowed.

Disguised as new members of the faculty, Pajammy

and Corndogger entered the laboratory of the Slutty Professor. They were just in time: looking over a pile of dirty beakers and used petri dishes, they spied on the Slutty Professor's latest project. It was a test of the effect of sexual stimuli on the human memory. Yes: there was the Slutty Professor, in his white coat. It was stained with rotten egg and tomato, thrown by despairing students. The two people in the experiment were a teacher named Mr. Twiddle and the captain of the football team, Race Treevor. Both were nude in this peculiar school.

"The subject will repeat the following semiotic cluster," said the Slutty Professor, consulting his clipboard. He read out groups of letters and numbers, and Mr. Twiddle repeated these correctly.

"Now Race will fuck you and we'll see the effect."

Race fucked Mr. Twiddle stand-up style. He was quite rough. He said, "This will be revenge for that C-you gave me on my paper on the decline of the Marais from Paris' aristocratic *quartier* to a slum during the Revolution because of the flight of the nobility."

"Oh, come on," I said.

"That was Tom-Tom," said Cosgrove. "You know how he loves French stuff."

"I say it's stupid," said J.

"Virgil, would you like another cocoa?" said Cosgrove. His use of J.'s former name so shocked him and me both that there was silence for a good thirty seconds. Finally, J. shook his head. It was a transaction of some kind, but who knew what. I returned to the text:

As Race pumped harder, Mr. Twiddle breathed out, "This is like Donkey Kong!"

"You can try my layaway plan," Race sneered.

The Slutty Professor announced, "The subject will repeat the following clusters: EG3Y9   X6AE4 7L5ZM."

"AEIOU!" Mr. Twiddle cried, as Race banged away at him. "Lemeneno P! Hee-haw! Hee-Haw!"

"Dear me," said the Slutty Professor. "That isn't even close."

"Get ready," Corndogger whispered to Pajammy in their spy niche. "Now!" They crashed into view with their seltzer bottles gushing, and no one was safe.

So that's how they cleaned up the school. Carboy and his revolutionary gang were so grateful they arranged to travel with Pajammy and Corndogger to Psycho City to defeat the sheriff. But first, our two heroes had to be initiated into the gang, in a touching ceremony in the nude.

"We stand for unity and brotherhood," Carboy intoned, as his cohort hummed quietly behind him. "We believe in honor, duty, and the taste of kissful lips. How often have we risen against the foe, our ideals our only armor."

The humming reached a lovely crescendo, then died back down in noticeable harmony. "Yes, yes," Carboy went on. He was so inspired. "We love the mission, the truth . . ." But wait. Seeing that Pajammy seemed to be coming close and holding something behind his back, Carboy asked what it could be.

"Oh . . . nothing," said Pajammy.

Carboy's gang started humming again, as Carboy made some more speech.

"Yes," he said, gesturing like opera. "As we close ranks around our dream of fraternity, it is 'Down with grown-ups!' that we cry."

Again, Carboy paused, noticing that Pajammy was putting something around Carboy's loins. It looked like buckskin shorts.

"Is that the Acme Patented Cockalizer?" asked Carboy, with a shudder.

"Set it to Piano Concerto Jizzboree," Corndogger advised.

So Carboy, too, learned not to test the patience of Pajammy and Corndogger. Then one of the schoolboys rushed in to say that Sheriff Slade and his deputies had captured the Smooth Boy gang!

"Those villains may be rugged," cried Carboy, who had been cockalized only a short time, as a formality. "But our hearts are true!"

"Hooray!" cried the schoolboys.

And soon all was ready for an assault on Psycho City.

Carlo came in just then, and I stopped for a breather.

"Reading that porn tale, huh?" he said, joining me on the couch. "I helped some."

"How's business?" I asked.

"Got that one date for New Year's is all so far." He shared a knowing look with Cosgrove, and J. noted this silently. "You know how some people just go along with you and some other people fight you on everything? This New Year's guy's a fighter. 'Why do you have to get half in advance? Why is it so expensive if *I* have to do the wine? Can I see a photograph of the waiters?'"

"He's joshing or something, right?"

"The hell no! And the more money they have, I've learned, the more they try to stiff you. Remember that construction job I had off and on, light interior modifications with Bill Duryea? Typical gig is this family's brownstone. They *own* it, right? Count more servants than *Meet Joe Black*, and while we're working we can hear the boss lady on the phone selling buildings. I'm telling you, *rich.* So she owes nine hundred dollars for three days' work—nagging and checking on us the whole time, of course, like we're going to cheat her the second her back is turned. Right, onook in borverkoard instead of brick. But when it's time to pay, she's got bullshit to lay on us why she can't that day. She's buying and selling New York buildings and she can't write a nine-hundred-dollar check?"

"I know that type," said Cosgrove. "They're living on the Planet Me."

"Yeah. Well ... I just think maybe we have another of those in the New Year's guy." To Cosgrove, he added, "You know? It's important to you, the first job. But this guy's giving off cheater signals."

"Has he paid the advance?" Cosgrove asked.

"Not yet, and he's late and full of bullshit."

The four of us contemplated this state of affairs for a bit.

"You can always tell a cheat right off," Carlo continued, in an oddly subdued voice. "Bossy, and suspicious, and arguing with everything. I told Bill Duryea that woman would try to cheat, and he sure had to keep at her before we got that check. Took two months. And she subtracted from it because we messed up her bathroom or something." He nodded. "Cheats. And you can't explain to these little freaks about playing fair any more than you can describe green to the blind. Because a cheat thinks everyone's like them."

As Cosgrove handed him a glass of the house beverage, Carlo asked, "Where're we up to in the story?"

" 'Return To Psycho City,' " I said.

"Yeah, read that. I like the ladies' umbrella wars."

It was a dark and stormy night, but in the Psycho City Shithouse, it was hot and light, and everyone was raring to go. The Smooth Boys had been trussed up and raised in harnesses fastened to crossbeams high above, and some of the deputies were loosening those cowpokes up for the Grand Shoot by eating out their plumbing as they swung in the ropes.

The Psycho City ladies were well turned out for the doings. Of course, they had left their clothing in neat piles and were sashaying around with only their parasols, to uphold social decency.

"I have Parasol Nescafé," said one.

"I have Parasol Carmen," said another.

"But I have Parasol Résumé," said a third. "And mine is best."

So the first two whacked her with their parasols.

"Ladies, ladies," cautioned Lady Clairetta Boothroy in her soothing tones. "This is a gala event in our town's history, and it deserves the utmost in etiquette and do-si-do."

So the first three whacked Lady Clairetta with their parasols.

One deputy was oiling up Johnny Mambo so the boy would dazzle under the lights. The sheriff was staring at Johnny Mambo as the ladies came near. One became obsessed with Johnny Mambo's triceps. As she felt them, left and right, she was heard to murmur, "This one will cream me oh so high."

So Lady Clairetta whacked her with her parasol.

The sheriff kept gaping at all the boys swinging in their harnesses. Pierce Mayplow warned him that too much looking at boys would lead to the dread condition of droolemia.

Flex Dumhed thought he should give a show. He mooched around in the piles of the ladies' clothes and put on bra and panties. So the ladies whacked him with their parasols all around the Psycho City Shithouse.

Sheriff Slade had not moved. He was standing in front of a Smooth Boy in the harness. The boy had the cutest elbows the sheriff ever saw.

"What's your name?" the sheriff asked. "You look like a Manfred, or perhaps Charles Shortzaroff."

"You can torture me," said the Smooth Boy. "You can oil me up like a muscle freak. You can vandalize my local *HX* giveaway box. But you can't make me come so you can get high."

"We'll see about that!" cried the sheriff.

Then our heroes burst in, and the onslaught began. In the confusion, Flex Dumhed grabbed a seltzer bottle and squirted Lady Clairetta Boothroy. The Psycho City Shithouse was awash in crazy seltzer. But soon the Smooth Boys were freed and the sheriff was the one dangling in a harness.

"Cockalize him!" cried one and all.

"Form a single line," Flex Dumhed announced. "No Confederate bills accepted after the bell."

"No!" the sheriff shouted. "No!"

"It must be yes!" the good folk replied.

But then Flex Dumhed stepped forward, to ask all assembled if they could give love a chance. "It is only lack of love that caused the sheriff to turn out so mean," Flex explained. "See how he longs for love."

And everyone who was not already engaged in ferocious rimming championships looked upon the poor sheriff. Their hearts were moved at the sight of the big hairy galoot swinging helplessly. Some of the ladies had to quieten a sigh of delight. All knew that Lady Clairetta Boothroy had first rights to him, for she was the town belle. She softly approached. With grease and condoms there displayed, the others broke into couples to fall in love that night and to bring peace to Psycho City. Lady Clairetta, meanwhile, was putting on her private set of Turandot fingernails, to point out the fine points of Sheriff Slade's body sculpture.

"The heavy upper torso," she noted, running one nail along the pec line. "Yet the tiny waist, as in a cartoon. The famous Sheriff Slade genitals, bursting with guilt. The thighs, big and gloomy as a forest. The poetic haircut."

"Let me down, okay, lady?"

"We cannot do so, Sheriff," said Lady Clairetta Boothroy. "Oh, not ever. We are saving you for the first human cloning experiments, for you are too magnificent a specimen to be surrendered to the cycle of life and death. You must live forever, my dear Sheriff, for you are fuck itself."

That's where the text stopped. A surprise ending, one might say. And, perfect timing, the buzzer went off just then. Cosgrove got it, saying, "Send him up."

"Who is it?" I asked.

Carlo was grinning at J. and Cosgrove. "It's not your daddy's porn, is it?" he said. "But it's somebody's."

The visitor was Davey-Boy. That was odd, because he and I had little to do with each other, and he seldom ventured north of Better Bodies or whatever they call that gym now.

Both Cosgrove and J. opened the door for Davey-Boy, crowding him with copies of their story, and gala reports of its impending publication, and the usual esoteric ad-libs. This was even odder, because they and Davey-Boy had never met.

On the other hand, Carlo and Davey-Boy had definitely touched base somewhere, because they nodded at each other in a surprised but acquainted way. When Davey-Boy doffed his coat, he was in a skimpy top that made him look like an anatomy chart.

"You must know Bud's cousin, right?" said Carlo, getting up to shake hands. "In that gang of his, I guess." Carlo couldn't resist running his fingers very lightly through Davey-Boy's hair; he alone would dare challenge the latter's highly inflected sense of masculine decorum.

Davey-Boy looked at Carlo as if he'd like to take it to the next level, but was distracted by urgent business. "If I'm interrupting, I apologize," said Davey-Boy, his eyes still on Carlo but his attention turning to me.

"You didn't interrupt," said Cosgrove, "but you missed our prestigious trilogy."

"Henry Wadsworth Longfellow had his day," J. put in. "Now the library files will tell of J. and Cosgrove."

True son of Chelsea that he is, Davey-Boy couldn't quite bring himself to turn from the hunk that is Carlo. He reached out and held Carlo's upper arms as if making a physical effort to pull away, so I went over and stood behind Carlo, thus getting into Davey-Boy's line of sight.

"What's wrong?" I asked.

Finally looking at me past Carlo's right shoulder, Davey-Boy said, "Ethan, I need your help."

8

THE
EMERGENCY
DOLLAR

OW, WHAT DID HE mean by that?

Most immediately, Davey-Boy wanted me to help him with a birthday gift for his only close friend who was not one of the Kens. No, this man was a show-biz buff, with the usual specialty in musicals; and Davey-Boy found it urgent to delight him; and this friend was facing a crossroads of life. He was within days of being twenty five years old.

"I want something special for him," Davey-Boy told me. "Something no one else can have."

That was easy. My friend Matt has a computer scanner and a...something, and...I don't know, a duodenum, which all together produce homemade CDs in jewel boxes with full-color covers. He creates all sorts of anthologies—imagine having the Streisand 45 singles that were never reissued in any form. But Matt's gems are his CD transcriptions of old LP cast albums—not the ones you love. The ones that don't exist, like *Let It Ride!* and *Donnybrook!*.

This is truly something no one else can have, and once I explained it to Davey-Boy he was eager to make arrangements. Matt obliged with *Seventeen, New Faces of '56*, and *Say, Darling*, all looking exactly as if Victor had CDed them. Davey-Boy was as grateful as he was ignorant of what these three little boxes of music represented. And of course this was the help he had asked for, but not the help he needed. Because what really was going on was not a birthday, though one's twenty-fifth is a very serious matter in a place like Chelsea. No, Davey-Boy's problem was that Jim Streeter had finally broken up with his boy friend.

We had left Matt's apartment with the three CDs and were on our way to E.J.'s Luncheonette on Sixth Avenue, my haunt in that neighborhood; Davey-Boy owed me a din. Matt lives just around the corner from it, and as we passed one of (this is my mother's term) God's unfortunates, I pulled out the dollar bill I always keep in my right back pocket and handed it to the one-legged guy in the wheelchair with his little cup.

"Ken does that, too," said Davey-Boy.

That's because Ken and I are products of a family that impresses upon its tender offspring the importance of service. Eventually, this would comprise a stay in the Peace Corps or so, but as kids we were expected only to carry an Emergency Dollar at all times. We could use it ourselves, of course, in dire need; back then, a dollar was worth seven or eight bucks in today's currency. But the Emergency Dollar was really there to hand out to anyone in dismay. Arguing that I myself was perpetually in need, especially of the next cast album, was useless. God had chosen unfortunates, and the rest of us had to serve.

At E.J.'s, Davey-Boy told me he really needed my help without actually saying so. "Why Ken never tried to score that flashy lunk," he said, as if announcing a topic. "Right, why. And passed him to Tom-Tom."

"You mean Red?"

"Red," Davey-Boy repeats, without inflection. "Oh, yes. Red": now a schoolmarm detecting mischief in the cloakroom. "Red": an ex-lover referring to his successor. "Red," Davey-Boy insists: Cézanne planning a barn. "Ken never cared about Red, because he was waiting for the availability of Jim Streeter. Which who didn't know was on the verge in any case."

"Who's Jim Streeter? Is he The One?"

"He'll make sure he is."

"I hear a 'but.' "

Davey-Boy gave me an okay-let's-settle-this look. "Who do you think runs our group?" he asked me. "Ken? This is how you think, and you're wrong. Ken is window dressing. He's the looks captain. Yeah, so who calls the plays, if you're way the wise one?"

"You do. But where you're wrong is you think Ken resents that. He prefers it, my very excellent Davey-Boy, who is always sparring in a challenge match, such as now."

He didn't deny it.

"Ken doesn't want to be in charge," I continued. "It takes too much out of him. Besides, command looks good on you."

The food arrived, and there was a Luftpause as we got set up. We ate for a bit in silence, Davey-Boy doubtless going over what I'd just said, because it was news. He thinks that he and Ken are locked in a dispute over who stands at the top of their order.

" 'Davey-Boy always struggles,' " Ken had told me. I said that aloud to Davey-Boy now, just those words. While he thought about it, I added on, "What's new with your porn project?"

"It fell apart. Nobody was serious about it but me."

"Were you really serious?"

He looked right into my eyes and calmly said, "Yes." Then: "Your cousin's wrong to date Jim Streeter. That guy's a catch, it's true. But so's Ken in the first place. He doesn't need the spike in his stats. And Jim's a handful. High-maintenance, they all say. It's like marriage, life with him."

"I think Ken wants an adventure."

"Why not with me? I could turn into whatever the gentleman needs. Did he ever . . . Is there some kink he's trying out that you could heads me up on? Or I suppose it's confidential—but you could pass along a clue. Because sometimes Ken has a purely physical conception, right? He's going for type. But what if this time it's a conception of fantasy? I could do that. Like a waiter when you order. Yes, I'll bring that to the table for you, sir, if such is your delight. Though, if I may take the liberty, if you weren't so fucking handsome with that wave in your hair along the part, you wouldn't get away with driving me crazy, sir."

He put down his fork, drank deeply of his water, and stared at me.

"A physical conception *is* a fantasy, anyhow," he went on. "I went out for wrestling in high school. Thought I was pretty neat, huh? We all did. We'd go round Robin Hood's barn to express our contempt for pro wrestling, because it was so freak. Of course, the others never guessed what a secret fan I was. My folks didn't allow a television in the house, nor any of my relations. It was hard to keep up with the shows. Yeah, I had to get the other guys on the team to tune in when I was at their homes. Have to be slick with a pretext, or they'll see right through you. They're very good at spotting a queer, did you know that? You go slow. Say it's just for a laugh. See what they're up to. Come on, what a joke. Sure enough, they turn it on.

"Pro wrestling today, now, it's so full of melodramas that it's talk and gawk. Boring. But in those days it was all action. Half the guys were the stars, and the other half were sparring partners. They never got interview time or turned up on bubble-gum cards. They'd show up or vanish without warning. And one of them sort of fascinated me."

He started eating again, calming down. He can prevail. "This one guy," he finally said. "Big Viking type, with that white blond hair. Not a day over twenty-two, and very, very big. Young and big. Six foot six, easily, and not so much gymmed up as . . . *grown* up. They called him Mike Justice. He didn't appear a lot, and maybe he wasn't so handsome. Clumsy, too. In the ring. But something about him spoke right to me, even as a teenager. Now we are the kids of Chelsea, and we know style. This guy Mike didn't know style."

"Isn't that what Ken's looking for?" I said. "A guy with no style?"

"Ken doesn't know what he wants. He makes it up from week to week. Like compulsive shopping, right? He's trying the whole store on, something'll fit. See, what I wanted to say about it . . . Ken's like me and this wrestler. I knew I wanted body contact—except what kind? Can I stroke his soft white hair and say . . . What? And how do we decide what happens on the date? Where does my mouth go and what do I touch? I could beat off to the thought of the guy, but what if he's in the room with me? So Ken's ahead of where I was then, because he knows what happens on a date. But he doesn't know who his partner is. Which is funny, wouldn't you say? Because usually you know who you want to do it with long before you know what you'll do. Didn't you have a guy on your mind when you were in high school? Someone total?"

"Yes," I answered, thinking of Evan. "He turned out to be an idiot."

Davey-Boy nodded. "It's never who you thought it would be. I mean, not in real life." Looking more serious, he said, "Tom-Tom reports far and wide that you figure everything out. Can you figure this out for me? How much does Ken like me?"

"I believe you are his best friend, Davey-Boy."

"I know I am. But how much does he like me?"

WHEN I GOT HOME, Tom-Tom and Red were in the listening room; the selection was Cosgrove's rarest cast album, the 1989 Australian *Anything Goes* with Geraldine Turner and Simon Burke. Matt has offered to run up some of his mom-and-pop reissues for Cosgrove, but Cosgrove knows that Demento would have a fit if one of his devotees was, as Cosgrove puts it, "collecting homemade."

Our record buff was in his element socially, I have to say, supplying Tom-Tom and Red with story continuity between the numbers and blandly rising above the fact that his two guests were, as always, staring at each other so intensely that the paint was fading on the walls. I dropped down on the shoelace couch for a bit, in time to catch the great moment during "Easy To Love," when the hero tells the heroine, "You love me, Hope. You're going to marry me."

"Yeah, listen," Red commented. "That singing boy friend's taking the trolley to Prisontown. Why do guys want to get married?"

"Or why do gays want to get married?" said Tom-Tom. "Since they never had to before. At least, straights always had to."

"I won't" was Red's pledge.

"I won't, either, Red," said Tom-Tom.

As they jumped up to shake on it, I wondered if Red had registered Tom-Tom's reference to a gay issue and how he reacted to it. But Red does miss a lot. In any case, the union of the two, taking their oath in the center of the living room, created so much extramusical content that Cosgrove buttoned off the CD.

"Did your New Year's client ante up with the advance yet?" I asked him.

He shook his head. "Mr. Smith is my new business manager. He's going to call about it."

And then, suddenly and casually, as if they were always this impulsive in exactly this way, Tom-Tom put his arms around Red and Red went along with it. It made quite a change from the last time they occupied the center of my living room, because not only was it not erotic: it was peaceful. It was a real-life gloss on *Anything Goes'* musical comedy. You like me, Red. You're going to be my friend.

Then Red got a beep on his pager and had to head for his gym to cover in some emergency, and Cosgrove went off on the Saturday errands. Tom-Tom was going to leave as well, but I delayed him with questions about Jim Streeter.

"Why him?" Tom-Tom asked, clearly surprised to hear the name.

"Aren't he and Ken about to hook up?"

"It's news to me. Of course, everyone in Chelsea wants Jim Streeter. But he's going with some rich Broadway guy."

"Apparently not for much longer."

"Somebody better tell Davey-Boy."

"He knows."

Tom-Tom's eyes widened. "Oh, he must be on the warpath for sure. Davey-Boy holds next–boy friend rights to Ken, and everybody knows it. You should see them when we have a threesome; I could be just some cameraman on the set. They draw high card–low card to see who's top, then they caress each other while they promise to go way rough. 'I'm going to snuff-porn you,' Davey-Boy says, in such a loving tone. Yes, c'est le choc! It's like those legends of the gay blades of early Stonewall. You know, where they invented sex with a crazed determination. Didn't I think that was all over by now?"

"It's still going on, Tom-Tom. My Harvard friend Erick just had sauna sex with a Mormon."

"Yes, but how did he know it was a Mormon?"

"The other fellow kept saying, 'It's just two guys getting off.' He said, 'It doesn't mean anything.' Then Erick happened to mention God during the patter, and the guy flipped out. 'Don't do the G-word,' he said."

"Yes, that's a Mormon," said Tom-Tom, with the authority of one who has bagged many a Latter-Day Saint.

"Now tell me about Jim Streeter," I said.

"Do you like franks and beans?"

Two beats passed as I figured it out, then: "I love franks and beans."

"Come to my place and we'll dinner it."

TOM-TOM'S APARTMENT IS VERY small, and he makes no attempt to refine or enliven it. He treats it as a dorm room: knowing that he'll be graduated out of it sooner or later, he sees no reason to tart it up. A can of beans, half a package of franks, and the biscuits that come in a tube went into one of those infomercially available cooko things that render everything ready for the table all at once. It's what I call "school food."

As Tom-Tom got out the plates and flatware, I filled glasses with tap water and asked him how he liked his new job.

"Oh, it's fine enough," he replied. "The main thing was to get away from that stress. And you know?" He stopped what he was doing to emphasize the wonder and weirdness of what he was about to tell me. "One of the boys from the old office invited me to a little souper. Aux chandelles, très galant. I asked him—in just these words—if *she'd* be there. And he said, 'Who's "she"?' Can you believe? After all that trouble, he just forgot?"

"He didn't forget, Tom-Tom. He's denying his knowledge so he doesn't have to deal with it."

My host absently folded a paper napkin into a triangle and slipped it half under a plate. "Why would he do that?"

"Most people don't side with the victim, Tom-Tom. They side with the aggressor. Otherwise, the aggressor comes after them, too."

Once dinner was served and Tom-Tom had set out an assortment of marmalades, relishes, and chutneys—"for the biscuits," he explained, "so each bite is a new treat"—we got down to the matter of Jim Streeter.

"Is this why Ken keeps failing to date anyone new?" I asked. "Because he was waiting for this Jim Streeter?"

"Ken tricks rather easily, you know," said Tom-Tom. "But he *dates* with a real sense of purpose."

I watched him cut off a bite of hot dog, carefully give it a topping of beans, and guide it into his mouth with a little kid's concentration. "How come Ken never mentioned this guy to me?" I asked.

"Don't miss the black-cherry marmalade. It's from St. Dalfour Frères, In the Aquitaine."

As he bladed some onto a biscuit, I said, "Do Jim Streeter for me."

"Okay." The biscuit. Then: "You know how sometimes you just wake up in the middle of the night for no reason and can't get back to sleep?"

"I always know the reason—Cosgrove and Fleabiscuit are building one of their dominoes steeplechases."

Tom-Tom reflected on that while ingesting more biscuit. "Isn't one of them a puppy dog?"

"Go on, Tom-Tom."

"It was when I had that problem at work. I went TV-surfing, and there was this adventure show about, like, Victorian English people in a jungle. But the jungle had dinosaurs and even sci-fi aliens. The good guys were broken up into different qualities, so an old guy was smart, and a classy brunette wised off to everybody, and then there was a young cute guy and a jiggle blonde. But most of all there was a kind of thirties hunk with an odd accent like it's not from England but it's not Crocodile Dundee, either. But he was from somewhere like that, because he wasn't gymmed up the way our hunks are. He was ... Well, what do you call it when they're masculine and strong but they don't have muscles?"

" 'Straight.' "

He smiled as he readied another bit of biscuit and jam. "Anyway, he doesn't have to pump, just stay trim and good-humored but very warrior at the same time. See, he doesn't have to *look* strong. He just *is* strong. He's got a secret method. And that's what Jim Streeter is like. See, it's not a kind of famous movie hero. What they have is canned strength. Jim Streeter is like those strangely interesting guys that would turn up in a B movie and never get famous. Someone with real power."

I kept my face politely blank, but he knew that I was wondering where he'd heard such an intriguing aperçu.

"Davey-Boy," he said.

I nodded.

"Although *some* of us would like to know why Ken's going after other guys when he and Davey-Boy are *so* destiny. But, anyway, that's your Jim Streeter. He's someone no one can have, like that guy in the gym last year. Remember? When we were all fighting? I don't believe we'll ever fight again, at least. We'll do good works. That's Ken's term, I guess you know."

"Yes."

"What good works have you done?"

"I used to read to the blind at the Lighthouse."

"That's too radical. Tell about a little good work."

"When I was a teenager going into New York for Saturday matinées, I used to lunch at the Automat on Broadway and Forty-sixth. Oh! How odd—because my standard meal was an oval crock of a frank with beans, just as we're having tonight. Way back then, it cost only thirty-five cents."

Charmed by the coincidence, Tom-Tom nodded happily as he devised a miniature hot dog dressed with Major Grey's chutney.

"The Automat was huge but crowded, and it was customary to share one's table. On this particular Saturday afternoon, right next to me, was an old woman. She had put sugar into what she thought was an iced tea, but it must have been something else, because it foamed up and overran the top of her glass. And she said she had spent all her money, and started to weep."

Tom-Tom stopped eating.

"Now, it happens that in those days I was on a fixed budget, with just enough for the train, lunch, and the cheapest theatre ticket, which was two dollars and thirty cents. And one piece of sheet music—a beat-up old operetta score, a song from the latest show, whatever. So I had in effect spent all my money by then, too. But there was always my Emergency Dollar."

"Just like Ken," said Tom-Tom, in mild wonder.

"Just like Ken, and so I broke it into change and bought the woman a new iced tea."

"But what if you had had an emergency after this?"

"The way I was taught is, somebody else's emergency comes first."

Tom-Tom sat still absorbing this. Then: "What's an Automat?"

"A firm called Horn and Hardart had chains all over the Northeast. They were cafeterias but also a kind of home-cooked fast-food outlet. You put change into receivers in the wall and a little window would open for you to take out your selection. A sandwich, or dessert. Your frank-and-beans crock. You see them in old movies."

"Those black-and-white classics you like? Do people help the old woman in such films as those?"

"Quite often. There was a social contract in America that has been gradually leached out by forces I do not comprehend."

"It's wonderful that you believe in something, at least. The Emergency Dollar, I mean. That you and Ken still do that."

"Don't you believe in something, Tom-Tom?"

"Yes, but I don't know what it is. Ken says you're good to talk to because you write stories, so you know how things will come out. Do you ever surprise people by using them in your books?"

While I prepared a weaselly evasion, he suddenly went on, "Because it's very helpful to me when Red and I go to the listening room. So far, I can't do any more than skin-eat him, or he lets me shop him when he stays over to avoid the subway all the way back to..." Here Tom-Tom simply waved his hand, thus suggesting some distant arrondissement of Brooklyn. "And he has to pretend to be asleep. Then when he comes, it's like Rambo's machine gun."

Getting up to furnish us with seconds, Tom-Tom got pensive. "Red's no trophy in the Jim Streeter way, I admit. Some of my gang hold it against him that he's short, because he's this kind of dopey top, so he should tower over me. Full or half portion?"

"Half, please."

Spooning it all out, Tom-Tom said, "He could never be one of us, but there's something about him I really like. It's partly because his feelings get so hurt a lot and you want to protect him, and it's partly because his upper torso gets so wide over that tiny waist. But I believe I love him somehow. I *love* him, cousin Bud."

As he set the plates down, I said, "Tom-Tom, you are one of the finest young fellows I know. You're extremely handsome, you've got a shockingly rich head of hair in the most amazing shades of light and dark brown, and you have one of the three or four biggest torsos in Chelsea. And I've grown very fond of you. But I'm not your cousin."

"Ken calls you that," he replied, joining me at the table.

"Ken *is* my cousin, Tom-Tom. His mother and my mother are sisters."

"Oh. I thought it was a new game we were playing, like carrying the football."

"Here's what's funny, Tom-Tom: two gay men are having dinner, and there's no gourmet chow or smart wine, no sharp dressing, no décor comme il faut. No anything but simple and uninflected. Yet the two of us are stereotypes. I'm the old-fashioned show-biz buff with The Knowledge, and you're the Chelsea muscleboy—and I hope that doesn't offend you."

"No, I like being a Chelsea Boy."

Making a little hot dog in Tom-Tom's manner, I asked, "What happens when you become old enough to be a Chelsea *man*, though?"

"There aren't any, haven't you noticed? Davey-Boy says they send a car around at a certain age and pack you off somewhere."

"The way they dispose of the villain in *The Mummy?*"

"Oh no, it's quite peaceful. Davey-Boy says wherever possible they let you go with your best friend."

"Where do they take you?"

He started pasting a biscuit with lime preserves. "I think Iowa," he said.

MEANWHILE, BACK ON EAST Fifty-third, there was trouble about Cosgrove's New Year's catering gig.

"I finally get hold of this guy," Carlo told me, "and that was not easy. They don't make it easy's the first thing to know about someone like this. I told him the usual things you'd say. 'We have a business to run.' Or 'If we bend the rules for one client...' You know. And all I get is these complications. If it was just me, I'd truly chuck it. Guy's a professional arguer."

"Just lose him, then," said Ken. He and I had been going over a report he'd had to write up for one of his jobs, for a firm in New Jersey. He wanted a grammar and punctuation check.

"The kid himself is running this outfit," Carlo replied. "Only he can..."

Carlo trailed off as Cosgrove and Fleabiscuit came crashing in with the news that they'd passed someone asking for money on Lexington Avenue. "He looked so sad," Cosgrove told us. "Sitting on the sidewalk, kind of keeled over, crying and even talking. He was talking to the world, saying Why? He's a young guy, and sort of nice, and everything's gone wrong for him. But he didn't have a sign like the others do. He isn't organized, and he's so leaning over that no one can pass money to him, and... I can't just give him *that*, can I?"

Because Ken and I had pulled out our emergency dollars.

I said, "Get a twenty out of my wallet. But it sounds as though money isn't really the problem."

"Yes, because why is he crying so badly like that?" Cosgrove asked, crossing over to the dish where I keep my money, keys, and ChapStick. "He says, 'Why is this happening to me?' He doesn't care who sees any more. What do you call that?"

"He's broken," said Carlo.

Cosgrove looked at us as he stuffed the bill into his pocket. "But how does that happen to him?" he asked. "And everybody just walking past."

"Go," I said; and off he went, Fleabiscuit hard by his side with a worried look.

There was a pause. Then Ken said, "Why do you people have what you want if I can't find it?"

"That's the most imposing non sequitur," I replied, "since Julia Roberts married Lyle Lovett. And who says we have what we want?"

"You know what I mean," he said. I didn't, and he noticed, but as he started to explain, Dennis Savage came in, and Carlo had to share the vexing news about Cosgrove's New Year's job.

"Guy now says he's adding two vegans besides his dinner for six," Carlo told us. "And why should he pay for them, 'cause they'll just eat anything. But that's not true, for starters. Those vegetarians do not please easy. *And* can we walk his dog, because he'll be so busy hosting? And does the fee include birthday cake, 'cause one of the guests... See how he works it?" Carlo shook his head. "And the big fun is, he still hasn't sent the advance. What are we supposed to do, pay for his party ourselves?"

"Yes but," I pointed out, "If Cosgrove doesn't make his own business decisions, he'll never enjoy having a business. So far, all he's enjoyed is picking out a pocket agenda notebook with a pencil that fits into tiny leather straps. He's always taking a note or two, and this gives him a certain enabling power."

"So far, so good," said Ken.

"Yeah, he sure won't feel enabled come New Year's Eve," said Carlo. "He's got too soft a heart for the cheats who come floating right in when you offer a service to the public."

To Ken I said, "We have what we want? I find that so strangely disturbing."

"But doesn't it look that way?" he countered. "Everything fits together here."

"That's probably because we're hiding everything."

Then we had to tell Dennis Savage about Cosgrove's errand of mercy on Lexington Avenue.

"There's a lot of misery around, isn't there?" said Dennis Savage. "Why get so upset today?"

"Seems this guy's young and cute," said Carlo, "so that breaks the rules. If it can happen to him, who couldn't it happen to? Maybe to Cosgrove, if he'd had someone else's luck." Very, very quietly, he added, "On the street and friendless." He was almost chanting now: "Why is it happening to me?"

Cosgrove and Fleabiscuit returned, deflated. After he put the twenty back in my wallet, he came over to us, and Dennis Savage impulsively riffled Cosgrove's hair. It was a bagatelle of a gesture, but Ken must have read it more weightily, because he asked if Dennis Savage got Cosgrove for birthday sex.

Carlo chuckled, and Ken explained this Chelsea custom to Dennis Savage.

"When is your birthday, in fact?" Ken asked him.

"This afternoon," Dennis Savage replied, with an outrageous simulation of candor.

"Sneak! Sneak!" I cried. "It's April twenty-seventh."

Carlo decided to mooch a nap at Dennis Savage's, and they went upstairs as Cosgrove and Fleabiscuit—and who was the more morose of the pair?—headed for the bedroom.

"What happened about that guy on the street?" I asked their backs.

"He was gone," said Cosgrove, passing out of view himself.

By then it was December, and the Christmas cards started coming in. I display them amid the new CDs laid out for listening and the old CDs pulled for further enlightenment. I love the unique cards—the Rodgers and Hammerstein office may send a *Pal Joey* set design, Allan Mason Smith another of his scenic photographs, my longtime pal Clint Bocock an erotic study with his latest boy friend. Hetero acquaintances send family shots, complete with golden retriever. Is he Kendall? Joker?

Christmas also leads up to my New Year's party, which I've been attending since college. Matthew's the host, and Matthew's in opera, so there's a musical theme. It's fancy, with waiters filling your champagne glass, and soprano Sheri Greenawald and I center the fun with a concert of Broadway curiosities in a kind of camp espressivo.

The concert was inaugurated years ago, when Carol Neblett and some crazed loon improvised the second act of *Tosca*, with the man singing Tosca and Neblett Scarpia. I liked it, but Matthew said it was "tactless." He suggested that Sheri and I preempt any further action by espontaneos with a clearly demarcated vocal set—everything from Victor Herbert to Stephen Sondheim, some of it with scurrilous new lyrics or blended into intricate medleys in which themes from one number slip into another, and aided on occasion by my puppet friend, Barkis the Impedient Dinosaur. Devoted to raucous commentary and sabotage, Barkis will demand a kiss from Sheri in the middle of a jazzing DeSylva, Brown, and Henderson salute. There's a sing-along for the whole party, to Fanny Brice's "If You Want the Rainbow (You Must Have the Rain)." And there's the annual encore, "Meine Lippen, Sie Küssen So Heiss," from Lehár's *Guiditta*, to my English translation. In the years when Sheri was unavailable, Barbara Daniels, Lauren Flanigan, and Susan Graham stepped in.

It's the only time in the year that I get to make music in public, so the holidays become for me even more of an event. As New Year's approaches, I gad about like everyone else, wondering why some people claim to hate this time of year. Aren't there a lot of amusing things to do, like concocting a medley out of the Walt Disney *Snow White* score, or at least picking out crazy presents? I was at home resting up when Davey-Boy came buzzing by again. Cosgrove decided to take notes for possible use in his next porn story, so as I ran around doing an Emergency Tidy-up Cosgrove commanded Fleabiscuit to fetch Cosgrove's notebook-and-pencil. Fleabiscuit yipped obediently and ran into the bedroom.

"I could make some sly observations about Davey-Boy," Cosgrove explained. "He's canned heat."

Fleabiscuit ran back in to deposit a small rubber ball at Cosgrove's feet.

"No, Fleabiscuit. Fetch master's *notebook*."

Fleabiscuit yipped and ran into the bedroom, returning with his Shrek squeeze toy.

"No, Fleabiscuit—"

The door. Davey-Boy marched in with those shoulders of his, saying, "Don't play music, and I don't want that stupid water. I know what goes on here."

I reintroduced Davey-Boy and Cosgrove as Fleabiscuit came running in with his plastic windup Mickey Mouse.

"No, Fleabiscuit—"

"You," Davey-Boy told me, "sit down right now. I have something important to discuss with you. It's a very nice apartment, with extremely books. You couldn't read all these in a hundred years. I respect you, but if you play with me I'm going to get edgy."

He said this while taking off his dress coat, and—I swear, boys and girls—he was shirtless as he threw it onto the Fleabiscuit shoelace couch. That same canine worthy came running back in at the same moment with an old steak bone. Cosgrove got but halfway through the word "no" when Davey-Boy turned his cool eye upon them, and master and faithful companion slunk off.

"Ever so handsome Davey-Boy with the tightest physique in Chelsea," I said. "To what do I owe?"

"You will please help me some more."

"You enter like Captain Ahab and continue like Oliver Twist."

"That's just my way, because I know you like me."

I said nothing.

"Right?" he went on, sitting on his outflung coat.

"Everybody likes you."

"I poured out my feelings to Tom-Tom, and he said to come to you for the true analysis."

"You're the gang's theoretician, though. You lecture on The One. If you can't solve it ... This is, I presume, about a Streeter named desire?"

"Yeah, I'm jealous. I never minded the clowns and wastrels our wonderful Ken will deceive me with, because they're no more than deceptions. Jim Streeter's different. He's real."

"This will sound flip and bourgeois, but isn't your bare back against the couch uncomfortable?"

"It's never uncomfortable showing skin."

"Good, that's settled. Is Jim Streeter The One?"

"Yes, but not for Ken. I don't care if that's arrogant."

"It's arrogant but correct. You and Ken are born partners."

Some might be seen to ease up at hearing that concept. Some might even smile. Davey-Boy's expression did not change.

"What's your proof?" he asked.

"Some of it occurs in confidences I can't betray. Some of it I've picked up as I watch and listen, because after the first twenty stories or so you're out of invention and have to steal from life. And some of it's because Ken has exceedingly good taste and you are the most attractive man on his beat."

Davey-Boy cannot be flattered. He's just absorbing the information.

"I know looks are all that matter," he says. "But they don't reflect personality, do they?"

"I wish you hadn't put it that way. Some of my readers exasperate easily on the subject of looks."

"Tell me what Ken sees."

He was looking quite seriously at me, as if the question were coherent as asked. Well, maybe it *was*. "The fine black hair with the center parting and the floppy commas at the forehead?" I guessed. "The cobalt eyes. The light dust along the chest overlooking the hairless tummy. You even have beautiful ears."

"Ken is more handsome."

"Ken is beautiful. But you're so sexy it's scary."

"Ken thinks I'm too complicated."

"You are."

"And Jim Streeter is easy?"

"You tell me."

He leaned forward. "What have you heard?"

"Tom-Tom says he's a little girl-friendy."

Suddenly energized, Davey-Boy jumped up to pace and let off verbal steam. "Not a little," he began. "Jim has a whole system for staying in cell reach, and who makes dinner or do they café. He has to know what you'll be wearing tomorrow. 'So we don't *clash*'!"

Now he stopped short, looking right at me.

"And Ken loves it. He *says*. He wants to go steady, after all that sneaking around."

"Have you ever thought that Ken might simply be teasing you?"

Davey-Boy pantomimed looking here and there about the room, his way of saying, *"Duh."*

"Well, then—"

"But he's not a player," said Davey-Boy. "He's our Ken. I'm the one who games around—and I only do it to keep him online. It's hard to get that boy to focus."

A thought hit him.

"What was he like before?" he asked, sitting down again. "When you were kids."

"I blush to say that we weren't. I got to college before he was born, so we didn't—"

"Give me something, at least."

So I recalled the Christmas when my father, for unknown reasons, presented my brothers and me with recorders. They were oversize and made of a strong dark wood. Very impressive looking: but only Tony could play. Of course, the advantage of recorders is that they sound pretty much the same whether you have mastered the art or merrily pipe away in chaos. So we took our recorders to the big family party at Aunt Agnes and Uncle Mike's, and we would burst into a room as I called out, "Yes, it's the Christmas Fiddlers, playing their latest hit, 'Lo, How a Rose E'er Blooming.'" Then we'd tootle away for a bit, crash into the next room as I announced "Jingle Bell Rock," and so on. Tony's sense of musicianly professionalism got offended, however, so he dropped out. And Ken had been following us from room to room, greatly enjoying it, so when Tony quit, Ken asked if he could use Tony's recorder.

"To play with the Christmas Fiddlers?" Davey-Boy asked.

"It's called 'sitting in.' Ken was about five years old, I guess, very cute and rather dressed up. He may have been in a suit. The recorder concert was just a momentary goof, so we all gave up soon enough. But Ken kept coming up to me later on, looking so boyishly sharp in his duds, still carrying that gigantic recorder, begging for more stage time."

Davey-Boy looked like one of the 9/11 Commission witnesses after Joe Biden finally stopped asking one of his thousand-year questions.

"Is that what you're giving me?" Davey-Boy said, after a while. "What do we learn from it?"

"That somewhere in that strutting icon is a sweet little kid who wants to show off. So you—"

"Smother him with cell calls? Imprison him with dinner plans? That's Jim's way, you know. He's total relationship, they say. Ken can't want that."

"Nobody wants to be controlled," I said.

"I want to control him," Davey-Boy told me. "Yes. Oh, yes, I will! Do you know what I want it to be?"

He paused, and I clearly saw him wondering if he should keep this nugget to himself. Go on, Davey-Boy, because this is my last volume in this line of work, and I want lots of content.

He did go on: "I want him lost and disoriented, in a cave someplace. Bones cracking under his footsteps. This must be where the ogre lives. And now he appears."

"You're the ogre."

"Right, he appears, and he can't distinguish between loving and snuffing. The ogre has had men every which way already, so now he can only love on the most ultimate level. He feasts to love."

"You know, there is such a thing as being too alarming."

"Is he a teaseboy?" Davey-Boy went on. "Shall I tenderly whip him for his crimes? I'll put the blue cuffs on him, those Chelsea sex toys that come in merry colors, like ice cream. I'll fall so lovingly for him for the very last time, and in the movie there will be scenes of us laughing on the beach, oblivious of vivisection and world hunger. We'll be in contact by cell at twenty-minute intervals."

Cosgrove and Fleabiscuit were standing in the doorway, trying to look sophisticated yet inconspicuous.

"They can come in," Davey-Boy allowed.

So they came in. Fleabiscuit availed himself of a shoelace opportunity, and Cosgrove told Davey-Boy, "If you were four inches taller, you'd be God."

"Thank you for this talk," Davey-Boy said to me. "Tom-Tom is right about you, Ethan."

"You don't use my nickname," I answered. "Why do I have to use yours? Can I call you 'David'? Because you're not a boy any more. You're one of the most manly guys I've ever known, and that's counting Jack Dempsey, who used to live in this building."

Luftpause. Davey-Boy thinks it over. He finally says, "My name's Isaiah," rhyming it with "De Falla." He tells me, "My family have been Pentecostals for four generations. I had to break with them to come here and turn into Davey-Boy."

Joining Davey-Boy on the couch, Cosgrove felt his left biceps and asked, "Is it your birthday, by any chance?"

Davey-Boy was lost in thought, however, and did not reply. After a while, he uttered the term "girl-friendy" all by itself, in echo of Tom-Tom's comment on Jim Streeter. "We're having a dinner to all meet this guy," Davey-Boy finally told me. "It's at Sebastian's, because he has the biggest apartment. Get the flags out and come armed. You're invited."

Davey-Boy said Cosgrove could come, too, but Cosgrove said that, instead, he would like to be shipwrecked on a desert island with Davey-Boy, Cosgrove's portable CD player, and his twenty most beloved discs "for a period lasting no more than five weeks."

Throwing on his coat, Davey-Boy nodded once at all of us and left. As if at his signal, we all began to do things. I organized the New Year's music for a Sheri rehearsal. Fleabiscuit began to transfer the rubber ball, Shrek squeeze toy, plastic windup Mickey Mouse, and steak bone back to his den under the bed in the other room. Cosgrove decided to reexhibit the Christmas cards, moving some here and some there.

Then he said, "I've always liked your cousin, and Tom-Tom is very nice to me at all times. But that Davey-Boy is dark and crazy and strangely wonderful. Is that a type?"

"No, Davey-Boy's his own genre. Before I go—what happened about your New Year's gig?"

"My business manager told the guy he wanted the entire

amount in advance in a bank check by a certain day and no more requests for substitutions and extras. So I guess that's that."

"You seem to have a very healthy outlook about it," I said, retrieving my Sheri "Loveland" medley from the piano. It's the *second* "Loveland," and as "My Romance" ends I quote the main strain of the *first* "Loveland," thrilling the Sondheim buffs.

"Mr. Smith said, 'If you can't win, don't fight,' " Cosgrove quoted, creating a mini-display of the family photo cards. "I'm not really disappointed, because the next thing is just about to happen, whatever it may be. You know?"

"Yes—they call that 'gay life.' "

IN THE END, COSGROVE decided to give the New Year's dinner for Dennis Savage, Peter Keene, Tom-Tom, and Red, with Carlo and Nesto serving and guesting. I went to Sebastian's, where I met Jim Streeter and got to see what he and Ken were like together. Dennis Savage calls this "Who is the boy friend and what do they do?"

The boy friend was much as Tom-Tom had pictured, what the personal ads describe as "straight-appearing." (But then, who isn't nowadays, except straights?) Jim Streeter was certainly masculine as opposed to effeminate; his salient quality, however, seemed to be less an abundance of hetero than a lack of homo. It's not that he was straight-appearing: he wasn't *anything*-appearing. He functioned without giving clues. Perhaps that was his secret method.

He was certainly extremely handsome and in beautiful trim, though not Michelin-pumped in the Chelsea manner. I have since learned that his physique is termed "L.A. style"; it emphasizies abs over chest-fill and demands gaudy upper-arm separation between biceps and deltoid.

As for what he and Ken do, they were neither all over each other nor did they go the other way, into the cagey affinity of two men who shared the same lifeboat on some long-ago ocean disaster. More interesting by far was the behavior of the Kens. Tom-Tom sent me eye-faxes at every remark Jim Streeter made. Davey-Boy was cool and unobtrusive, but in the rococo Davey-Boy way: a congested cool, as unobtrusive as a Ming Dynasty mandarin whose eyelids flutter to signal the start of a holocaust. The rest of the party, loyal to Ken, were pleasant to Jim, and Jim was pleasant back.

At one point, Tom-Tom, in charge of some platter or other, passed behind me with the stage whisper of "Meet me in the kitchen." But we had nothing to say that would color in the line drawing of unpredictable Ken outfoxing all our expectations. Jim seemed to me another of those emptily charismatic guys who let the rest of us see in them whatever we wish to, need to. They're actors and we're dramatists: we imagine them.

I said as much to Tom-Tom, who replied "It's so profound" even as he was wondering whether to set the plastic container of whipped butter on the table comme ça or ferry the stuff into a serving dish. "How serious is this dinner?" he asked me.

"Butter-dish serious, I'd say," I replied.

He thought it over, frowning at the sacrifices etiquette demands of us, then transferred the butter while casting the odd look beyond us at the dinner table.

"I feel sorry for Davey-Boy," he said. "He doesn't really want to boss Ken, you know. Even if he does bark at people. Could you hold that for me when I . . . Thanks. It's a waste of butter, though, isn't it? Because in the end we'll just throw out whatever's left. And here Davey-Boy has to sit and toast the happy couple."

Picking a knife out of Sebastian's cutlery drawer, Tom-Tom

went on to "It isn't even like Ken to shack up. He only tricks. You know—the call of the wild."

I said, "It's nice the way you and the guys hold the keys to one another's lives. You know where everything is, from a butter knife to sex."

"Oh, it's easy knowing how your friends fuck. What's hard to get is when they mess around with the 'L' word."

"You're smart, Tom-Tom," I told him, and he rewarded me by flexing his right biceps for me to feel. "Bravo," I cheered.

"Now, back to our show," he said in a conspiratorial tone, as he led the way to the dinner.

Actually, there was precious little show out there till Wilkie asked Ken if he was free for video night on Saturday and Ken said yes. Because then Jim said no.

"No?" Ken asked him.

"Saturday's our supper date with Edward and Crosby," said Jim. "Remember? I said I'd get the flowers and you'd bring the wine. They're serving red snapper, so be sure it's white."

The table froze. Tom-Tom silently mouthed "supper" at me, as if Edward and Crosby tended to respond with "Let them eat cake" when told that the working class has no bread. Morgan turned to Ellroy to say, "If you return the tuxedo by ten A.M., they don't charge for the extra day."

Jim started to answer that, but Ken cut in with an easy "White wine it is, Jim."

Then the Kens looked at me—I mean, every one of them from Tom-Tom to Bradin—as if I had the next line.

Oh, yeah? "If everybody doesn't immediately look somewhere else," I threatened, "I'm going to recite Chaucer's *Canterbury Tales* in the original Middle English."

They did look away. Then Anders announced the topic for the usual after-dinner roundtable: What Gay Life Most Desperately Needs. Ellroy led off, with a plea for a gym with a looks code. Bart spoke in favor of a ban on gay realtors at dinner parties, because, he said, some jackass then asks a question about The Market and the evening becomes overwhelmed by the most boring subject on earth, apartment prices. Then it was Jim Streeter's turn.

"Well, isn't the answer obvious?" he said. "What could we need more than gay marriage?"

Ken had gone to the belasco, so he missed this, along with succeeding entries by Anders and Sebastian anent, respectively, calamitous gaps in the Undergear catalog and the limited menu at F.J.'s Luncheonette. Now it was Davey Boy's turn.

He got up and did a thing with his shoulders. Hiked them, something. His smile would gladly murder you. And, he announced, what gay life most deeply needed was an end to the wish to imitate straights.

Such as trying to make their parents proud. Such as leading the kind of life that, say, Dick Cheney would call "useful." Such as the stupidest idea of all:

Gay marriage.

The mild reactions that the company registered told me that this was an issue of no interest. However, Davey-Boy did not care what his cohort thought. He was speaking to Jim Streeter.

"Who *wants* gay marriage?" Davey-Boy intoned. "Real men wouldn't, because only a woman wants to be married. Who else, boys of mine? Well, those stinking politicals want it, because they're so stupid they won't work for useful issues. Like integrating the military. No," he insisted, drawing his right hand flat across the screen of view, a kind of real-life computer gesture. "No, they like gay marriage. Why, my boys? Because it's insane, and gay politicals like insane things.

"Don't they?" Davey-Boy added, hurling this at Jim Streeter, who simply looked back at him with a message undecipherable to the naked Chelsea eye, or mine.

"The pathetic little femme gays like marriage," Davey-Boy went on, "because then they can be what they really wanted to be all along: women. Oh, yes, my boys! Who else, we ask? Hetero businessmen want it, because then they won't have to offer us partner benefits—we'll have to *marry* to get healthcare. And divorce lawyers want it," Davey-Boy husked out, sweeping the table with his smoothly blazing eyes, "so that decent, hardworking gay hunks like me can go bankrupt."

He paused, as Ken made his way back to the table. "Have you scoped those silly drips lining up to get married—just like *real* humans do, Mommy! What meager specimens they are! And even, what *is* gay marriage? It's spending all your time together. You never go out, except to work and to attend your own funeral. No, marriage is staying in, because your wife controls you. You catch videos. You cook muffins. You secure the flowers and wine for those intimate . . . Tom-Tom, you'll have the term."

Tom-Tom filled in with "Ces dînettes en fag," while all stared at the couple of honor, then at Davey-Boy, then back, as stabilized as a line of Tiller Girls. Ken's face could not be read; believe me, I checked. Nor could Jim's, even when Davey-Boy came to "Losers is what they are. Not because of bad luck or they chose a wrong path on their map. They're losers because they deserve to be. Because gay marriage is for twerps who don't want to do anything with their lives."

Davey-Boy has huge hands and long, spidery fingers. He likes to show them off, extending the palms out at one as if bearing treasure: the portrait of Davey-Boy in cameo, or notations on his Pilates routine, or his beating heart.

I'd no idea that Davey-Boy cultivated a political viewpoint. All

I'd ever heard him speak of was people he knew and feelings he had, and his gay sociology never abandoned physical taxonomy and seduction technique. Davey-Boy isn't an intellectual; Davey-Boy is performance art, and now he thrust his right hand onto the top of his vest and flipped open the buttons in one ceremonious drop. Then he pulled the vest off of his skin like an adventure hero in the final reel, because sometimes he is nothing less than the movie of Davey-Boy and must stand before you, magnificent.

Ken, you are with the wrong man, I thought. I know that Davey-Boy's a show-off, but there are worse things to be. If heaven does await and I get to it, the first one I want to meet is Beethoven. Or— no. First I want to meet the Dolly Sisters. The *next* one I want to meet is Beethoven; and I have the fantasy in my mind that, through the vast holy ooze of the Beyond, he's going to seem like Davey-Boy.

Did my mind wander? Davey-Boy had finished, though he was still on his feet, staring at Ken and Jim. The latter was rubbing the back of Ken's neck, concentrating on him, tuning the rest of us out, ready for their private video-and-muffins evening.

And everybody else was looking at me again; it was my turn to discourse on the thing that gay life most desperately needs. " 'Whan that Aprille with his shoures soote,' " I began: because I've no idea what gay life needs. But Davey-Boy wasn't finished, after all. He cut in on me with "Only faggots like that one want gay marriage."

"That one" was of course Jim, who rose to complete the confrontation. Immediately, Ken got to his feet and grabbed him, calmly saying, "No, we're going now."

Davey-Boy again hiked his shoulders up and dropped them. A muscle thing, terse, defiant. Like an animal rivalry in the forest. I *will.* I *am.*

I have to say, Jim Streeter was not intimidated. Maybe he's used to this; I have since heard that he only goes with men whom third parties regard as already taken. Among his confidants, he calls this "cheatsex." I've *even* heard that Jim can't get off unless he's cheating.

But I digress with pleasantry. What happened was that Jim tried to defuse Davey-Boy's anger with a shrug, and Davey-Boy told him, "You're a wife, you stinking squish."

So we had jump up and pull them apart, which was easy because the dinner table stood between them. Still, there was some real danger for a bit, because neither Jim nor Davey-Boy wanted to be seen pawing the ground and bellowing yet securely held back. They really needed to fight.

"You want some, Topless Pete?" Jim cried at Davey-Boy. To the rest of us, he added, and none too gently, *"Let me get to him, that's what I ask!"* And he was grinning all the while—not a joker's grin: a killer's. He even shook off his guard momentarily and tried to crash over the tabletop—"Allons-y, les gendarmes!" cried Tom-Tom, charming to the nth degree—but the standoff was immediately reinstituted.

"You *loser!*" Davey-Boy shouted.

"You *straight!*" Jim replied.

And somehow somebody got the indicated coats as Ken bustled Jim out into the hallway. It wasn't over yet, though, because now Davey-Boy threw everybody off, pushing past those of us who were milling about or protecting the dinner things to get to Ken and Jim. Or no: to Ken. Angling around a corner, I saw that Jim had got locked outside on the far side of the door, while Ken held Davey-Boy special-close and whispered into his ear, four or five words at most. Ken caught sight of me over Davey-Boy's shoulder, winked at me, planted a deep one on Davey-Boy's hungry mouth, and left.

All the Kens now burst into applause behind me, as I slipped down the few feet to Davey-Boy. He had not turned back to the interior of the apartment, where the party was. Rather, he was just standing, facing the door through which Ken had just passed. I fancied seeing the door fly open for the entrance of a fantasy icon, something out of Tom of Finland or A. Jay. He would take Davey-Boy in his arms—or, wait, isn't Davey-Boy his own fantasy icon? What does the icon need?

"Ken," said Davey-Boy to me. "Why did he wink? Was it at you? You know something, don't you?"

"Everyone's dating," said Tom-Tom rhapsodically, coming up to us with the entire party behind him. "It must be like spring in Franche-Comté, where the Cascades du Hérisson gush like a porn star in the money shot, and tourists gape at Le Corbusier's chapel of Notre-Dame-du-Haut."

The guys looked at him for a moment, then turned back to Davey-Boy.

"You won" was Wilkie's opinion.

"No contest," Morgan agreed.

"Although I question," said Bradin, who has a somewhat academic way of expressing himself. "One must. We want tolerance from the straight world—should we not display tolerance among ourselves? And by this magnificent example—"

"You're lucky Pajammy and Corndogger aren't here," I told him.

"I have to get to cousin Bud's for a second dinner party," said Tom-Tom.

"And me to make music at Matthew's" was my rejoinder, as the Kens began to peel away to return to the main room. Tom-Tom offered to drop me on a generous detour to the West Side, though he was staring so hard at Davey-Boy that he may not have known what he was saying. Not yet cooled down, Davey-Boy had the fierce hot wetness of a prizefighter after the gong. One gets so used to the sheer style of the Chelsea Boy that one never knows how to take it when one of them gets real.

"Did I win?" Davey-Boy asked me. "You always know."

"It was a great speech," I told him. "I'll be getting hate mail for months."

"That guy Streeter—is he The One?"

"Don't ask me. It's your concept."

"I wasn't sure if I liked you before," he said, putting a hand on my arm as if bucking me up. "But I almost do now."

He did that shoulders thing again, as Tom-Tom made Hand Display Gesture at Davey-Boy's square-cut pec line like a model on an old TV commercial presenting the advantages of a new refrigerator.

"He's my irrepressible Davey-Boy," said Tom-Tom, pulling a leather jacket out of the closet and handing me my dress coat, muffler, and the attaché with the sheet music. Tom-Tom and Davey-Boy enjoyed a major hug as I held the door, and Tom-Tom and I were all but gone when I stopped him and turned back. Davey-Boy was still there, that gleaming shirtless darkhair, still panting from the recent action, just there, just standing there.

Then he smiled at me, so I asked him where he was recruited.

"In the parking lot after a Christian League softball game," he said. "The umpire."

In the cab heading uptown, I asked Tom-Tom if he had programmed any resolutions. He said he had a few minor ones relating to his gym routine, but this very night he was putting a major resolution into action.

With a confidently understated determination, he said, "I'm going to have what no one else can have. Somebody's going to take off more than his loafies tonight."

☾ ☾ ☾

Matthew's party was, as always, the highlight of my holidays; after the Sheri concert it gradually wound down to a little thissing and thatting: baritone Paul Whelan picked up some cute chick; a wondrous mezzo who has the honor to be the only person in all five of these books to remain nameless tried to decide if the charming twenty-three-year-old Puerto Rican waiter was straight; and I invented an act with opera director David Alden in which I put on a German accent and David was mute and referred to as "the Bar*on*." We fooled conductor Christian Thielemann. I *think.* I told him the Bar*on* and I were heading to Hamburg for *Der Freischütz.*

"Who sings?" he asked.

"The usual Nazis," I replied, then, faking embarrassment, I changed that, in a confidential tone, to "Strictly local cast."

The party always dwindles intimately down to Matthew, David and his twin brother, Christopher, and myself—the four of us college buddies—along with Sheri and a few kibitzers of honor. At length, the waiters split, the sun comes up, and I go home. I came in, very quietly, to the sight of Carlo dozing on the couch, Fleabiscuit nestled between his legs. The dog looked extremely partied back (as we used to say in the old days). His eyes opened as I switched on a light, but he didn't move; his frame shuddered with a sigh and he went back to sleep. Now is the time when I gather up the Christmas cards and throw them out to start the new year.

Something stirred behind me, and I turned to see Cosgrove holding up a ssh finger.

"It's okay," I whispered, "Rip's a heavy sleeper. How was the dinner?"

He smiled, and also whispered, "The perfect New Year's special. Mr. Smith and Nesto served, and Red didn't know what the food was and had to have a peanut butter and jelly sandwich on toast. Peter was quite amazed, I noticed. But, after all, it's just your three main food groups. There's your toast group. Your peanut butter group. Your jelly group."

We shared a silent giggle, and he produced his own pocket comb, so I could neaten his hair.

"How is Red getting on with the guys?" I asked.

"Well, he's sort of like Space Godzilla. Like, he hears his name and turns too fast, so his tail crashed into a building. But his heart is good, and his rap is so strange that he's fun to listen to."

Nodding at Carlo, Cosgrove added, "I think Mr. Smith wants to give Red a spanking with a wooden paddle, but since Red's with Tom-Tom, Carlo's too much the gentleman to say so."

I thought that altogether too advanced a concept for my traditional early New Year's Day soothe-down, but before I could reply Tom-Tom came out of the bedroom wrapped in a blanket, and I did a take.

"You're still here?" I asked, keeping the volume low.

"It was too late to go home. I felt like those people in…" Once again, he waved at some fabulous, even imaginary place. Eldorado, Metaluna, Bay Ridge. "You know. The ones who have to stay with you on Friday nights and they get affectionate and suddenly it's more sex with straights, which seems to be happening a lot lately. No wonder the heteros think marriage is endangered. I told them about Davey-Boy's action at the other party. Like in World War II: an *action*." Tom-Tom went into a tremendous yawn, but he kept on talking with "Then we had a magazine…" till the yawn overwhelmed him. Shrugging like a little kid, he concluded with "a magazine party is what, with dramatic readings."

I turned inquiringly to Cosgrove. "A mood of historical wonder descended upon the guests," he explained. It sounded re-

hearsed, to say the least. "So we had a look at your old *After Dark*
and read aloud from the interviews."

"I loved it," said Tom-Tom. "What's an 'actor-model'?"

I said, "Someone who charges one hundred fifty in and two
hundred out."

Peter now appeared; he was nude. "Everybody has a boy friend
but me," he merrily announced. "First, I attempted to create my
own brand of . . . well, *niche* sex by turning the couples into three-
somes. Finally, this spectacular specimen"—he gazed fondly upon
Carlo, still sawing a log—"took pity on me. Laddies, I can turn
straight at last. No—spare me your pity, for I've had sex with
Zeus. Everybody watched, too. I feel like a porn movie."

"Red put his hand over his eyes," Cosgrove reported, "at the
moment of . . ."

"Action," Tom-Tom put in.

"You had an orgy?" I asked.

"Fleabiscuit and I didn't," said Cosgrove. "But those others . . ."
He trailed off as Dennis Savage and Nesto joined us, one blanket
enclosing the two of them.

"You perv," I called Dennis Savage. "You bawd. You have
turned my bedroom into a circus clown car, plus I can't help but
notice that everyone had sex and all I did was socialize."

"You got to make music," said Cosgrove. "You once told me
that was the greatest pleasure of all."

After all the kidding, that solemnly joyful remark silenced the
room. Then Tom-Tom piped up with "I can't wait to tell you,
cousin Bud. Because I got sexually promoted tonight in my quest
of Red's heart and mind. Nous allons causer, mon vieux. But Red
is embarrassed and won't come out. The suspense is awesome.
Could you . . . ?"

"Why do I always have to be the one?" I asked.

Carlo had awakened at some point in all this. Still stretched out on the couch, he was petting the adoring Fleabiscuit. It struck me, right then, that some of us on this planet are simply loved. That's all: loved. The rest of us are umpires.

You know? Anyway, I went into the darkened bedroom, where Red was standing in a corner wearing my old Yale sweatshirt and nothing else.

"I knew they'd send you in," he said. "Will you play music?"

"Take this simple test, Red. You're alone and uncertain because, one, You've fallen into something and can't handle it. Two, You just wish it weren't moving so fast. Three, Other: please specify."

He thought about it for a moment, then said, unhappily, "That sounds like school."

"Second Approach," I announced. "Let's not worry about what to call it. It doesn't have a name, okay?"

"It does, though."

"The Third Approach is no-fail," I went on, with my usual overconfidence. "Given the rules of the place you come from, you don't realize that everyone in *this* place likes you just as you are. We're not laughing at you or locked in a lifelong rivalry that pretends to be fun-filled. We want to know how you feel about things so we can learn from you. We're curious. And we notice things. We recognize patterns. And, fine, let's call it what it is: *gay*."

I paused to gauge his mood, but he was simply listening and not, apparently, reacting.

"I hear you ask, Why do we recognize patterns?" A little dry humor. "It's because gays have to identify hetero in order to imitate it, out of self-defense. At some later point, we enter the gay world and don't have to recognize patterns any more. Because anything a gay man does belongs to gay culture. We're self-inventors. But note the irony—when straights come into the gay world, they're completely lost. Because they haven't acquired the ability to spot the patterns. Or I guess they aren't really straights, because..."

It's a valid concept, but it suddenly felt so irrelevant.

"What's wrong, Red?" I asked him. "Just tell me."

I could see that he was trying to piece his wording together, so I waited. Finally, he said, "I'm not a great-looking guy, and I know that. But Tom-Tom likes me for some reason. So we can joke around. And I really like that, when I tell him how I feel about things. And then come these...ideas. You know. To do stuff."

"You're a major type, Red. You don't know that, because everything in the world has been telling you that it's all about pretty. That's true of chicks, Red. Chicks can be hot in only one way—Marilyn Monroe. But men can be hot in variety, because it *isn't* all about pretty. It's also about power. You're a hetero-culture power dude who doesn't know his own valence."

"You must be right, because I don't understand any of it."

I gave his right shoulder cap a light bonk of my fist and suggested we join the others.

"I always knew I had to, sooner or later," he said, not moving.

"Come on, then."

He came, half-nude as he was, and the others raised a yay for him. Allured by the Pre-Raphaelite symmetry of Red's exposed bottom, Peter drew near, but Tom-Tom warded him off with a look.

"Speech, speech," said Cosgrove.

This time, Red actually did say "Gawrsh," followed by "Let Bud do it."

But I was fresh out of invention by then. Instead, I simply recounted the greatest story ever told, that of The Mechanic and the Librarian. The latter's car breaks down in the small town of . . . Tom-Tom helpfully thrust out his arm for me: somewhere in that direction. The Mechanic needs a spare part, how long will that take?, perhaps tomorrow, you can bunk with me tonight. The Mechanic is kinky and the Librarian ambitious, and they're still together as we speak, in that small town of . . . Tom-Tom threw out his arm again, now letting it rest on Red's back. Red looked down. Dennis Savage and Nesto grinned at each other in their blanket. Peter Keene was mainlining a bottle of seltzer.

"Each one can choose who to be, Mechanic or Librarian," I noted. "So it's the perfect gay story."

"If *that's* the gay story," Peter pointed out between gulps, "you would have had nothing to write about."

There was a pause as Carlo started to move, Fleabiscuit leaped off him, and Carlo rose to take some of the water off Peter.

The other guests drifted off to the bedroom, so Cosgrove asked, "Where's everyone going to sleep, I wonder?"

"No time for that," I replied, "as we finally hear from the sinner's own lips of his physical contact with a certain Virgil Brown, currently known as J."

"Never." The little traitor didn't even bother to seem defiant.

"It's my throughline," I insisted. "We can't conclude without it."

"I don't feature that for your throughline," said Carlo. He set down the empty water bottle and crossed the room to stand behind Cosgrove as if they were a pair of something. "More like some guy from nowhere cuts into this world of, like, arts and sciences. Maybe I got the phrasing wrong, but that's your throughline. Because otherwise that guy might well have ended up in police trouble with the ladies, where they invent charges against him and he goes to jail. Because the one who first says 'He did it to me' is the winner. Guys don't know that about women. They will lie to send you right to jail."

"Why?" I asked.

" 'Cause they want to be married, and you're not marrying them. See, they don't have sex the way we do. They give something up with sex, or they truly think so. And you have to give something back, which is love."

"It's the mystery of the universe," said Cosgrove, glad of the distraction and still standing directly in front of the lecturing Carlo.

"And there's society, too, isn't there?" Carlo went on. "Making you turn into what they want. But then..." He rested his hands on Cosgrove's waist, brother to brother. What are they, a valentine? "Then you wander into this strange location where everybody is in charge of his freedom. No control. No one saying, 'You have to be my husband. My son. My slave.' You reject them to be yourself, and your new friends will guide you. They play you music, take you to the show. You could have been a criminal. Instead, you're everybody's friend."

"Who are you talking about?" Cosgrove asked, his head tilted up at Carlo's face. "Me or you?"

"Both, my boys," I said.

Fleabiscuit came crawling around at this point. Snuffling and whining, he planted himself among us, afraid to listen yet welcoming it as youth must welcome the wisdom of frost.

"In *Les Mis*," said Cosgrove to me, "when wonderful Gavroche died, he left those two younger brothers all alone. Who can save them then? They just want nice guys to like them."

"We have to help the newcomers," said Carlo, a hand atop Cosgrove's head.

"Who will help me someday?" I wondered, gathering up the Christmas cards for filing in the new throwaway. The old one looked so old and wrecked that I sent Cosgrove to Bed Bath & Beyond to replace it, and somehow he managed to return instead with a giant antique B. Altman's Christmas-themed shopping bag, which is what we use. "What if I need an umpire?" I asked. "Or even just a grown-up?"

"Look what I have," said Cosgrove proudly, pulling an Emergency Dollar out of his pocket.

Happy New Year, boys and girls. Thank you for listening.